RAVE

Born in 1961 in St Georgen in the Black Forest, Thomas Strittmatter now lives in Munich. He has written a number of plays and film scripts, and received the Kranichstein Literature Prize in 1989. This is his first novel.

'There are wonders in this book. Its dislocating power – which seems inseparable from the knotty, sometimes tortuous style and the the sly deadpan humour – defies easy analysis'

Harpers & Queen

'Enticing flow of its prose and sumptuous characterisation ... This is a funny book with a brutal side, elegantly written'

Independent on Sunday

'A grotesque and often hilarious pilgrim's progress ... Quickly paced and energetically written ... an effortless read'

Time Out

'A brooding, witty first novel of great promise'

Times Literary Supplement

Thomas Strittmatter

RAVEN

VINTAGE

VINTAGE
20 Vauxhall Bridge Road, London SW1V 2SA

London Melbourne Sydney Auckland Johannesburg
and agencies throughout the world

First published in Great Britain by
Chatto & Windus Ltd, 1993

Vintage edition 1994

2 4 6 8 10 9 7 5 3 1

Originally published in Germany 1990 as Raabe Baikal
by Diogenes Verlag AG Zurich

Printed and bound in Great Britain by
Cox & Wyman, Reading, Berkshire

ISBN 0 09 999800 9

Contents

How Does Death Work?

ON A COLD autumn night, Raab had fallen asleep to the sounds of the fountain in the yard and the light, rapid steps of the sisters. During that night he was to experience for the first time how death works.

Even though he, like all the others, had already seen dead people in photographs in the newspapers, on television, and had even taken an inquisitive look – from a distance – at a corpse lying on the road, covered by a plastic sheet, he had, however, never witnessed death at close quarters. Who in the world would have thought that, a short time later, Raab himself would come within a hair's breadth – or, to be more precise, to within the breadth of a handful of hair – of death, and that, only two years later, he would kill a man.

He woke around ten o'clock, when a dull bellowing started up, at longish intervals at first, but then more and more intense, ever louder, and it was unmistakably a roar of pain.

Raab listened to his room-mate's regular breathing, and he himself was breathing like someone in a deep sleep. His eyes were wide open, he was staring into the darkness. The noise had wakened both Fever and Raab, yet neither wanted to admit to being awake. One of the sisters could come into the room at any moment, and anyone caught awake always had to get up first next morning and give a hand with preparing breakfast. So it was that the old caretaker who came into the room to rouse them was aware of two shining pairs of eyes which snapped shut with amazing speed when he switched the light on. But he had mellowed, softened, over the passing years. In a quiet voice, he told them to get up, put on something warm, but, most importantly, to put on their wellington boots. They weren't to wash, they were just to hurry.

Almost thankfully they left their beds, everyone in their class was emerging from the other rooms, the bellowing had apparently prevented them from sleeping too. They dressed quickly and excitedly and followed the janitor to the headmistress of the boarding school's office, where she was waiting for them, dressed as usual in her plain tailored suit, although this time she, like them, was in gumboots. When Andre, the youngest of them, saw the headmistress standing there like that, she suddenly burst into tears and admitted that, a week previously, she had, in a fit of temper, kicked in a glass door near the refectory. So dismayed and frightened by the cow's bellowing was she that her guilty conscience now wrung an unexpected confession from her. They would go into that in the morning, said the headmistress with a look of satisfaction, happy to see in this confession a further indication of increasing maturity in this child under her care. And to the others she said that they were now of an age where they had to be enlightened about a variety of matters. Now they were not to be afraid, if there was anything they wanted to know, they were not to hesitate to ask, and if one of them was to feel unwell they had to say so right away. So they left the building and followed the headmistress, who was carrying a large torch, to the neighbouring farmyard; there they were met by the farmer's wife, whom they all knew from those times when it was their turn to fetch the milk. Any moment now, she said, and led them into the cowshed. The farmer was already standing there with his strange brother, who frightened the younger children, while the older ones made fun of him. This man had been deaf from birth.

Raab timidly shifted his gaze away from the Deafman and

went round towards the cow's hindquarters; its tail had been tied to the ceiling with a length of hemp rope. A transparent slime, mingled with blood, was dripping from the animal's tightly stretched genitals. On the floor stood a bottle of disinfectant, and there were several pieces of rope lying around, with bits of wood secured to their ends. He and the other boys flinched with every cry the animal let out, it was a dreadful noise. And even the headmistress, who had intended opening the discussion long before this point, was watching events with a mixture of fascination and alarm. The farmer's wife, observing them all with a smile of unconcealed amusement, explained that in this case it was taking an unusually long time as the calf was no doubt lying in an awkward position, hadn't turned itself round completely. With that, the animal began to tremble, it was breathing heavily and was already exhausted. The farmer rolled up his sleeve, rubbed down his hand and arm with disinfectant and, to the horror of the boys, reached into the animal's insides. A large part of his arm disappeared into its womb, groping for the calf's body. It hasn't turned itself round properly yet, it's going to be difficult, he said. The headmistress added the explanation that everyone came into the world head first. So long as the forelegs come first, then we can pull it out, said the farmer's wife. And all this time, the Deafman was watching Raab.

And so they waited, saying nothing and listening to the cow's breathing getting faster, hearing how it gradually became too weak to bellow. Little by little its breathing turned into a wheezing, a rattling groan, which sounded so pitiful that the farmer went off to telephone the vet. Raab had no idea how much time elapsed before the farmer came back. He hadn't been able to contact the vet. But hardly had he entered the byre when the animal's forelegs buckled and it rolled slowly over on to its side. Perhaps as a result of the pressure being exerted by the weight of the cow's body on the calf lying inside it, the tip of a tiny hoof suddenly slipped out of the vagina, and right away the farmer bound it with the rope he had laid out ready and pulled on it with all his might. Immediately afterwards a second hoof appeared, and the farmer's wife pulled on the second rope, to drag the calf into the world it obviously did not want to see. As if it already suspected that it was never going to gambol about among ruminating cows on flat meadows, would never once penetrate the restrictions of the ticking electric fencing so that someone would have to come looking for it in the sparse little spruce forest, that it would never plod across damp Alpine pastures, but was instead destined for a brief life in the artificial light of the cowshed.

The Deafman drew from his pocket a school exercise book, to which he had tied a ball-point pen with a length of parcel string, hastily wrote something in his precise hand and passed it over to the headmistress, who was staring spellbound at the dying cow.

Emergency slaughterings, and the slaughtering of animals whose general condition is impaired, must be undertaken in the casualty slaughter-hall of public abattoirs; where no casualty slaughter-hall is available, and in the case of slaughterings outwith public abattoirs, these may be undertaken only at times separate from normal slaughterings. On completion of the slaughterings described in paragraph 1, the place of slaughter and the implements employed therefor must be thoroughly cleaned, she read out, in that voice she also used in her biology and physics lessons, whenever she had to talk above a noisy experiment or the vacuum pump or the drone of the generator.

And during all this time, the Deafman watched Raab. The more violently the cow panted and the more relentlessly the blood flowed out of it, the more the farmer's wife tried to talk about other things to prevent the children becoming too alarmed. She told them about the various breeds of cattle: Appenzells, Friesians, Oberland cattle, Bavarian cows, the advantages and disadvantages of each, their various characters and what their milk yield was, which can climb the slopes best and which can run fastest. Meanwhile, the cow had stopped bellowing and was now giving out, at increasingly long intervals, only gasping, whistling breathing noises, which sounded so distant that they could hardly be coming from a bovine body, however huge. The farmer was slaving away, pulling and straining at the calf, helped by the Deafman.

No one spoke a word now, there was almost complete silence, even the sounds of the other cows, the pigs, became hushed and muted, then the cow itself stopped panting, it came almost as a relief, for it had been so painful to listen to that everyone had almost had to hold their hearts at every sound.

The farmer took up a sharp knife, so quickly no one could see where it had come from, cut an enormous slash in the cow's perineum and, in one final gush of blood, the calf was flushed into the world. Well now, you've learned something new, the headmistress said, ushering the children out of the cowshed. Even she herself was feeling queasy. She didn't want to put on another visual lesson like that in a hurry.

Some of them had nightmares and screamed in their sleep, Fever woke up feeling sick, The Victim cried in her sleep, Andre seemed to sleep as if in a dead faint, and Raab remained awake all night, staring into the darkness.

The headmistress reproached herself for having exposed the children to such an experience. She intended to deal with a different topic in her next biology lesson.

Hoar-frost

ON THE FOLLOWING autumn morning, when hoar-frost lay on the meadows and the icy ground-mist hovered in the hollows, the janitor awoke just as he had done every day for the past thirty-six years. He waited for a few seconds after opening his eyes, and gave a satisfied smile when the alarm set up its clatter. He sat up, perhaps a little too quickly, for he felt a slight giddiness, there were signs of some approaching indisposition and a vague lack of enthusiasm, a feeling of having had enough, which was something new to him. He got up, shuffled into the empty washroom, tooth-brush and glass in hand. He washed, and then he rinsed his false teeth with Odol and cold water. From the kitchen he fetched a wicker basket, went back into his room and dressed. He reached for a clean shirt, but then left it lying where it was and pulled the old one on again.

He went out of the building, tried to clear his throat, but neither his nose or throat nor his bronchial tubes seemed to want to unblock properly, his breath came through them rather laboriously and there were audible indications of resistance.

He walked the five minutes to the neighbouring farm, where they were already at work, the farmer's wife saw him approaching, slipped quickly out of the shoes she wore in the cowshed, beckoned him into the kitchen, the dog barked, briefly as ever, and then wagged its tail. In the kitchen lay some seventy eggs, brown ones and white. As was his wont, he selected his eggs himself and counted them into his basket in a husky voice. The process took rather too long for the liking of the farmer's wife. The old man took hold of each egg with such care, as if there were a tiny child inside it, in fact he became so agitated by his own exaggerated caution that he began trembling with increasing intensity. He made his way back, went down into the cellar where the science lessons were held and laid ten eggs on the headmistress's desk. Outside he heard the loud noise of an engine and shook his head. Who's that making such a row out there? Do they really have to? he thought.

Then he locked the door behind him, went up the stairs into the kitchen, where there was already a strong aroma of coffee, and drank half a cup. It was not going to be a good day, he thought, and left the rest of his coffee standing.

Meat

THE HENS SCATTERED in alarm, for the Meat Inspector was coming clattering past the boarding school on his extremely noisy moped. This tiny machine set up as much racket as a racing car or the farm boys' re-bored and souped-up mopeds, on which they regularly ran their moto-cross races in the woods. But the Meat Inspector's moped had not been re-bored, it had just rusted, its exhaust had been eaten away by corrosion, and every now and then bits would detach themselves and fly off in a wide arc and land on the roadway. Then the Meat Inspector would have to brake, a manoeuvre that took some considerable time, since his brakes were not gripping any more either, then he'd have to turn back to retrieve the pieces. More than once, his carrier, complete with its basket, the black microscope-case and the box packed with chemicals and three, maybe four apples, had come flying off in similar fashion.

The microscope was an impressive model, made in Leipzig, which had already seen service with several generations of meat inspectors, schoolteachers, doctors and anatomists. It was apparently indestructible. Not two world wars or the division of Germany nor, for that matter, the moped trips with the Meat Inspector had managed to do anything to impair its precision. Besides it, the box contained several chemicals and an assortment of razor-sharp knives, as well as glass slides, a thing called a trichinoscope, glass containers for holding tissue samples, some gauze bandages, sticking-plaster and iodine in case he cut himself, alcohol for disinfecting, his apples, a hip-flask full of kirsch, a small box of Sumatra cheroots (sub-standard quality because of their discoloured outer leaf) and a bundle of plastic freezer bags in case his dissections would not fit into his little glass jars, or perhaps against the time when these same jars might finally shatter as a result of a fall. Riding his moped, he always wore a black rubber mackintosh cape, no matter whether the weather was stormy or, as was all too seldom the case, sunny, and, in hail and snow, a heavy black motor-cyclist's jacket. Underneath these, day in, day out, he wore a greenish-blue pin-stripe double-breasted suit; while this did indeed bear the traces of his profession, its colour had been so cleverly chosen that the stains became apparent only on very close inspection. In fact, you would have had to scrutinise it with the same meticulous care and precision that he himself applied to the examination of his sample slices of kidneys, liver, lymph nodes, intestines and muscles. Not many people looked at the Meat Inspector as closely as that.

Yet the more comical the effect that this stumpy meat inspector made on other people, with his crooked walk, black bobble hat and black horn-rimmed spectacles as thick as your thumb, the more respect and admiration did the Deafman bestow on him. Whenever the Meat Inspector had driven up and was being treated to a welcoming schnapps in the parlour as a preliminary to unpacking his professional box of tricks, this amounted, for the Deafman, to far more than a mere arrival, it was a grand entry, it was a theatrical turn. Hardly had he swallowed his schnapps when he would pull out of his jacket pocket a half-smoked cheroot, half of a discoloured Sumatra, which, even before it was lit, already emitted such a pungent, biting stench that it would have sufficed on its own to sterilise his whole array of dissecting knives. But once he had actually lit it, there arose such a stink and such a fug that eyes began to burn and any admiring spectator was unable to see a thing for a full minute. And so it was always like that moment after a successful trick by a magician, when a rabbit, a dove or his assistant appears out of a cloud of smoke, as if emerging out of thin air, from some boundless magical beyond; as if by sorcery, there stood the Leipzig microscope beside the bottles and the brilliant-green, phenol-red, lactose-milky petri dishes, and next to them again the trichinoscope, made in Wetzlar, the ever-present kirsch as well as the freezer bags, the iodine, sticking-plaster and gauze bandages.

Then he got to his feet and, with the apparently spellbound Deafman at his heels, set off with his crooked walk towards the scene of the slaughter, his little leather bag with the knives in one hand, the bottles in the other and the fuming discoloured Sumatra in his mouth. It was obvious from the tortured, miserable expression on his face that he was repelled by the sight of slaughtered animals and their entrails and the steaming smell of blood. The fact was, he hated his job; hardly had fate dealt him the blow of landing him in the profession of meat inspector when he became a strict vegetarian and an alcoholic. The purchase of this once-expensive and handsome suit helped him, to some extent, to get over the years of revulsion and dissatisfaction. At that time, shortly after the Second World War, he had bought it from the widow of a doctor killed in the war, with the aim of investing himself with the aura of a respectable, caring man of science. He had spent his last penny on this suit, so he could never bring himself to admit that the sleeves were too short and it was just that uncomfortable shade too tight across the shoulders. Unconsciously, he accustomed himself to a posture which camouflaged the deficiency in the length of the sleeves and through time made the ache across his shoulders at least bearable. The constant drawing together of his shoulder-blades had no doubt shrunk the muscles, so that now he could walk only with his shoulders tensed, which explained his slight stoop; he carried himself as if he were hanging from an invisible rope tied round his waist. Though just why he always had to wear under this tight jacket not a shirt but a green pullover was a mystery even to the Deafman. He's probably got trouble with his kidneys, he thought, as he noticed that he cut the kidney sample out of the animal with a particularly excruciated expression on his face. Now the Meat Inspector had not failed to sense, down through the years, the degree of respect in which the Deafman held him. In 1960 the regulations governing meat inspection were revised and a new edition of these ordinances was published, so, since he was unable to carry on a conversation with him, he presented him with his old copy. He had been looking forward for weeks to giving the Deafman this present, and he handed it over as he sat in the parlour with the butcher, drinking schnapps and coffee and eating a piece of plaited yeast loaf and an apple, while the others got stuck into their *Kesselfleisch*, fresh boiled beef slaughtered that day. He wanted everyone to see what a kind-hearted soul he was. And in fact the Deafman took the book, left his boiled beef and his cabbage standing and ran off to his room, incapable of giving expression to his gratitude. The butcher, who was suspicious of people who couldn't talk, said, D'you think he can read at all?

So now the Meat Inspector came to view the cow that had had to be put down. As soon as he stepped into the byre, he said, There's something sick in here.

And in fact, after a routine examination, he was unable to pass the meat even for sale as substandard. So the cow ended up as animal fodder.

He's always got an air of death about him, said the farmer as he watched the departing moped.

The Meat Inspector had hardly rattled away out of the farmyard when they slaughtered the little calf and put the cuts of meat into the big freezer cabinet.

The farmer was convinced that any bacteria and germs would be killed off by the shock of the cold. However, he was alone in putting his faith in this theory and eating the meat. As things turned out, it was to do him no good at all.

Egg

THE CELL AS fundamental element of life, the headmistress wrote in green chalk on the blackboard. The distinguishing signs of life, the protozoa, the amoeba.

In blue chalk, she wrote: The egg cell. The egg as model for the cell.

She drew a cross-section of a hen's egg in white.

The egg shell, calcium, up to one millimetre thick, depending on the hen's diet, the albumen, in which the yolk floats, enveloped, held together by the flexible yolk sac, protected and nourished, the chalaza, a kind of umbilical cord, if you like, and here, she said, something that is often forgotten: the air space inside the point of the egg, for an egg breathes, too.

Before the headmistress broke the first egg into a glass bowl, with pointed yet gentle fingers, she tied on a white pinafore, to protect her grey tailored suit from splashes. Either she owned a large number of these suits or just the single one, for Raab had never seen her dressed in anything else.

Now she handed round a plastic dish containing the other eggs, white ones and brown ones, which the janitor had fetched that morning from the neighbouring farm. They sat in groups of five, each one surrounding a small glass bowl. Raab used a ruler, reinforced down one edge with a metal strip, to open the egg with a sharp blow. Undamaged, the yolk and the transparent slime of the egg-white flowed out of the brown shell.

Andre was too tentative in opening hers, she went about it as if she were trying to peel the raw egg, digging her small fingers, moist with excitement, into the faint cracks; a hole appeared, through which the yolk squeezed out. The skin stretched, but just before it reached breaking point, it plopped into the little dish, quickly followed by the slippery white.

As for The Victim, somebody had pinched her just as she was breaking her egg open and it seemed to explode in her fingers, giving her even more of a fright, the white of the egg spurted on to her blouse, seeped through the linen and ran in a slow trickle down between her breasts. The yolk slithered past the edge of the dish, but she was able to slide it across the table top with her warm hand and gather it safely into the bowl.

Fever had to take a deep breath and gulped audibly as he picked his egg out of the bowl; he didn't trust his fat fingers which tended to make a sudden grab at an object, sometimes squeezing it, sometimes pressing it, only to end up by dropping it. The last thing he wanted was to have to break open an egg, but it was he who had pinched The Victim, the headmistress, as usual, had been watching, and now came his punishment. He tried to smile, tried to save face with a joke by making as if to throw the egg at Raab, but as he did so, it very nearly slipped out of his trembling hand. He was just able to hold on to it and take it towards the bowl, but he was holding it too firmly, hit it too hard on the glass rim, and both the pressure of his fingers and the weight of the blow were too heavy and the yolk sac burst and the whole demonstration egg was scrambled. The chalaza floated on the top, and a red seminal stain showed that the cock, whom they all detested, must have mounted the hen and taken her again by brute force the day before yesterday. They examined the eggs and drew them with coloured pencils, yellow, blue, ordinary lead-pencil grey for the whites and, for want of white, green for the little string of the chalaza.

What came first, the chicken or the egg? Well?

The egg, because reptiles existed long before there were hens, said Raab. At last he got an answer right for once.

Then, in order that nothing would go to waste, one out of each group was to sup up the raw egg. The teacher showed how it was done and slurped her egg; the white separated from the yolk and disappeared into the headmistress's sucking, puckered mouth. With obvious relish, she bit gently into the skin of the yolk to break it and then, with a satisfied expression, she let it slide over her throat. This convinced no one but Fever, however, so the two of them were left to slurp up five raw eggs each, one after the other, and then they went to great lengths to assure everyone how delicious that was and how good it was for them. Next, replete and quite pleased with herself, she turned to the construction of the human cell. At this point, Raab put his hand up and said he had heard that pigs and humans were so alike that surgeons practised operating on pigs. And besides, he had read that human cells and pigs' ones were capable of mingling. So if somebody ate a lot of neck of pork, the pig's neck cells and the human's neck cells would mix and interbreed, so that very quickly the human would have more and more pig's neck cells and sooner or later would have a complete pig's neck between his head and his shoulders.

What nonsense, said the headmistress and went on with the lesson.

All the same, the pupils were now far more preoccupied with pigs than with eggs.

Sow

THEY WERE SITTING in a history lesson, hearing about the buried town of Pompeii and sneaking the odd glance at the pictures of the last clients of the brothel with their lady-friends, preserved by the rain of ash like Chinese thousand-year-old eggs, when Fever recognised the approach of his brother's Ford Capri by the unmistakable defect in its gearbox which caused a grinding noise at every gear change.

So he stood up, asked permission to go to the toilet and ran to the car park behind the building where he could not be seen from the classroom window.

His brother was bigger than Fever, his features oddly soft and flabby. Perhaps this was a result of the fact that, during his training as a chef, he had put on some twenty kilos, then he had broken off his studies and subsequently managed to get his weight problems under control by drug abuse. The family had effectively disowned him, so that all their hopes were now focused on Fever, although the elder brother did still receive a small monthly allowance, which he supplemented by all sorts of illegal and semi-legitimate activities. Every three or four weeks, he visited his little brother to enjoy the feeling of respect and admiration that, for some unfathomable reason, the latter still evinced for him. Now and again he would bring little presents, which Fever stowed away in his medicine-pouch. This time it was a handful of home-grown marijuana. All right, he advised Fever, he could be generous with it if he liked, but only towards those he could trust implicitly. If any of his schoolmates should want to buy anything from him, then he was to get paid in advance and never say a word about where the stuff came from. He was then simply to hand over the money to him. They smoked a small joint together, the brother promised to come back very soon and, with grinding gears, drove off.

In the next lesson, the teacher talked about the saying, 'Man is what he eats.'

In the PE lesson, Fever, who was normally a lethargic character, struck everyone with his over-exertions and, in the changing room after showering, he was still talking sixteen to the dozen.

Now, after school was out, they just could not get away from pigs. For lunch, there were pork sausages with sauerkraut, Fever's favourite meal and a dish that appeared on the menu at least once a week.

Fever had always been an impulsive lad who found it almost impossible to keep his feelings under control, far less conceal them. But he had never been as uninhibited, never as ruthless and yet as cunning, as when the pork sausages were being given out, when they lay steaming and fragrant on the big serving dish, curved and huddling together as if they had been caught in the act of some gigantic orgiastic party and, as a punishment, roasted on the spot like those people trapped in the brothel at Pompeii by the hot ash raining down after the eruption of Vesuvius. And a similar, overwhelming lasciviousness arose in the staring, sweating Fever as the dish came within his reach. His brain went into action, and parts of it that he otherwise never used sprang to life and transformed him into a calculating strategist.

Even before his schoolmates, who were eyeing the lecherous sausages with equal longing, could stick their forks into them, bringing out a spurt of bright red juice, he had formed a plan. Normally, when he spoke he seemed inhibited and ponderous, but now his speech was a hot, passionate stream.

In the farmyard they've got great big sows, the words came tumbling out of him, that eat anything and everything, even their young; if we don't keep an eye on them, they bite each other and eat each other up. They're stupid and they can't keep anything in. They just shit everywhere and wallow in their own mess. But they've got little pigs there too, and they're choosy about what they eat and so they don't stink, they only crap in one corner and they don't roll about in the muck, they don't bite each other, they're intelligent and listen when you talk to them. Whenever you go up to their sty, they stand up on two legs like a human and stretch up and look at you and prick up their ears and listen to you.

The cannibals in New Guinea, Fever went on, nowadays they're only allowed to eat pigs. The word for pig is just that, pig, but the word for human isn't human, it's long-pig.

And that's why, with little pigs, if you were to put a suit on them, they could pass for people.

In the winter it was so cold, so they say, that this farmer took a piglet that was sickly and put it in bed with his wife, who had just had a baby, to keep it nice and warm and get it better soon. And then the neighbour came to pay the farmer's wife a visit and bring her some wine and she saw the piglet next to the new mother and said, Well well well, look at the little fellow, he's the spitting image of his father.

The diners' appetites seemed to dwindle rapidly, one fork after another was laid down next to its plate or merely poked around in the sauerkraut, until Fever unearthed another big chunk of greasy bacon fat and set about it with gusto.

The subject took such a hold on the children's minds that some of them refused for several weeks to eat any pork. Fever, on the other hand, became increasingly gluttonous and couldn't get enough roast pork and pork sausages. He grew fat on everything the others didn't want and soon needed a new, and bigger, pair of trousers.

Bulldog

WHETHER IT WAS because of having eaten the veal or because of the cold draughts as he drove the tractor, he was finding passing water more and more difficult with each day that went by, and at night his wife had to expend an increasing amount of effort to kindle any conjugal activities.

If only you had listened to the Meat Inspector, she said as, yet again, he forced out a few miserable drips of urine and groaned with the resultant pain.

Fine thing, the farmer groused, can't even have a proper piss any more without the Meat Inspector's permission.

That day, he decided to buy a new tractor with a heated driver's-cab.

For four nights he hadn't slept, because the pains were getting worse all the time. In the privy, he had gone through agonies, bellowing like an animal, and his wife made him one camomile tea after another, which he drank down in the belief that the warmth would undo the knot, until he thought his bladder would burst. Then, drop by tiny drop, small amounts did indeed trickle out of him, but so little that it was as if some invisible, malicious hand was squeezing his member to let out just enough to prevent him from exploding.

In the evenings he sat in the parlour, armed with a pocket calculator, a pencil and his tax assessment, studying the information brochures from the farmers' association and from the Raiffeisen building society, from the banks and savings banks, calculating and reckoning this way and that, until he had convinced himself he could afford a real marvel of a tractor, for he saw this as his only hope of a cure. He still hadn't been to the doctor, because he hoped the trouble would disappear in very short order once that accursed old Bulldog was no longer able to ill-treat him, and he developed such a hatred for the good old Bulldog, as if it were a human being instead of a machine. No, there had to be something in that diesel engine and that heavy green sheet-metal, in the leather seat on its nicely curved leaf-spring, something that wished him ill, wished evil upon him. And now he even cast a febrile, suspicious eye on his wife, watching as she worked in the kitchen to see whether she wasn't secretly putting something in his tea. He went about, fearful and fevered, glancing furtively and forebodingly all around him.

Whenever his wife begged him to go to the doctor, which she was now constantly doing, he would say that he hadn't been to a doctor these thirty years now and it hadn't done him any harm. Whenever the pains became unbearable, she would say, Go and see him, why don't you? To this he would reply that he hadn't anything decent to put on and he certainly wasn't going to go around looking like the Meat Inspector.

So his wife tried to persuade him not only to go to the doctor, but also, and this was almost every bit as difficult, to buy a new suit.

But first and foremost he put his trust in the new tractor – a FENDT FARMER TURBO, that was the one, there was no doubt in his mind. He would be the only one in the whole region to drive a FENDT FARMER TURBO, all the others had splashed out their savings on new tractors years ago, but he, he now insisted, had waited until something worthwhile came along.

Early in the morning he drove in his old Bulldog, with a sheepskin over his knees and a blanket under them, to the Central Agricultural Cooperative for a demonstration of the latest tractors. Along the way, he cursed and swore out loud, his urethra was on fire, as if there were some kind of acid in it, his bladder was full to bursting and couldn't be emptied. That's because of this cold, you bloody old Bulldog bastard, he fumed, and pushed the machine to the limit in an effort to cut to the minimum his exposure to the cold and the airstream which, he was convinced, was getting stronger and stronger and was aiming directly between his legs.

Startled by his customer's wild, feverish expression, the head mechanic showed him the FENDT FARMER, which stood shining and freshly painted in the garage.

Indeed, this machine was completely different from all previous tractors: its front wheels came up to his shoulders and the rear wheels were almost taller than he was, the hollows in the mighty tread on them, over which he lovingly ran his hand, were a good ten fingers long, it had double rear wheels and, best of all, the driver's-cab was enclosed and luxuriously appointed, equipped with a heater and even with a radio. Just like in an aeroplane, he thought, and even the head mechanic, who kept going into raptures as he demonstrated this vehicle, referred not to the cab but to the cockpit. And sure enough, there was a kind of small joy-stick there. That was for the accessory equipment, all hydraulically operated and hitched up before you could so much as blink. He jumped from the cockpit, hauled a tarpaulin off an implement in the corner, climbed in again and started up the engine. And in fact he had attached a front loading-shovel in a matter of moments. Words like pressure hydraulics, electro-hydraulic lifting-gear and enormous hoisting capacity flitted through the huge shed like little birds of temptation, cooing and fluttering round the customer and sounding sweeter and sweeter to him the less he understood them. He raised and lowered the shovel again and again. If the driver takes his right hand off the steering wheel, the foreman was quoting the brochure by heart, then it will land almost automatically on the very operating lever he's looking for.

There was no stopping the sick man now, he would have liked nothing better than to scrap the Bulldog on the spot and drive the FARMER home. And already, he believed, he was feeling better, practically from the moment he had made his decision.

Brothers

NOT LONG AFTER his birth, the Deafman developed into a big, strong child who could cry at the top of his lungs. He grew at a great rate, yet, by the time his brother was born, he was still crying like a new-born babe, in fact he screamed louder than the new arrival. While the brother had long since learned to reach out and grasp everything that was held out to him, the Deafman would still be taking a long look before stretching out a hesitant, groping hand, and often he would first have a thorough sniff at things. The fact that he did not react to sounds was something they noticed only very late on, since he would always be screaming, the milking machine would be running, the dog barking or the cattle moving noisily around in the cowshed. The brother grew steadily, for a time he was bigger than his elder, but that soon sorted itself out. Jealously, he would watch how the deaf boy was given more care and attention than he himself got. The Deafman could draw better, and he looked at books. While his brother reluctantly learned to read in primary school, the deaf boy had achieved astonishing success in reading at the special school which he attended for a short time. This special school was in the county town, so that the Deafman's schooldays were short-lived since, for one thing, he could already do everything they tried to teach him and, for another, he had a very long walk to get there. When his mother passed away, his father followed her only a few days later. By this time, the Deafman had come of age, and his brother was consumed by fear that the other one might now dominate him and that he would have first claim to the farm, but none of this came about.

The Deafman became very withdrawn when his brother married, in fact he became downright strange, and people were not quite sure whether he was suffering from some mental deficiency as well or whether his slow reactions and his weirdly garbled speech stemmed from his hearing defect. The brother's attitude towards him was always strangely distant, it was almost as if he were ashamed of the handicapped member of his family, and although he well knew that the Deafman was in no way mentally handicapped, indeed that he was on the contrary a very sharply observant and astutely contemplative man, he nevertheless treated him at times as condescendingly as he would a child or an adolescent. It may well have been that there was a kind of similarity between the two which went deeper than mere physical resemblance. Perhaps, too, the farmer suspected in his brother certain traits which he sensed to be present in himself, but which he could never countenance. By contrast, the Deafman's sister-in-law was an honest, kindhearted and affectionate woman who often reprimanded her obstinate husband for treating his brother badly. On no account was he prepared to let the Deafman drive the new FENDT FARMER, no one other than himself was to operate the machine, and although the old Bulldog was far more complicated to handle, he acted as if the new tractor were some kind of mechanical miracle that few people were clever enough to manage. This, of course, hurt the Deafman, but he soon came to terms with it. He carried on driving the Bulldog in masterly fashion and was in fact the only one who really knew this vehicle. Second gear was forever jamming, and there was nothing for it but to drive continually in a circle until, by wrenching, caressing and shaking in turn, you persuaded the gearbox to release its grip on the obstruction inside it. Don't let me catch anybody going out on my FENDT, the farmer kept saying, long after everyone had lost interest in arguing with him.

Whenever the children in the boarding school wanted to annoy the deaf man, they would shout Deafman after him. If he was able to make out the corresponding lip movements, he would become wild with rage and chase the children, but he never caught them, since he would not have known what to do with them if he had.

Raab felt sorry for him and never annoyed him, but on the contrary tried to be friendly towards him. This aroused only suspicion on the part of the man, who reacted dismissively to any friendly approach and pretended not to notice any sign of greeting. If he was offered cigarettes, he would pull them out of the packet and throw them on the ground, only to smoke them gratefully once he thought he was on his own. To Raab, the stern rejection in the man's gaze was thoroughly unjust, because, for some reason unknown to himself, he wanted to be liked and trusted by the Deafman. He even went so far as to buy cigarettes with what little money he had and to leave them on a bench at the edge of the wood, a place where the Deafman liked to sit, and to leave a comic-paper along with them. They were sure to give the deaf man some pleasure, because, in them, sounds were represented in words. For example, if a bell was ringing, then next to the drawing of the bell the word DONG would stand in heavy black letters. If someone was caught by an uppercut or got a black eye, the word WHACK appeared next to the picture in which the fist thumped into the chin or eye. And if a shot was fired from a revolver, of course there was a BANG.

One evening, at the time when the Deafman was working in the cowshed, Raab went to see if the cigarettes were still there and found the packet, filled to the brim with fresh cow dung. And the comic was gone.

Dew

AS IF DEATH were an aura that gently falls like dew on a house, a village, a town, and remains there and does not go away until still more dying has been done, two days later, quite unexpectedly and seemingly snatched away while in the best of health, the amiable and kindly caretaker gave up his last breath with a faint rattling sound.

He, too, died in the night.

A doctor on the emergency service came from the distant town; long before reaching the boarding school, he had both the siren and the flashing blue light switched off, not only because there was no longer anyone out and about on the road to impede his rapid progress, but also because the headmistress had asked him to avoid creating a stir. Fever claimed later that he had seen the ambulance drive up and had also seen it leave again without being used. And, an amazingly short time later, he had watched the undertaker's hearse arriving at top speed and, he related with a shudder, the men – one of them was the Meat Inspector who did indeed occasionally earn a bit of cash on the side as a funeral attendant, backache permitting – carrying the corpse out of the house in a coffin, minus its lid to cut down on the weight.

In the morning, the sad news was announced, and since the janitor had no relatives and the school effectively constituted his only family, the headmistress, along with one teacher and a representative of the senior pupils, had the task of choosing a suitable headstone for the man's grave. To this end, an old stone-mason rode up on his bicycle and, cursing at the infuriating and roundabout new detour cyclists had to negotiate since the arrival of the motorway, produced an A4 ring-binder with photographs of sample stones set out in transparent plastic sleeves. In addition, he invited the selection committee to visit his workshop, where they could view the stones in their natural state.

Raab declined the chance to go along, for he believed that, in a monumental sculptor's workshop such as that, not only the stones were piled up and stored, but the dead bodies as well. He convinced the other pupils of this, and so it was agreed that they should select a headstone from the photographs.

The Complications-Notebook

IN THE EVENING, Fever and Raab went to their bench at the edge of the wood for a secret smoke. Fever walked a few paces ahead, in case it might come to a race for the only dry spot. And Raab saw him picking up something lying under the seat and hastily stuffing it in his pocket. What have you got there? he asked, and Fever, like it or not, had to pull the package out of his jacket again. It was a comic, neatly wrapped in plastic film. That's mine, said Raab and pocketed the comic.

That same evening, after dinner, he went back to the spot and laid another comic under the bench. He had already turned and gone a few steps when he hesitated a moment before turning back to light a cigarette. He sat down on the arm of the bench, as it had got rather damp, and rummaged in his pockets, but he had been in such a hurry that he had forgotten his matches. In his annoyance, he was about to get up and head straight back to the school, but he was startled, as if struck by lightning, when, right next to his face, a lighter sprang to life in an enormously long tongue of flame. Without a sound, the Deafman had crept up behind him and had probably been standing there for some time. He realised that he had given Raab a fright, slapped him heartily on the shoulder, walked round the bench and sat down beside him. The two of them sat smoking and staring into the darkness. Their faces glowed reddishly in the light of the two tiny burning points of their cigarettes. Raab had no idea how long they had been sitting there like that before the Deafman thrust a school exercise book into his hand.

He had seen an exercise book exactly like it that night the calf had been born. The Deafman, for his part, gathered up the comics from under the seat, thumped him on the other shoulder and disappeared into the night. Raab watched the red dot as it receded, like some glow-worm, becoming smaller, tinier, and abruptly disappearing as if it had been extinguished. He hurried home, took himself off to his room and examined the blue-covered exercise book.

On the front, in large letters that looked as if they had been copied from those in the comics, were written the words COMPLICATIONS-NOTEBOOK.

Inside, after numerous quotations from the regulations governing meat inspection, which the Deafman seemed to know almost by heart, there were drawings, some of them with speech-balloons, some with thought-bubbles growing out of their heads like clouds of smoke. The Deafman had done an extraordinary drawing of himself, with huge ears and an enormous nose, but no mouth; the heavily outlined figure with the paunch must be Fever, the matchstick man with two tiny breasts and tousled hair was unmistakably Andre, the one with the big breasts was The Victim, and he himself had been drawn completely in black, his clothes as well as his face, so that neither mouth nor nose nor eyes could be made out. All the same, Raab immediately had the feeling, that's me.

All of them were wearing wellington boots, the headmistress had on a dress, coloured in with an ordinary lead pencil, and large spectacles, and in front of her stomach the Deafman had drawn, to Raab's particular amazement, a mixture of a phallus and a floating egg.

Now he understood why the Deafman had written COMPLICATIONS-NOTEBOOK on the cover, for he saw people as being not simple but complicated, and what he was trying to say was not easy to convey, but complicated, and the way he viewed things, they were not straightforward but complicated.

Raab pondered. Would the Deafman, since he could neither hear nor speak, ever be able to understand complicated things, and, if not, would this inevitably cause him suffering? This thought made Raab infinitely sad, and in that state he fell asleep.

The next morning, Fever had a look at the Deafman's drawings. He said, You look like a raven, all black like that. Quite right, the others agreed, Raab looks like a raven. There's something dark about him, they said. From that time on, the pupil Raab was known as Raabe – the Raven.

Bad Luck

THE HEADMISTRESS OF the boarding school drafted two advertisements and handed them in at the newspaper office. On the Saturday, people throughout the region were able to read: Established boarding school requires caretaker (janitor). Three pages further on, the second intimation announced: Taken from us in the midst of life . . .

No later than the Sunday, an enormous automobile – the pupils had swarmed round it immediately – drew up in the school yard. One or two of the children did have rich parents or relatives, but a car like that had never driven in here before. A small man got out, attempted a shy smile and hesitantly pushed his way through the crowd of youngsters.

His face looked as crumpled as his clothes, he smelt of a

night's sweat, and in his car could be seen blankets and the traces of several nights having been spent in it. Apart from the clothes he stood up in, a tube of brilliantine and twenty-four litres of 4-star petrol, the car was the sum total of his possessions. Excuse me, could you tell me where I can find the headmistress? he asked.

Everything will be all right, it will all turn out for the best, things will run their proper course, and there's a reason for everything, even if it is often a long time in revealing itself.

These and similar observations the new caretaker had off pat for the pupils whenever they seemed to be in despair about something, whenever they suffered some mishap, whenever they felt they were about to be overwhelmed by unhappiness or whenever misfortune dogged them most cruelly.

He – his name was Glück, or 'Good Luck' – was the very man to know all about that sort of thing, for within only a few days it was common knowledge how desperately he needed his unshakeable optimism. He had told part of his story to the headmistress, to arouse her compassion; the rest was well known to some of the pupils already, since Herr Glück's fate had been the talk of the town for some time.

Just once in his life, this little man, who used brilliantine to fix his hair in a quiff, had had good fortune heaped upon him. As a result of a surprise inheritance, he fell heir to a medium-sized car business. He was a passionate motor enthusiast, a passion which, for lack of money, he had been unable to pursue. With suitable dedication, he set about managing this hitherto flourishing business. At first he even made small profits, which encouraged him to indulge his passion to an increasing degree; he was consumed by a deep, almost sexual love of American limousines of the fifties. The angular, aggressively jutting tail-fins of a DE SOTO FIREDOM

SPORTSMAN, with their triple tail-lights, sent a shiver through him, and the soft top of his FORD FAIRLANE SKYLINER, which folded back as if at the bidding of some magic hand, afforded him moments of rare pleasure. He acquired the first of his cars, and was in a state of bliss for weeks. He set the vehicle up on display in his showrooms and watched, in ecstasy, as little knots of customers walked round this car while they forgot about the small or middle-of-the-range one that they had had a mind to buy. He bought himself a second, a third car, each one of them a veritable cruiser, which made every other vehicle in what was in fact a spacious showroom seem superfluous and out of place.

Sales declined rapidly. Figures moved from the black into the red, profits became debts, so that his monthly interest payments themselves amounted to the price of a small car such as was no longer to be found on his premises. Soon he was forced to put the first cruiser in his fleet on the market at a collector's price – and then to sell it well below its real value. Its loss affected him badly, as if someone close to him had passed away. He grieved, for weeks on end it was as if he were paralysed, life seemed to him pointless and grey. Soon, because his despondency had rendered him unfit for work, he had to put his second leviathan up for sale, a move he was driven to by the bank's inability to comprehend his passion for these mobile pieces of real estate. His mental state became as ruinous as his business situation.

With his spirits at their nadir, he was forced to consider giving up the business. He wanted to dispose of his firm with the minimum possible loss, though here he was thinking not in terms of financial losses but of his limousines. He was prepared for the worst, and swore to himself, if I can keep my Cadillac, I'll be the happiest of men for the rest of my life. He managed that, even though he had to sacrifice everything else to do it. His family ostracised him, his flat was repossessed by the bank, his reputation was in tatters.

When he pulled up at the school to be interviewed for the vacant caretaker's post, people at first thought, this gentleman must be joking, for he had grown up there and had been enrolled at the school as the son of the rich car dealer, Glück. Since a pupils' committee, who quite fancied the idea of borrowing a car like that now and again, had a say in the choice of candidate, and since he was a former pupil, who could not be refused such a request, he was given the job. From that moment on, he was indeed the happiest of men, come what may, he took the view that everything would be all right, it would all turn out for the best, things would run their proper course, and there was a hidden reason for everything, which, in the fullness of time, would be revealed. The man groomed his Cadillac and his brilliantined quiff, and was known to all as Bad Luck.

Reputation

TEN, FIFTEEN YEARS previously, the boarding school had enjoyed a reputation for exclusivity, so that numerous wealthy parents belonging to so-called better circles had sent their children to it. Year by year, however, this special reputation dwindled. Rumour had it that, since the old headmaster's death, common people had been accepted as boarders. The headmaster was an old army type who had had the good fortune, thanks to his having a Jewish cousin, to fail to make a career for himself under the Nazis. Thus he was regarded as beyond reproach and he maintained the best of relations with the occupying power. Men of his stamp were few and far between in those days. He would have been happiest wearing a uniform at all times, but that was out of the question then. So he acquired through an acquaintance, a British colonel, two bales of best Scottish tweed and had three suits made, all identical and interchangeable. This, then, became his camouflage uniform. Thanks to his reputation and his connections, the boarding school prospered, but after his death from a stroke brought on by an astronomical cholesterol level – he knew then, all right, why he would have been better to lead the spartan life of a soldier – his daughter used the remaining bale of tweed to have three equally identical suits made and stepped boldly into her father's shoes.

Now the footprints that the closet general had, metaphorically speaking, left behind were the kind and size made by hob-nailed army boots, whereas her feet were shod in flat-heeled college-girl shoes. Insecure, irresolute and confused, she hopped from one footstep to the next and soon had the feeling herself that she would never make an adequate successor to her father. Yet the iron discipline of her good breeding forbade her ever giving up the position she had assumed, the legacy she had inherited, the task imposed on her by her father. *Vorwärts, Vorwärts*, had always been her father's exhortation, Advance, Advance, whenever she had approached him with a problem.

The first sign of the decline of a private school, the general once said, is the acceptance of day pupils. The second sign, he said ten years later, is the merest suggestion of the intellectual baggage of a mixed-sex school.

Dutifully she strode on, then, the pupils dwindled in number year by year and came from less genteel families, the income from fees, which were fixed according to parental earnings, continued to diminish. Only a few pupils were now so-called boarders, the majority were day pupils or went home at weekends. Then the boarding school was converted to a co-educational institution, as the changing times dictated.

Since the headmistress was a classic example of a spinster – the pupils could tell just from looking at her that she had never slept with a man in her life – many a rumour was spun round her lifestyle.

In fact a particular incident did occur, which caused something of a sensation. There was one sixth-form boy with brown eyes and jet-black hair, with whom all the girls, without exception, fell in love. He had a soft voice, and when women were near him, they felt the urge to touch him. Apparently the headmistress was not immune to this; the enraptured glances, the bouts of confusion during lessons, the moments of absent-mindedness, the sudden pauses in the middle of sentences, all those were enough to trigger off a dreadful rumour. The headmistress of the boarding school had fallen in love with a pupil. No one who knew her thought her capable of laying a finger on him, yet the spiciest rumours soon detach themselves from fact. And it all got out beyond the confines of the school, it reached the ears of the boy's parents, and the parents of the other pupils, and now there was a minor scandal when the boy's parents sent him off to another school shortly before his final examinations to save his soul from harm. At his new school, everyone knew of the reason for his transfer, he was made fun of, the teachers, especially the female ones, were inhibited in their dealings with him, he became the butt of jokes and ridicule, felt insecure, became nervous and could no longer concentrate and ended up by failing his *Abitur* and having to resit the examinations a year later at yet another school.

In such so-called better circles, word of an occurrence of that sort spread with the speed of a bushfire. Only Fever's family were too *nouveaux* among the *riches* to get the message, and so Fever was now really the only son from a wealthy background to attend the boarding school.

The Correct Measure

WHEN, AFTER HIS first early morning attempt at passing water, the farmer came back into the bedroom in a state of shock, looking like death and with a cold sweat standing out on his forehead, it was because he had found streaks of blood in his urine.

Right! Tomorrow you're going to the doctor, his wife ordered.

I'll go tomorrow, he said.

The next day, he put off the visit to the doctor until the following one. Then again he said he couldn't go into town in these old clothes, not to the doctor's, not to be seen among people. And the farmer's wife finally convinced her husband that he had to buy himself a new suit.

The procedure was as follows: the wife had to drive into town and go to the gents' outfitters to pick out four, maybe five suits which were not to cost any more than a certain amount and were on no account to have tight-fitting trousers and were not to be any colour other than somewhere between grey and black. With this collection, she made her way home, although it had been no easy task to convince the shopkeeper of the necessity for such a rigmarole.

For several days, the man had to be left alone with the suits for a few hours, until he was at last ready to try on two of them in front of his wife. Even then, he opened the bedroom door no more than a crack and hastily beckoned her in. There was not a scrap of material to be seen as he did so, indeed he behaved as if he were stark naked and was trying to hide some dreadful rash from view. Finally he decided in favour of a pin-striped model that in fact looked extremely good on him, only the trouser legs had not been taken up and stitched. So how was the tailor now supposed to get the length right without a fitting? The farmer's wife tried to measure it off with a ruler, but her husband would not stand still. They got all mixed up, and when she brought the trousers back, they were a good hand's breadth too short.

Anyway, the Deafman got his brother's old suit as a hand-me-down.

His sister-in-law did her utmost to impress upon him that he was to take care of the suit and, above all, not to wear it in the cowshed or the pigsty. But the Deafman was so fond of the suit that he forgot to change out of it before doing the mucking out. So he did the next best thing and took the jacket off and hung it on a nail. He mucked out the pigs, first the big ones, then the small ones. And when he was finished and went back to fetch his jacket, the big sows had chewed it away right up to the breast pocket.

Ashes and Frost

RAVEN'S FATHER WAS due to return home after working abroad in the fur trade, but what came instead was a black-bordered registered letter announcing the imminent arrival of his father in the form of ashes sealed in a zinc box. His mother reacted with composure, her bearing was impeccable, it almost seemed as if she had had a premonition of her husband's death. But her world collapsed when the promised urn failed to arrive. Somewhere, along the mail routes between Quebec and London, Father had gone astray. He had completely dissipated, dispersed into black and grey dust, grains with a few particles of bones mixed among them, and nobody even knew whether he was completely or only partially missing, or was renouncing his family, or for that matter what parts of his body had remained behind in an alien land, a land that gets extremely hot in summer and extraordinarily cold in winter, where people are reluctant to bury bodies in winter, but prefer to cremate them, since the permafrost does not begin to relent until June, and then only for a month or two. It often happened, so they said, that the frost would force coffins up out of the earth like wooden mushrooms.

So how could Raven ever comprehend that a death had occurred? Even now, his memory of his father still had an odour of naphthalene clinging to it, the smell of the pelts, redolent at one and the same time of life, of something wild, and of death, decay and embalmment.

And as for the story of his father's career, he knew nothing of that either; had he started out as a dresser of furs, rising to be a dealer, or had he been a hunter, setting snares, a trapper? How he would have loved to counter Fever's boasts by saying his father was a trapper.

Fever would not have been prepared to accept that Raven's father might have had such an adventurous profession. He took a peculiar, oafishly malicious delight in persistently telling Raven stories about his father. According to these he was supposed to be living abroad and had been unfaithful to both wife and son and had deserted them. Or again he had been killed in a gunfight with the police, an unheroic bank robber who had taken a helpless old lady hostage. Deep down, Raven did not believe a word of all this, yet these stories did not pass through his mind without having some effect.

Pleasures Shared

When Raven had first got to know him, Fever was a fat, quiet child who disliked any kind of exercise, was reluctant to leave his bed of a morning and was inclined to give even the slightest obstacle a wide berth. He was a whiner, an idler, with an excessive need for tender affection and warmth. His surname was Liebherr, and he came from a well-to-do family, his father owning a hotel. But Liebherr was soon to be known to everyone only as Fever.

At first he attracted attention because at every opportunity he would spend all day in bed; at the slightest hint of a cold, he would insist he had a bad dose of flu, he was dizzy, he was hot. He would be threatened with having his temperature taken, because no one believed him. Initially, they made do with putting the thermometer under his armpit, but later, after he had sorely tried the patience of the sisters, they would insert it, with the aid of Vaseline, into his backside, allegedly in the interest of greater accuracy, but really because they wanted to put a curb on Fever's malingering. Raven felt sorry for him and taught him how the mercury could be made to climb just by rubbing the thermometer, and this met with considerable success, but soon Fever found even the rubbing too much bother and helped things along with a cigarette lighter that he had cadged off his brother for the purpose. The result was that one of the nuns told Fever they would have to call a priest right away, for nobody had ever survived running a temperature of over a hundred and twenty. From that day on, the pupil Liebherr became known to all and sundry as Fever.

Fever had taken a great liking to Raven, for he was very placid, didn't bully him, didn't tease him and often even passed him his leftovers at table. For a while, Raven was Fever's hero. Whenever Raven wanted to go for a walk on his own, Fever would beg to be allowed to go with him. And when Raven tried to explain to him that he really wanted to be alone, Fever, too, started to take solitary walks. When Raven no longer got any pleasure out of his walks, Fever lost the notion of them as well. He also liked touching him and tried to involve him in bouts of rough and tumble, just to have him close, but Raven was the one person in the whole place who did not enjoy these scuffles and, to get things over with quickly, he would concede defeat at once, which in turn gave Fever the impression that he was strong.

Raven would always get up early in the morning, to hear what birds were first to sing at whatever time of year. Hardly had he dressed and left the room without a sound and without looking back at the sleeping Fever, when the latter would open his eyes, dress too, and follow Raven. Raven moved as lithely as a cat, twigs and bushes seemed to fall back and yield before him without him touching them.

Fever created a noise when he walked, sounding like a cow crashing through the undergrowth. He stepped on branches, which broke with a loud crack under his weight, he managed to conjure noises out of the dry leaves on which he trod that made it sound as if the forest was burning like a torch, he talked loudly and a lot, sang and whistled so much himself that the birds fluttered up in startled swarms instead of getting on with their singing and whistling.

Raven quickened his pace, went deeper into the wood and said nothing. Fever followed him like a dog, trotted clumsily after him, broke even more branches, and his torrent of words was unceasing. He took Raven's silence for close attention and recognised in it a facility of which he was not possessed and which, albeit in secret, he admired, since he himself, even when he made an extreme effort to pull himself together, could never hope to achieve it. If he was examining an object, first his toes would begin to twitch, then his fingers twitched, then his thoughts twitched and then his eyes and his whole being would twitch off to the next thing, which he would abandon just as quickly and twitch on towards the next again. So his ponderous body was in a state of perpetual fidgeting even if nothing was visible to the watching eye and he would break out in a sweat for no reason at all, his breath becoming a panting, without any outwardly perceptible signs of exertion manifesting themselves. More and more, people thought he was weak and sickly, but could find no cause, and thus they fostered his malingering. In the end, Raven felt increasingly uncomfortable in Fever's unwanted and, as time passed, more and more insufferable company and he became irritable and waspish – which Fever did not notice, since he never listened and thus never gave a second thought to anything anyone said to him. Raven became really nasty, but Fever remained unaware of it, every unpleasantness bounced off him, since Raven's malice was much more refined in style than Fever's coarse brand of it.

Now he wanted to outwit him, so he got up even earlier, when it was still pitch dark, and he managed not to bump into anything and to leave the room soundlessly and in complete darkness. But when he had at last succeeded in hearing the birds wake up, just once, Fever crashed out of the bushes soon after, shouting loudly and scaring off everything that could fly; from then on, he watched like a lynx to make sure that Raven did not shake him off again.

Wanted to give me the slip, didn't you, he said, panting and grinning. You'll really have to be up early for that, he gasped, and hid his wounded feelings behind a high-pitched giggle that was supposed to sound superior.

Later on, when Raven had to go for long walks to be alone with the turmoil in his hormones, his testicles, his penis and his thoughts, he went so far as to rebuff Fever gruffly, thump him in the midriff and chase him off with digs in the ribs, even to throw stones at him, when he insisted on accompanying him. And yet it came about that Fever, who over the years had learned to creep along surprisingly quietly, was suddenly sitting there, two bushes further ahead, eavesdropping on his solitude, his thoughts on his busy preoccupation with his penis, and Fever watched briefly in amazement, reflected for a moment before taking out his member, too. As he did so, he turned slightly to one side, away from Raven, so that he would not be able to see something that was of absolutely no interest to him anyway.

From his big brother he had heard a saying that he hadn't quite understood: masturbating's more fun, but with screwing you meet a lot more people.

Fever watched carefully what Raven was doing, and followed suit exactly.

The Strong and the Silent

THREE DAYS AFTER a visit home by the girl – her father was dead and her mother was married again, to a man who was himself a widower and had two children – the headmistress noticed an odd change in Andre's behaviour. For two whole days, she had hardly spoken at all, although that was nothing out of the ordinary. But now she seemed to hear nothing either. Her eyes stared into space and when she was spoken to there was no visible response whatsoever. She refused to leave her bed, and when the sister, who had put her strange behaviour down to some act of defiance or a piece of bad manners, took her temperature, she was running such a high fever that the headmistress got out her own car and drove her straight to the district hospital in town.

Quite unwittingly, the girl's very absence had the effect of making Raven notice her. Because she wasn't there, he found her pretty; because she, who never said much at the best of times, was now completely silent as she was no longer there, he found her mysterious; because she was ailing, he took her to be delicate, and because she had chosen her own name for herself, he regarded her as being strong. He told all this to Fever. All he said was, there's nothing strong about leaving out an A, I'll show you what strength is. Fever, who had hitherto tended towards lethargy, was becoming aware of his cunning, his size and his physical strength and now attempted to demonstrate to anyone and everyone what strength was all about.

Down among the Mushrooms

ON THAT SUNDAY morning when the Deafman was going to teach Raven all about mushrooms, the church bells were chiming for early Mass. The farmer's wife placed a large pail of milk by the door of the white-tiled dairy for the janitor to collect later, the milking machines were humming and sucking, the cat snuggled up, shivering and purring, against the warming, gleaming chrome machine.

Bad Luck had parked his Cadillac in the forecourt and was happily washing and polishing and sucking too, with his vacuum cleaner; he lay under, in and on his limousine. These were his happiest hours.

The Deafman amazed Raven by saying DONG every time the big bell chimed, and it was a puzzle to Raven how he could be aware of it. The Deafman made Raven put his hand on his stomach, until he thought that he too could feel the vibrations caused by the stroke of the bell on the Deafman's diaphragm.

Humidity lay heavy in the air and was sucked up by hair, clothes and plants alike. On such a morning, then, the Deafman went into the wood with Raven to give him his introduction to the mushrooms.

The farmers never ate mushrooms, they mistrusted these treacherous plants, but the chemist had given the Deafman a handbook on mushrooms as a present and the Deafman had picked up all he knew from this book, although he never had complete confidence in his knowledge. More than anything, it was the names of the mushrooms that intrigued him. Like the Ringed Flame-Cap, where you could tell by the sound of it that it was inedible and would cause a burning in you, just as the Flat Cripple's-Foot, its colleague the Club-Foot with its gelatinous flesh and the Tripe Fungus aroused more pity than appetite, while the Jew's Ear had something deceitful about it and the Yellow Brain Fungus had an unapproachable ring to it. Nevertheless, from time to time he sold a chip-basketful of them to the chemist, who was a mushroom enthusiast but no lover of fresh forest air and left his camphor-smelling house only when he absolutely had to. They had no idea whether he ate the mushrooms or made medicines out of them, but certainly, every time the Deafman brought him mushrooms, the chemist was highly delighted and quite happily paid a pretty high price for them, throwing in a few throat pastilles or a nasal spray into the bargain.

The time of year and the humid weather were driving the mushrooms out of the ground so quickly you could almost have watched them grow. The maggots and snails could creep around and feed as greedily as they liked, they still could not keep pace with the sprouting mushrooms that year. The Bronze Boletus with its velvety, church-bell shaped cap was the first they found. The Deafman swung it to and fro, for Raven to memorise the colour, and he invented names that fitted the fungi even better.

1. DONG, he wrote in his notebook.

Very close by, but hidden behind a bush – the Deafman must have smelt them – stood a whole family of Bay-capped Boletus. The Deafman showed Raven how the flesh stained blue when you touched it and broke a piece off.

2. CRASH, he wrote in the notebook.

Striding out purposefully, the Deafman led the way to a large clearing, on which two oak trees stood, with thousands of droplets falling from their yellowing leaves and creating a gentle yet busy kind of sound which mingled with the light sighing of the breeze. In the grass there was a group of round-topped white mushrooms, which the Deafman examined minutely. They had pretty white gills and exuded a pleasant aroma of old potatoes, the farmers' staple diet. Their stems were ringed by a little frill of skin as if they had put on a collar. Some of them had already spread their caps, others lay in the grass like eggs. They looked very sweet and trustworthy. With great care, the Deafman picked one of the mushrooms and scrutinised the bulb that had been stuck in the earth and overlapped the stem a little. With a look of alarm, he dropped the fungus. He put a finger to his temple like a pistol, pressed the trigger and wrote

3. BANG.

Raven was amazed that a mushroom that smelled so good and looked so harmless should have such lethal effects, and made a mental note of its appearance.

The sounds had changed, the wind was no longer rustling, all that was to be heard was the multiple dripping from the autumn leaves, it was getting a little darker, heavy clouds were pushing their way across the sky. It seemed to Raven as if the birds had all at once stopped singing. Uneasily, he looked around. The Deafman too had noticed a change, his nostrils flared, he looked to the sky and frowned.

Both of them were seized by an overwhelming apprehension. So they decided to head for home. Hardly had they left the wood when the sky was lying almost on top of them as if they were walking along the bed of some cloudy-green, filthy lake. The cat was no longer lying next to the milking machine. It was running up and down with its tail steeply erect, the tip whipping around in the air, the fur on the back of its neck standing on end. If it had been bigger, it could have been quite frightening. Raven went over to pick up the waiting pail of milk and take it to the school, but when he lifted the lid, the smell immediately told him the milk had turned.

The water level of the lake that was the sky dropped and pressed down on the landscape, the houses, the animals and on the people as well as on the mushrooms and the milk.

Bad Luck had switched off his vacuum cleaner and was looking apprehensively at the sky, at the surface, for he too stood on the bed of the lake, and he feared for his car. He made a hurried attempt to close the soft top, but in his haste it got even more thoroughly snagged until it was impossible to disentangle. He leapt into the car and drove it over to the old shed that stood near by, a crooked, dark building constructed out of heavy, almost blackened oak beams. There his defenceless car would find shelter, for what was about to come, it was now quite obvious, was a storm, the weight of which was already crushing heavily down on everything, things creaked under the brewing trouble, and suddenly the wind rose violently after the dead calm. The sky hung only a few metres above them, it was now sea-green, sulphur-yellow and grey-blue, and birds, already being tossed about by the gusts, flew low over their heads. There was an evil smell in the air, it quickly turned to a stench. The foulest odours were wrung from the remotest corners by the atmospheric pressure and they rose up and hung in the confined space, the lake between heaven and earth. Just as a relieved Bad Luck had left his car and hurriedly run over to the school building, the rain started. It was the kind of rain that did in fact threaten to submerge everything in an actual lake. The thunder made the windows tremble as they reflected the lightning flashes, and people were only too relieved to be sitting under their roofs. The leaves swirled like a heavy fall of snow and, the next instant, were stamped to the ground by the massive drops. Anything not nailed down was swept away and the crooked shed began to tilt, the rusty nails snapped and the enormous weight of the oak beams forced everything to collapse in on itself, crushing Bad Luck's Cadillac absolutely flat.

Temper

THE GREAT STORM was followed by three muggy days. Then it turned cold. For four nights in a row, there had been an unusually early frost. A thin skin of ice had formed on the pond when Raven believed he had fallen in love for the first time. He was not quite sure, for he had always taken the view that you could only fall in love in the spring. After her return from hospital, the girl was still extremely taciturn, more than that, completely silent, for she did not exchange a word with a soul throughout the first few days. She was small, delicate, fragile, and she hid her thin body from the world under a heavy motor cyclist's jacket which seemed about to drag her down with its weight and yet at the same time appeared to keep her upright with its stiffness. She was very pale and where her straggly hair hid her eyes and touched her forehead, she had a lot of tiny pimples which she worked incessantly at eradicating. And Raven loved her for every one of these little pimples, and he would have loved her still more if the expression in her eyes, which only occasionally flashed from behind the curtain of hair, had been even more timorous, even more mistrustful. The first word she uttered after her arrival was her name. The headmistress introduced her at the evening meal. This, she said, was Andrea. But the girl cut in with a startling, violent rage in her voice. Andre. At all costs she wanted to be called Andre, she detested the name Andrea. She went into tantrums, tears sprang to her eyes and, once already, driven by a towering fury, she had thrown a pair of scissors at Fever who, to tease her, had called her Andrea. The small, blunt scissors stuck, still quivering with the power of the girl's anger, in a door that Fever had managed to close behind himself in the nick of time.

Next time, you're dead, she added. From that moment on, no one ever called the girl anything but Andre.

During that time there were several other outbursts of temper in the boarding school. Fever had a nasty habit of dealing out unexpected clouts with his knuckles to people's heads. After he had been caught by it a few times, even Raven felt the first spark of anger glowing within him. These knuckle-raps on the head were less painful than the bitter taste they brought to his mouth for some strange reason, a taste which in turn reminded him of an occasion when a teacher had boxed his ears in a most humiliating way. Raven threatened Fever that if he clouted him once more, he would do his business in Fever's bed when he least suspected it. Fever considered the threat for a day or two, but then either forgot it or reckoned that Raven wasn't serious. In the RE lesson, he gave Raven's head a rattle with his knuckles. Two days later, he found, on waking from a deep sleep, an evil-smelling pile in his bed. In a rage, he ran to the headmistress and said Raven had shit in his bed. For his choice of vocabulary, he received a strong reprimand. And on top of that he had to wash his bed linen himself, since the headmistress was convinced he had soiled his own bed, which appearances certainly suggested.

Fever loved to get Raven irritated by his ability to lock and unlock doors. On one occasion Raven went down into the laundry cupboard in the cellar to fetch fresh tablecloths. The door to this store was never locked, but Fever, by way of a joke, locked it with his skeleton keys. Raven, faced by a locked door, turned around and went to ask the caretaker for the key. Bad Luck never handed out keys, so he came with him to open up. In the meantime, Fever had unlocked it again and now watched with glee as Bad Luck gave Raven a cuff round the ear and accused him of playing silly games with him.

This was witnessed, with a thoroughly disapproving eye, by the headmistress, who warned the janitor never to lay a finger on a pupil again.

Bad Luck had exchanged his Cadillac, which was fit only for the scrap heap, for a motor-bike, on which he wanted to go for a brisk spin that evening to work the reprimand out of his system. But there was a nail as long as his thumb stuck in the rear tyre.

Fever wore a leather draw-string bag hanging round his neck; in it he kept everything of value to him, for just as he entertained a most unconventional view of property and was consumed by a great curiosity, an urge to rummage about in other people's cupboards, he also regarded his room-mates with considerable suspicion. This pouch he called his medicine-bag, and in it he had collected a few small stones and two broken quartz watches which he treated with a superstitious reverence, as he also did his skeleton keys which he had got from his brother. If ever Raven wanted to threaten Fever, then he would say he would take this bag from him.

Animals in the Far Distance

LOVE, MY TREASURE, is manual work in our case; two hands, the man has, and the third hand is you.

That little dolly drips like a gravel lorry, said Fever about the girl known to all as The Victim.

Because of the tendency of some of the parts of her body to expand even in her childhood, she caught the eye, for her breasts were the biggest in the place, and she set the boys' imaginations aflame with her conspicuously feminine figure. She was well-rounded and good-natured, simple and none too bright, and saying no was something she had never learnt. She never wanted to draw attention to herself, and she would have preferred to take up as little space as possible, she had no wish to possess anything, to keep anything and, least of all, to make a fuss over anything. For a long time, no one wished her any harm, and Fever was the first to lay hands on The Victim. It all happened in an overheated basement room, in the fug of many cigarettes, under the influence of sweet drinks like apple schnapps, cola with cherry brandy – Fever called these drinks leg-spreaders, a phrase he got from his brother. And later, any time she spoke about sexual topics, she would do so with extreme indifference and would say, And then I did you-know-what.

The music came in a distorted, agonised scream from the small radio that was gradually self-destructing through regular over-strain, and bounced with a clatter from the concrete walls of the room, on which the grain of the wooden moulds was clearly visible. That was why Bad Luck had painted one wall of this cellar brown, in an attempt to create a cosier, warmer, timber effect. He was trying to make the best of a bad job. Just like wood panelling, he would say, gazing with pride at the wall.

Fever had developed the habit of going up to her, seizing her round the hips, making a grab at her breasts or between her legs and not really kissing her but mechanically shoving his tongue into her mouth, the same way all his graspings and gropings were performed with unvarying, robot-like movements.

The Victim was used to Fever's sudden attacks and had done you-know-what for him on several occasions already, becoming progressively more apathetic about it each time. She felt neither arousal nor desire. Nor did she experience disgust when she did it. Only some hours later would she sniff her hand and then wash it, wash it again and again, yet despite her efforts, she felt, there was still a peculiar smell clinging to her fingers. Soon Fever boasted he could stick his tongue right to the root into her throat and lick her uvula, 'the dangler in her throat', which, he maintained, tasted of malt sweets, without making her gag, and he went so far as to claim she also took his dick in her mouth.

Go on, show us, some of them shouted. Fever's a pig and that's why he's got a pecker like a pig's, like a pig's curly tail.

Fever flushed and kept quiet, the others laughed some more but soon they also fell silent, staring in shock at Fever's face which was still bright red, with the muscles around his chin standing out gruesomely. His neck, too, seemed to have gone completely rigid, and Fever was breathing quickly and loudly and his hand rubbed against the brown concrete wall, running over the grain of the shuttering wood, until drops of blood stood out on the torn skin. He was afraid of losing the respect he had gained through his acts of impudence and aggression. If he had previously believed he would never be able to earn the respect and certainly not the affection and admiration of the others because he was listless, awkward and immobile like a walrus on the rocks, now he felt he was about to forfeit all he had achieved at such laborious and cruel cost to himself and to others unless he immediately pulled his thing out of his trousers. In fact he was afraid of having an ugly cock, but all the same an ugly cock was better than none at all and he certainly didn't have a curly pig's tail of a cock, and if anybody tried to say he had, then he'd tell them, Anybody that doesn't like it, I'll stick it in them. None of them would dare to make fun of him, that was for sure.

All this rushed through his mind, inside his head where all the blood was gathering, making his face redder and redder, and the thoughts themselves, he felt, were flashing, circulating and gathering in his neck, which he thought he could feel turning into a pig's neck, for he was a pig, he was now beginning to believe it himself, and so he felt compelled to grab the girl by the hand again and pull her towards him, to look round the silent company with his watery eyes, to push his cigarette into her mouth and pull it out again and throw it away and, with his other hand, grip her chin and pull it towards him, towards his mouth. Her lips opened slightly under the pressure of his grip between her jaw-bones and again he stuck his tongue into her mouth and claimed the dangler in her throat now tasted of HB cigarettes and malt sweets. And in fact she didn't feel the urge to gag, since, under his grip, she had turned off all her senses, as if she had some hidden switch within her. So he looked round them all, still holding the girl with his thumb and index and middle fingers between her jaws. He was watching to see whether he would have to go further.

They were all silent, only Raven gagged quietly instead of the girl, and he camouflaged his choking as a gurgling laugh, at which Fever was uncertain as to how he was supposed to interpret it. Was he laughing at the stupid girl or at his joke? So his gaze became irresolute and his brief triumph began to waver. How had the others' expressions changed when Raven laughed? Were their eyes now on Raven instead of him, or were they staring into space, were they nauseated or horrified? Were they fixed on his neck, which was a pig's neck, had turned into one and from this moment on would always remain a pig's neck?

He tried to count the pairs of eyes and could only count eyes, there were too many of them and he could no longer make out the expression in them. So he would have to go on, to distance himself from them and to be able to count them from afar, once they had become smaller. Until the pairs of eyes had become one eye, one dulled eye, an animal's eye, and then he could smash them all down, for they were far away from him, little animals, animals in the far distance, the cellar was a cave, damp and overheated, swathed in clouds of smoke and exhalations from the bodies in turmoil that the confined space forced to rub against each other, exchanging warmth or drawing warmth or giving off intense heat. All the warmth of these bodies, which for him had become animals' bodies, all this he added together until an enormous heat generated itself in his insides. He still held her jaws in his ever-tightening grip, her mouth opened wider and she felt pain that, unlike the nausea, she was unable to control. She gave a groan, quiet but audible to all, and Fever, who no longer realised how hard he was gripping, could not understand why she was groaning, she who usually never made a sound; in his state of inflamed excitement he would have been incapable of understanding anything at all, neither anything within himself nor anything about the others. His being at the mercy of the situation, the igniting of his senses, came to him as a pleasurable pain which he could share with no one. In that instant he was no longer aware that pain was a sensation which could strike everyone, he, he alone, he felt, was capable of experiencing pain; everything else was a lie, the cry of pain an empty cry, an animal cry.

So there was nothing left for him but to try to thrust his left hand into her trousers, which were too tight, tight blue jeans, and to feel for her knickers, to draw his moist hand back to the buttons on her trousers, to open them and to pull down the zip with his hand, shove his fat, increasingly clammy fingers back into her knickers, to feel her pubic hair, and beneath that to fumble for the opening, which, under his grip, had closed, and he knew and expected that this slit should have become damp by now and given off a secretion that was supposed to make penetration easier, but no secretion would come. And even though he was aware of everything else at a hazy distance, he registered this fact in all clarity and with the insight of the man of action, for he knew that he couldn't force his member into her, since her body had closed itself too tightly against him. He realised he had to carry out this demonstration of his strength another way. He opened his own trousers and pulled out his penis, for he had the feeling that it had to be brought out and shown to the world. He took her hand and led it to his member and worked it so that in a short time his semen spurted out over her thighs. And that, he said, that's what I'll do to any one of you; anybody that wants it, just say the word.

Feeling incredibly tough, and without the slightest doubt as to the keenness of both his gaze and his desire, he swept the basement with his eyes; they were all silent, as if they realised that one word, one sound, would call forth another demonstration of his strength. He was staring at his half-limp penis when Raven said, That's enough of that.

Don't you believe it, Fever retorted. D'you know whose turn it is now?

The neighbour's big sow.

Fever pointed to Andre. Raven stood up, sat down again.

Fever leaned forward and made a grab at Andre. Raven tore off the medicine-bag dangling in front of his chest and said, Pack it in, or else I'll throw this in the pond.

Fever made a lunge at Raven, Raven jumped to his feet and ran out. Fever was after him, the others following, until they formed a circle round the recently frozen pond.

Raven held the bag in his hand, Fever stared at him, turned towards Andre. Raven threw the bag out on to the ice, into the middle of the pond.

Fever's rage crumbled instantly, all the strength that he had wanted to display had been expended. The only thing he was worried about now was his bag. Raven saw that Fever was almost in tears, and stepped out on to the ice.

Death, a Machine

NOW IT'S CRUNCHING, cracks are appearing, spreading out from me like a cobweb, now there's some water forcing its way through the cracks, now my shoes are soaked through, at last I'm sinking right in and can feel, to my horror, how cold it is. Now the cold water is pushing into my nose, how beautifully the light is refracted in the ice above me. I can't expect any help, they want to watch as I drown, and it's my own fault, I didn't pass that one final and conclusive test. Can I break through the ice? How deep the pond is, I hadn't imagined it to be so deep. Will I be looking fish in the eye? Will I lose consciousness? I push against the ice, it's so thin that I fell through it, but it's too thick for me to break through it again. So this is death, this is what death is like. How clearly I can think. I'll be dead if the water gets into my lungs, so I'll shut my mouth, there would be no point in shouting, not for nothing are fish mute. I'm delaying death a little. Death is a machine made of ice and fish. It comes nearer and rumbles and chugs like a diesel engine. How does death work? Does it take on the shape of a fat man whom nobody knows? It certainly is not in the form of a skeleton stripped of flesh. No, death is a machine made of ice and fish, the whole works crowned with algae. Gently it's pushing its way into me and it's beginning to work away in my insides.

So this is what it's like when you die, thought Raven, once he found himself under the slabs of ice. He was astonished at how clearly his mind operated, how he could weigh up whether he could break through the thin ice and then reckon he would not manage it because he could not get a footing. Will she let Fever stick his tongue in her mouth? Will she caress his tongue with hers, will she allow him to take his dick out of his trousers and rub it until, despite the cold, it stiffens, will she let the stiff dick lie in her hand and become very warm and gently throb to the rhythm of his heartbeat? Will she stroke it until the white milky stuff sticks to her fingers and gives off its smell? How did my father beget me, did my mother get any pleasure out of it? When you die, do you get a stiff dick?

His imminent death seemed to him – one final conceit – exciting and beautiful. His father had slipped out of life so unobtrusively that Raven was never able really to believe that someone close to him had passed away; the loss of his father had never been able to trigger off any tears. Soon he had the feeling that his father was still alive and had simply left his mother and himself in the lurch. This wounded him, and his hurt robbed him of any yearning ever to see his father again – assuming he was still alive.

After his father's death, after his disappearance on his travels, his mother was no longer in a position to keep her son at home with her. In earlier times she had liked a drink, now she drank steadily and much more, and on top of that she often took medicines. Her uncle, who ran a chemist's shop with a drug dispensary, provided her with the appropriate pills when the doctors were no longer prepared to prescribe them for her.

First of all it was sleeping tablets, so long as she hadn't had a drink, then tranquillisers, then stimulants and then back to alcohol. Raven loved his mother more when she had been drinking. She didn't laugh so much at other times. How droll visitors always found it, when the barely five-year-old lad would offer to fetch wine for his mother and then use every trick in the book to get her drunk.

From very early on, Raven was pretty worldly wise. His mother was therefore able to explain to him that his time in the boarding school would be the best chance for him to get his youth behind him, so as to be no longer dependent on anyone. That was the thing she was always dinning into him: Be dependent on nobody.

The chemist had recommended the boarding school out in the country, not too far from the small town where he had his business. That way he'd be able to keep an eye on the boy, too.

With some bafflement, the Deafman, who was clearing away the debris of the collapsed shed, saw the children standing motionless around the pond. They were staring at the hole out of which bubbles were rising, getting smaller and smaller. He tried to crash out of second gear – it was still jamming – to bring the Bulldog to a halt, but to no effect. The engine refused to stall or shut off, so he leapt from the old rattletrap as it dawdled along, seized a plank with an axe stuck in it, tore the tailboard off the trailer and was at the pond as quickly as his burden would allow. Roughly, he shoved the bystanders aside, threw the plank down on the ice, gripped the axe and, lying flat on his stomach, pushed himself out towards the middle of the pond.

Raven still had his eyes open and was looking upwards. This is it, he was thinking, when something dark slid across above him, he heard noises and then he could remember only a short, sharp pain as he was grabbed by the hair.

With a few blows of his heavy axe, the Deafman had broken a large hole in the skin of ice, he reached in and managed to grip Raven by the hair; with all the strength that desperation lent him he pulled and heaved the dripping victim to the surface. A good handful of hair flew ownerless on to the ice as the Deafman brought Raven back to life with a thump from his great fist. He vomited up several litres of water and, coughing and spluttering, regained consciousness in the arms of the Deafman who was clasping him round the chest and squeezing him repeatedly to try to pump the last of the icy water out of him.

The tractor had already uprooted three young apple trees in the school garden and was heading towards the caretaker's motor-cycle, his pride and joy; it was an old BMW, and when the tractor had trundled over the machine only the fuel tank and the front fork of the solidly built chassis were damaged and the mirror, a recent addition, broken off. The drive shaft and the gearbox were not even so much as scratched. *German craftsmanship*, the Deafman wrote in his little book after he had brought his own vehicle to a standstill.

Vague Uneasiness

BAD LUCK HAD not yet recovered from the blow of the shattered Cadillac and watched enviously as the chemist's VW Beetle drove past him and pulled up outside the playground. The Deafman, who was doing some sweeping up there, courteously opened the car door for the chemist. The two of them disappeared into the building. Shortly after Raven had fallen through the ice, an article appeared in a medical journal about a sensational operation which had enabled a deaf man to be cured with the help of two hearing aids. The chemist had cut out the article, intending to pass it on to the Deafman's family and alert them to the possibility of a similar operation.

It'll be the same story with you as it was with the cow, the farmer's wife wrote in the Deafman's notebook, at which they all laughed, and no one other than the chemist took the suggestion seriously, and yet, for a few days, a vague uneasiness crept into the Deafman's life. The chemist, who was only too well aware of the aversion to the healing arts among country folk, had to join in the laughter, and he left with the words, I'll be in touch.

What's Chopped off will Grow again in Another Place

On certain days, when the heavy sky pressed down on all odours, when the smells crept out and rose up from the silos and the cowsheds, the brackish pools and muddy ponds, all the decomposition, the exhaust gases and the methane, the silent farts of growth and decline, on those days the Deafman did not know which way to turn, where to point his sensitive nose. If he sought refuge in the cellar, he was convinced he could smell the breath of the earth, the lewd sprouting of the potato shoots, the factory smell of two hundredweights of coal-eggs stored down there in case the wood supply should run out. His sense of smell was cauterised by the fermentation gas rising from the must-barrel, the exhalations of the cattle in the byres as well as the slimy trails of the snails in the cellar, as thick as a child's arm and completely tarry black, and the diesel fuel that had seeped into the ground. The smell of all this came to him in such an overpowering way that he felt assaulted by it, threatened with the loss of this sense as well.

If he then went out into the open, into the fields, it was the clouds of some chalky, pungent fertiliser, the mummified stench of ammonia, that drove him away again, chased him deep into the wood to let the tang of resin rise to his nostrils. Yet it seemed to him that he was smelling not only the wholesome fragrance of the resin but also the pitch, the tar, the turpentine, all the mysterious essences that lay hidden within the resin. Many a time he suffered because of this marvellously acute sense of smell, which had developed in him like a missing limb growing on in another place. Indeed he feared that nothing could conceal itself from him any more in the way he himself liked to hide away, regarding this as a kindness towards himself and an act of politeness towards others. He was afraid of being able to smell and see everything in its concealed form and of never being able to see things as they wanted to reveal themselves, but only the way they really, and of necessity, were. You can hide, he thought, behind many things, but not behind your smell. All these dodges, lotions, essences, strong-smelling soaps, perfumes and deodorants, of course they can overlay a real smell, but no matter how blended with, and adulterated by, all these alien fragrances the real smells might be, they would only emerge all the more distinctly, more unmistakably than people like to smell them. What stinks, stinks more foully and what is fragrant begins to stink.

His manner of sensing things was so different from that of all the other people about him that, to some extent, the best description of it would be the somewhat old-fashioned word, apprehending; just like expressions such as to tarry, to behold, one's countenance and to descry something and even to snatch an evanescent glimpse of something fugaceous.

Every two weeks, his sister-in-law drove into town, and every twelve weeks, he would accompany her. How fascinated he was the first time he passed the Italian's shop, which had opened fairly recently. The Italian ran his business after his day job, when he worked in the plastics factory. All the rest of the day, his wife stood in the almost deserted shop, for the customers, too, came in only after work. Of course, the Deafman and his sister-in-law never set foot in the shop, but just walking past it, those seventeen paces, seemed like a voyage to the Deafman. He felt as if there were half a continent to be discovered in there: you could smell garlic, something he had never eaten before, yet his mouth watered in instantaneous floods. He was consumed with curiosity as to what the farm animal, the plant, the herb, the drink, the fish or whatever it was that smelt so delightfully, actually looked like, what colour, what shape it was, was it hard to the touch, or downy and soft. This odour moved him to such a pitch of excitement that his normally well-developed logic deserted him; it was only after his tenth or twelfth visit to the Italian's that it struck him that the smell of garlic had to be related to that of onions, leeks and, first and foremost, chives and ramson.

How badly, he thought to himself, your mind can become muddled when you are missing one sense. The lack of that one sense confuses the brain.

All the greater, then, did his desire now become to purchase on the spot that fragrance that he had classified in its family and categorised according to more or less accurate degrees of relationship within it. He had come to regard garlic as such a gift that he now felt an intense need to lay out money for it. He set aside a portion of his meagre earnings to save up for garlic, and after two hundred and sixty-four weeks he acquired his first bulb of garlic, which he had eaten so often in his imagination, without knowing, however, whether he should put the whole thing in his mouth or bite a piece off first.

The Lost Melody

THE INTENSIFYING AGONY inspired in the Deafman's brother such fear, and the growing fear such apprehension, that he could no longer sit still. He scurried around and looked for things he had owned and used years ago and then put away without giving them another thought.

With an especial stubbornness bordering on frenzy, he was now looking for his Hohner accordion, which he hadn't played for years and which, he remembered clearly, he had then thrown into the furthest corner of a lumber room. And it was there that he found the book of music from which he had tried to play a piece but simply could not get the hang of it. If he succeeded in playing the melody with the right hand, then his left did what it liked on the bass notes. But if he kept an eye on his left hand, his right went completely berserk and there was not a recognisable shred of the tune left, all that emerged from the instrument was the most tormented and distorted sounds. And all at once the old rage flared up again at the memory of his previous failure, mingling with his annoyance at not being able to find the instrument.

Just as he was often seized by wrath over an innocent object, an inanimate machine like the good old Bulldog, so also had he put all the blame for his past failure on the beautiful instrument made of mother of pearl, goatskin and ivory.

Today, then, driven on by his fever, he searched, rummaged and foraged around among the junk and found it at last in its black case, which he impatiently opened, almost had to burst open, since one of the catches had jammed as a result of it having been violently hurled into the corner.

Sitting in the dark closet, he began to play, without the music-book, a jagged and insistent rhythm, which would have been agony for any audience, and his wife closed the bedroom door in terror, this music seemed scary, remote and incomprehensible. The sounds brought him an altogether new sense of relief. The pain became insignificant, an otherwise ever-present tension seemed to be released. What he actually played had nothing to do with what he had unsuccessfully attempted in the past, he was playing something completely new, something altogether his own, but if he had had to repeat it, he would have failed utterly. He was aware of this, and for that reason he was determined not to stop, no matter how long he played or how overcome by exhaustion he became. He played well into the night and his wife waited for him anxiously, but he never came, he fell asleep as he played, bent over his instrument, and for the first time in a long while his dreams were not about something painful, not about powdered glass or iron filings, or mill-stones, or needles falling from the sky like rain. When he was wakened in the early hours of the morning by the return of his pains, he tried to play the tune from the previous night, but he could not find it again.

He decided to make a present of the instrument to his brother and to go to the doctor that very day.

Basil

ON ONE OF the first, and one of the few, really hot summer days in this barren, cold region, the Italian had put a bunch of basil in his display in front of the shop. Today the sun was shining all the more generously on it, the fragrance developed, became heavier and descended at first before being caught by light draughts of air and wafted upwards, climbing and hovering over the street. It outdid the garlic, eclipsed the smells of cars, the oil from the barrel of black olives and the stink that heralded the arrival of the clouds of diesel smoke from the tractor chugging nearer and nearer. The Deafman had sensed the tractor's approach long ago, feeling in the pit of his stomach the rhythm of the rising and falling pistons, in fact he knew already who it was that was coming. The tractor was a FENDT FARMER, and only one farmer in this district owned this kind of model with a hydraulic shovel. The pleasure this shovel brought the poor man was short-lived, the raising and lowering of the shovel according to his whim was a substitute for the corresponding movements of his penis, he was suffering from cancer of the prostate and was in fact supposed, at that very moment, to be undergoing an operation, albeit one with little prospect of success. Thanks to the arrival of this poor, pitiable man – this was the idea that flashed into the Deafman's mind – he could secure for himself, could acquire and could consume in its materialised form, another new fragrance, namely that of basil.

His sister-in-law and he could communicate with each

other without the slightest problem; a mixture of gestures, signs, noises and touch achieved this as quickly as other people could converse. He liked to play games in which he could prove a cripple's superiority. Now he knew a full three minutes before his sister-in-law who was about to appear, and into the bargain that it was someone who should have been lying under the surgeons' knives at that very instant. Here's your husband coming, he communicated to his sister-in-law.

Get on with you, she answered scornfully, he's in the hospital. No, he's just coming. And he offered her a wager on the subject. They spat on their hands and shook on it. His stake was a cubic metre of solid wood, an enormous amount, a mountain of timber. The Deafman was betting on the fragrance. What's that smell? he wanted to know, but his sister-in-law couldn't say.

So they both stepped inside the Italian's shop for the second time in their lives, and he greeted these two exotic customers warmly. Right away, he plucked a bulb of garlic from the plait hanging next to the counter, but the Deafman shook his head, grabbed the Italian by the wrist and pulled him outside. There were in fact two bunches of basil inside the shop too, but the sun had not got to work on them, so their fragrance was not so overpowering. In the meantime, the husband on his FENDT had drawn appreciably closer and his eyes were shining, for he was convinced that the vibration of his machine would drive the cancer away, with lasting effect and without resort to the doctors' knives, without any nasty wounds.

I'll not go this year yet, I'll keep myself warm, then it'll get better, he called, and his eyes flashed, his cheeks glowed with pride in his new tractor.

Do what you like, you stubborn ass, said the farmer's wife.

The Deafman put his nose close to the little bouquet, a cloud of diesel stench formed an umbrella over the tomatoes, the fennel and the cucumber-like plants unfamiliar to folk hereabouts and the broad-leaved Italian parsley. The Italian sniffed in disgust, then the Deafman held the bunch of basil under his nose and pronounced, in his strangely articulated, clipped way, one of his favourite words, which he only very seldom considered appropriate – EXCELLENT.

A bet's a bet, said his sister-in-law and paid for the herb. That was the last day she was to see her husband.

Three Moles

AFTER THEIR RETURN to the farm, the Deafman set up his little plant in his room, bestowed one more tender glance on it and locked up, so that none of the precious aroma should escape. He went into the cowshed, mucked it out, then went to the woodshed and chopped kindling. He went out to the fields to see that everything was in order, checked his mole-traps and released three moles, all of them with wounds in their necks; only one was completely dead, the other two were still alive, their breath gasping and loud, almost like some larger animal or even a human being. The racing of their little hearts was visible under the beautiful black velvet skin, one of them was only just moving its stubby head with the pointed snout, the other was still able to make weak movements with the little shovels on its front paws, further down it was paralysed, its spine snapped. How was he to kill the two of them, he didn't have a spade to hand, didn't want to use a stone, for he might not strike accurately and the animals would have to suffer even more through his clumsiness. Perhaps it was again his sense of smell that drew his attention to the two figures sitting smoking on a bench at the edge of the wood. On Raven's head, a tonsure the size of a coin gleamed where the Deafman's rescuing grip had torn the hair out. In his moment of need, and because he was driven by curiosity, he went down, still carrying the two animals in the traps, towards Raven and Fever who sat there rolling and smoking big fat cigarettes. As he watched, bewildered, they hurriedly tried to hide their cigarettes in the hollow of their hands, which proved too small, and then Raven gave the startled Fever a dig with his elbow and singed the palm of his own hand with the burning tip of his cigarette. An odour rose to the Deafman's nostrils, a smell that was at the same time heavy and yet light, its heaviness was captivating and seductive, its lightness was like a whim and a passing fancy.

When Fever's eye fell on the two dying animals, panting their last, his own breath came faster. What he found hard to bear was the sheer volume of the moles' death-rattle; Fever's own breathing became louder, his forehead, his hands became moist, he felt a tightening in his gut, somewhere between pleasure and pain. If he were to kill the moles, he said, it would be doing them a kindness. When a horse breaks a leg, its rider shoots it with sadness in his eye, but he is and remains a hero. Killing, he said, isn't a bad thing when there's nothing else for it.

Well, go on then, said Raven, who could sense Fever's rising agitation.

Desires and emotions swirled up in Fever, they spun around, receded and converged again and finally coalesced into a touch of bloodlust. He got to his feet, gripped the first mole and beat it on the stony ground until it was quite obviously dead. It took a long time.

Fever's hands were stained, and he felt the first surge of nausea. He killed the second mole by stamping on its squat head with his boot, again and again, and in doing so the overweight lad developed a surprising elegance, like some dancing bear.

Once he had finished his killing and had noticed the revulsion in the eyes of the other two, something snapped inside him. His stomach contracted, in his mouth there was that rush of saliva that presages vomiting, his brows started to twitch, and then his belly, the insides of his thighs and his back, everything about him was twitching and, within minutes, he was covered in red spots that rapidly swelled into blotches of repugnance. He could, he was sure, never feel more wretched. He would never kill anything again, he said.

They sat smoking in silence for a while, Fever scratching himself and struggling against the rising vomit. Raven passed the big cigarette to the Deafman, who inhaled carefully, for he didn't know this brand. He seemed to like the taste, for he raised his eyebrows in appreciation and drew the smoke as deep into his body as it would go. The intense inhalation made him slightly giddy, but apart from that it was all quite pleasant. And when Fever could hold out no longer but stood up and sprinted away, stopped beside a spruce to retch and finally ran off home, the two of them were greatly relieved. Fever had left his medicine-bag behind; Raven opened it up to show the Deafman the dried weed they had been smoking. That must be what basil would look like if it was dried, the Deafman thought to himself. Fever got the leaves from his brother whom he was trying so hard to resemble.

Back in his room, the Deafman plucked a few leaves from his basil, heated them briefly over his lighter, crumbled them and smoked them. It tasted so good that he went through to his sister-in-law, who was still awake, and let her have a draw too. Like grass, she said.

She was worried, because her husband had driven off on

the FENDT, he hadn't gone to the doctor, he wasn't wearing his new suit, not even the jacket of it, and had stopped coming home. She had received a few telephone calls from relatives and acquaintances, who reported that her husband had driven into their places on the latest thing in tractors, had lodged with them for a while, only to disappear again. He had hardly talked at all, other than to plead urgently with them not to say a word to her about his having shown up. Since he had obviously not been in the best of health, they had been concerned and so had not complied with his request.

Every time she received such a call, she went into the bedroom and looked at the accordion standing by the bedside, and the note lying on it, written in his shaky, rarely practised hand. It said, FOR MY BROTHER.

Upheaval

IT WAS A windless day, with the faintest of odours of drizzle, damp tar and urine in the air, when a great upheaval occurred in the life of the Deafman. Such a long time had passed since the chemist's visit, and as no one had said another word in his presence about the possibility of an operation, he had come to believe that they had forgotten all about it and did not consider him worth repairing anyway, or maybe they were sorry for him because he had been more afraid then than he could ever remember. The upheaval in his life came in the shape of a brown envelope containing a letter, almost ten pages long, which explained the possibility of such an operation and described life in the home for the hard of hearing before and after the operation, the way the hearing aids worked, the care offered by the home, the possibilities for rehabilitation and the happy lives led by those who had undergone both the operation and the re-education, and the medical insurance companies' recognition of the methods employed. A possible date for the operation was offered, and that seemed to the Deafman to be a long way off. What was required from him for a start, though, was a recent photograph. At first he merely laughed – *Am I supposed to be going to have my ears put right or to enter a beauty contest?* he wrote when he read that.

Neither would do you any harm, wrote Raven.

Then I'll go and have my beauty put right and enter an ear contest, the Deafman wrote.

Can only be good for you, wrote Raven.

But now, how was the Deafman to come by the required photograph?

Once, a long while ago, his sister-in-law told him, there was a photographer's shop here. But because nobody wanted their picture taken, the photographer soon gave up the business and went to work in the plastics factory. There, he ended up five years later with bronchial and lung troubles, because they didn't have the prescribed breathing protection or proper ventilation in the place. A health cure at a spa on one of the North Sea islands seemed to make the whole thing worse and after he came back he took early retirement and so, if he was still alive, he would no doubt be delighted to take the Deafman's picture. His sister-in-law looked for the man's name in the local telephone book, found it, called the number but got only the recorded message, NUMBER UNOBTAINABLE. The telephone directory was coming on for ten years old, so this was not altogether surprising. All right, I'll ring the chemist then, she said after a moment's thought and almost immediately she had his assistant at the other end. The man's got the usual factory worker's disease, his lungs and his bronchial tubes are bad, so he needs various medicines for the rest of his life, and he gets them from the chemist, she explained to the amazed Raven.

Ah, he said, speechless at such a display of sharp-wittedness.

And of course the chemist, who had quickly come running to the telephone and so was now talking rather breathlessly, knew right away who they meant. The photographer, yes, he's still alive, after a fashion, the cortisone is making his skin brittle and his flesh spongy, but he is still in the land of the living. But it would be advisable to get the picture taken soon. And yes, he also knew where he lived, after all he himself often delivered the necessary medicines personally since the photographer didn't like leaving the house for fear of the poisonous vapours from the plastics factory. He gave them the address and promised to look in on the invalid that very evening and ask him if he would be so good as to take the Deafman's likeness.

The sister-in-law thanked him and passed on regards from Raven and the Deafman, even though neither had asked her to do anything of the kind.

Then she looked the Deafman over from head to foot and said, Wouldn't do you any harm to have a shave. You'll have to spruce yourself up a bit.

No matter how hard he tried to think back, he couldn't remember when he last had his picture taken. He supposed there must be a photo in his identity papers, but he hadn't the faintest where they were, and in his moped-licence there was only a picture of his brother. All the same, he must have been photographed at some time or other in his life, otherwise he wouldn't be a real person at all.

You have to look your best for a photograph. So you borrow one of your brother's suits. His wife bridles a bit at this but then, after a great deal of haggling, she says, Well all right, but for a half-length portrait the jacket will be enough. Then you get someone to let you have a tie. You wash, comb your hair and put on something that smells nice. With the styptic pencil you speed up the clotting of the blood in the cuts on your chin and your top lip. You seal them off with snippets of newspaper. After all, who's going to let themselves be photographed bleeding and, it follows, debilitated?

Getting his picture taken was, like almost every other novelty, an exciting, yet at the same time a worrying prospect. When someone is being photographed, the light hurled out by a flash bulb crashes against the sitter, it is then flung back by him, goes through the glass lenses of the camera and fixes the light of the sitter's image on the film. But why does it capture this light, why is it not thrown back yet again?

That was a question which, he hoped, the terminally ill photographer would be able to answer. If the sitter's body did not hurl the light back strongly enough, the picture would be under-exposed, but if it flung it back too violently, it would be over-exposed. This much was clear: the sitter had to be perfectly composed. And the best way to achieve this state of equilibrium, as the Deafman well knew from experience, was to have practised a thing many times before you have to do it for real. Nevertheless, the trial runs must not inadvertently become realistic themselves, otherwise the actual first time would no longer be real, and so would be bound to fail. And he didn't want to be either over- or under-exposed, to come across either too feeble or too fierce while he was being photographed, otherwise he might end up damaging the lens or maybe even the whole camera and having to pay compensation for their replacement, and besides, he didn't want to give the doomed man an unhappy send-off into the bargain. So he had to rehearse having his picture taken so that nobody would come to any harm and the best possible photograph of himself would result, for who could tell how badly they might cut him up later on if he were to send in a poor photo right from the start. If you look too handsome, then the doctors are jealous and let the knife slip, and if you're too ugly they don't pay attention and botch the cut then too. So the whole thing had to be properly thought through and rehearsed thoroughly, but not too realistically.

Practise being photographed, he wrote for Raven in his Complications-Notebook. And practise he did, whenever he thought nobody was looking or when he thought his absence had gone unnoticed. In the middle of the cowshed he would suddenly stand bolt upright, brush his hair back from his ears and try to smile, as if he were being photographed. In his room, he set up a large mirror on the floor next to the light switch, sat down in front of it and, by switching the light on and off, imitated the flash bulb, which was the thing that made him particularly nervous.

Miracle of Photographic Art

BECAUSE THE PHOTOGRAPHER had put up a sign, on what had then been his shop, bearing the legend Pictures by Flash, people had started calling him not by his proper name of Hellinger, but simply Flash. Pictures by Flash, however, offered a service only for those in a hurry, people who needed, as quickly as possible and within half an hour at the most, a passport photograph or a wedding picture or a likeness for a visa. In this neighbourhood, however, weddings were carefully planned well in advance, there was no rush for passport photos, since nobody travelled anyway and so they didn't need a passport, far less a photo for a visa.

Flash enjoyed little success with his business, but the name stuck.

The sign still hung in the same spot, the writing had been partly covered over by the posters from numerous local election campaigns, partly faded by the elements and partly it had crumbled away.

His studio was used by the next-door gentlemen's outfitter as a store for boxes full of ties from bygone days, suits with extra wide lapels and trousers with 24-inch flared turn-ups, extremely elegant discontinued lines in non-iron man-made fibres, pure new-wool underwear and a complete matching set of uniform jackets for the local Volunteer Fire Brigade which he had bought years ago at a knock-down price and had meant to remodel – into what, he could not remember to this day.

Outside Flash's place, where he now inhabited a small room and kitchenette above his former studio, the Deafman rang the doorbell and settled down to wait, for he knew the man was ailing. A lot of elderly people and small children suffered from illnesses of the respiratory tracts around here, which was why neighbouring communities called the little town Coughers' Corner.

As soon as the bell had sounded, Flash had set off on his way, clinging desperately to the banister on the steep stair and wheezing heavily. Half-way down, he had to stop and use his asthma spray, then off he went again. The chemist had prepared him for the Deafman's visit. With perfect elegance, for in the days of Pictures by Flash photographers would have got nowhere without the best of manners, he showed him into the studio and around the junk and all the boxes. He started to clear the space around the camera and the sitter's chair. He was breathing so hard that he needed a double burst from his little spray bottle. The Deafman lent a hand, but carefully, so as not to disturb either his meticulously parted hair or his well-rehearsed expression, and above all so as not to perspire, for beads of sweat were the last thing he wanted to see on his portrait.

He looked round for a mirror, in order to check that the knot in his tie was sitting right – he had tied it using a coffee pot as a reflecting surface – but Flash beat him to it and made the necessary adjustments, picked off specks of dust and flicked two scales of dandruff from his collar before whipping out, in a flash, a clean comb – he had rubbed it down with surgical spirit the day before – and tidied up his parting. Gently, yet as firmly as all too few photographers nowadays are able to, he pushed him down into the chair, tilted his head to the correct angle and bent his spine into a dignified posture. His chin was tipped slightly higher, his cheeks lightly kneaded and pinched to bring out a fresh tone, something Flash swore by, despite the fact that this was to be a black and white photo and despite the Deafman's ruddy, wind- and weather-beaten cheeks which no amount of mere kneading could have made much redder. Behind the box with the Trevira ties, he found the electric socket for his floodlights, and then the whole process of picking off dust particles and removing bits of fluff had to be repeated after Flash had dealt with the layer of dust on the floodlight reflectors and lenses. And when he tried to bring the floods into action, they did not all three burst into life, but just one cast a feeble dribble of light on the Deafman who was still stuck in his most advantageous pose and was desperately wondering whether, when you were having your picture taken, you had to hold your breath as well. Since the lamps were not going to supply sufficient light, Flash had to go back up the stairs again, with a quadruple application of his asthma spray, fetch his 'Metz' flash-gun from his wardrobe and then negotiate the descent of the stairs again. While all this was going on, the Deafman arrived at the conclusion that holding one's breath was not an absolutely essential part of being photographed. As a result of his rigidly maintained upright posture, he soon became quite exhausted, his muscles began to cramp and finally, when Flash was somewhere half-way up or down the stairs, the dreaded beads of sweat appeared on his forehead.

By now, Flash's own state of exhaustion had reached such a peak that he was ready to sacrifice everything, even the ethos of his, now former, profession in order to bring these proceedings to the speediest possible conclusion. He mounted the flash-gun on the camera, took a fleeting glance through the dust-coated viewfinder, took a chance on the depth of focus being sufficient and pressed the button. The Deafman maintained his rigid pose for some considerable time before being convinced that that was all there was to it.

When, three days later, Flash had recovered from his exertions and set about developing the film, he discovered that the photo was not only out of focus but also under-exposed, and therefore completely unusable. He took himself off into the depths of his archive cupboard, hunted around and came up with the negative of a picture portraying the Deafman's brother as a young man, which, he reckoned, showed an adequate similarity to his deaf sitter. And so the Deafman was amazed, on opening the envelope containing his portrait, by the photographer's artistic ability which had not only succeeded in making him look ten years younger, but had also revealed him to be the spitting image of his brother.

In the Roll-front Cabinet

FOR HOURS ON end he lay without making the slightest movement. If he kept his eyes closed, he could see the roll-front cabinet in the headmistress's office. If he opened his eyes in the dark, then the image of the black cabinet loomed up again. In this piece of furniture, it seemed to him, the secrets of his existence, all their secrets, were locked away. In there could be found the explanation of why Andre didn't want to be a girl, why The Victim was a victim, why Fever was getting fatter and more shapeless, and in there he would also find the truth about his father.

He wanted to wait until it was so quiet that he could hear the others' heartbeats, but all he could hear was the rushing of his own blood, while the pounding of his heart seemed so loud that it must surely be preventing the others from getting to sleep. He tried to breathe as little as possible, so as to deprive his heart of oxygen and make its beating fainter and slower. And then he was seized with the fear that he might fall asleep and his breathing might suddenly stop altogether. They would find him, blue in the face, finally and really dead, for he had already put his life in forfeit. He was sorry that he would no longer be able to watch the horror on their faces. And with thoughts like these, time was passing.

Quietly at first, Fever was beginning to let out sounds, first a gurgling, which then turned into a regular snore. Raven could not remember Fever ever snoring before, and he reckoned this was a ruse on the part of his deceitful foe. Then he remembered that, for two days now, Fever had been complaining of a cold and probably that was what was making him snore. Let him suffocate then, he said to himself, but he immediately banished this thought from his mind, feeling ashamed and guilty. Was Fever maybe right, was there something vicious lurking and growing inside him? Was it not just as wrong to think such thoughts as to throttle him with your own hands? In the darkness, he drew his hands out from under the blanket and gripped himself by the throat, just to feel what it was like to strangle and to be strangled. The experiment convinced him that he was incapable of such a deed and he gave a start when, just at that moment, Fever stopped snoring, and immediately he slipped his hands back under the blanket. The sudden silence made him wary again, he waited, and only when Fever was once more moaning quietly did he let the blanket slide down slowly and get up, moving all the time at half his normal speed. From his clothes cupboard, the hinges of which he had greased that morning with butter he had saved for the purpose, he took a wire coat-hanger and left the room, convinced that he could not have been quieter or more careful. Out in the corridor, the lights were on; he hadn't reckoned with that. So instead of making his way slowly, step by step in the dark, along the route he had so carefully memorised, he had to run as fast as he could, so as not to meet anyone. Yet half-way along he realised his haste and excitement were totally unnecessary, for why shouldn't he want to go to the toilet in the middle of the night. If he were caught, he would just carry out his plan a few days later. Only the coat-hanger, which he was clutching to himself, would have been hard to explain away, and since he was wearing only his underpants, it would have been difficult to conceal. All the pictures and drawings that had been pinned up along the walls of the corridor, without exception, dealt with the birth of the calf. The headmistress probably felt it was important for the children to get the incident out of their systems in this way.

Raven was seized by anger towards Fever, and without even thinking, he tore down Fever's two bloody-red pictures, crumpled them up and threw them on the floor. Filled with a quiet satisfaction, he now stood at the door to the office, which was indeed locked. He bent the wire of the coat-hanger into a skeleton key and tried to open the lock. Again he was gripped by fear and excitement, because it refused to snap open as he had expected. He withdrew the hanger, examined the lock and bent the wire into the right shape again, until at last he heard a loud click and the door could be opened. It was dark in the office, he shut the door behind him, made sure the curtains and shutters were closed and felt for the cigarette lighter that he had hidden on the window-sill some days previously. He didn't dare switch on the electric light, a silly mistake as he later found out when he burned practically every finger on both right and left hand with the hot lighter. The filing cabinet was locked, too, and the wire of the coat-hanger was too thick for the narrow lock. He hadn't bargained for that. But on the desk he found a large paper-clip, bent it into a right-angle and, so quickly that it took even him by surprise, cracked open the old roll-front cabinet that for him, every time he had been in the office, had been the very embodiment of secrecy. With a grinding creak, the front slid downwards. There before him, in alphabetical order, lay all the files, as well as a bottle of cognac and a small packet of cigarettes, which had been correctly filed away under the letter C. Again and again he had to release the button on the lighter as he looked through the papers, and he had not yet got so far as to read any of the files when quite by chance he came across a dossier, the cover of which bore Andre's name. He hesitated for some time, then continued his search, only to come back and pull out Andre's papers after all. He was wondering why the file on such a young girl should already be so thick when he heard a click coming from the direction of the door. He gave a start and could tell that someone had thrown the lock from the outside. He cursed Fever and his own gullibility. The snoring had been a spiteful trick. Once he had got over his fright, however, it was obvious to him that Fever had not thought the thing through. For if he could open the door from the outside, then of course he could also do it from within. He took his coat-hanger and slid the hook into the lock. His brief triumph gave way to burning fury when he realised that Fever had forced some object into the lock and so Raven was now well and truly locked in. He reacted quickly. Carefully he restored the old cabinet to its original state, replaced everything he had touched in the office and even bent the paper-clip back into its correct shape. He would claim he had needed to go to the toilet and, half-asleep as he had been, had gone in the wrong door and then Fever had locked him in. I'll drop you right in the shit, he said out loud. Fever must have broken the door open, of course, because previously it had been locked. For a good half-hour he was in quite a happy frame of mind, and he wondered whether he shouldn't raise the alarm right away. Then, however, he was not so sure. If they were really to believe his story, would he not be behaving like a cissy and extremely dishonourably? Fever would certainly have to suffer some unpleasant consequences, but would he not then be able to stand before the others like some wily hero? And that was the part that Raven would have preferred to play himself. He took up the paper-clip, bent it again, opened the cabinet and spent the rest of the early hours emptying the bottle that had been filed under C. Of course they had often drunk a whole bottle of apple schnapps together, but that would be five or six of them. This was the first time that he had drunk such a quantity of alcohol on his own, and accordingly he quickly forgot that he had forced his way into this room to find out something about his father. He found the taste of the drink bitter and revolting, and he struggled with an overpowering desire to be sick. But he reminded himself that it had been the same sort of thing when he had first smoked. Then, after he had smoked five or six packets in quiet seclusion and racked with disgust and nausea, his body had got accustomed to it and some time later, when he was thirteen, he began to enjoy the taste. So if he drank enough now, he hoped, he would have beaten his nausea and it would do him good. To drown the taste of the drink, he lit a cigarette. After the fifth cigarette, he let the ash fall just anywhere on the floor. And the twelfth cigarette slipped from his hand, still lit, on to the carpet, where it burned a black stripe, which was the last thing he remembered before he fell into a deep sleep, or perhaps even a dead faint. He slept on, did not hear the noises in the corridor as the others headed for breakfast, heard nothing of the hymn they had to sing every morning and likewise did not hear the noise of the headmistress's bunch of keys as she tried to open her door and noticed that a large screw had been driven into the lock. In her annoyance, she pulled and tugged at it, breaking a finger-nail, and finally unscrewed it with a nail-file. She may well have let out a startled little cry when she found him lying on the floor, perhaps she made straight for the telephone to call for a doctor, but then again the sight of the empty bottle may have decided her against it; he knew nothing of all this, he never asked her about it afterwards and she never told him about it either.

The Thief's Awakening

THE FIRST THING he became aware of was the dripping of a tap. He came to on a camp bed in the school laundry. Then he could smell vomit and a distant waft of sauerkraut. He was naked; he tried to think whether he had ever felt worse in his life and retched at the sight of a basin that had been placed near the camp bed and was already well filled. He was thankful that the room was cool and light, everything seemed to be revolving slowly. His underpants were nowhere in the bare room, but on a washing line hung a bed sheet that was nearly dry. He wrapped himself in this, drank some cold water from the tap and headed off towards his room. He was not at all afraid of meeting the headmistress, because, he thought, things could not possibly get any worse for him than they were at this moment. He met no one, it was evening and the others were all at dinner. When he tried to open the door to his room, he discovered that it was locked. At that point he was sure he would have burst into tears if his body had not urgently needed every drop of water it could get. He had no alternative, in his pitiful condition, wrapped in a damp bed sheet, but to go and join the others in the refectory. He would be in no fit state to invent any story that might go some way to reduce the awkwardness of his situation. He would not be capable of taking his revenge on Fever. He went through the building and opened the refectory door. The others gradually fell silent, turned round and stared at him. Only the headmistress seemed not to notice him and carried on her intense conversation with one of the nuns.

His place had been set as usual. He reckoned that if he went and sat down, everything would return to normal and he would no longer be exposed to the others' gaze. The sight of the food on the plates aroused a further attack of nausea which he fought down with difficulty. My room's locked, he said.

Only after some time did the headmistress look up and retort that apparently he was able to go through locked doors anyway. Now that we are all here, she continued, she would like to seek everyone's assistance in the search for a small box which, for some inexplicable reason, had disappeared from her office. Everyone knew that she was referring to a green metal box in which she kept small sums of money. If anyone was ever sent by her on a shopping errand, or needed extra pocket money, she would open up the little box and take out the required amount. She noted everything on a list, which was also kept in the box. There was no more awful way of abusing her trust than by stealing this box. Raven stared at the plates, at the steaming sauerkraut and the roast sausages on them. He stared at a juniper berry and knew that he could not suppress his nausea much longer, his mouth filled with more saliva than he could swallow, he got to his feet and rushed from the room.

Even if a large majority of the others believed that Raven had committed the theft, the headmistress nevertheless knew full well that it could not have been him, for the box had already disappeared a few days previously. Her tactics were aimed at the possibility that Raven, in the confusion of his severe hangover, might perhaps let slip a clue as to the real culprit. The case was fully cleared up about a month later, when Fever suddenly came into possession of a radio cassette recorder which, as her inquiries in the only possible shop in the district revealed, he had not stolen, but bought. The money for it, so he told all and sundry, had been a present from his brother.

The thrill at the thought of being a bad person, a thief, a criminal, alternated with Raven's fear of the loneliness of such an existence and his uncertainty about the truth of Fever's assertion. Now and again, the possibility that he might have committed theft roused him to a state of almost heady excitement. In this and that object he thought he could make out a glance, a yearning that was directed at him. A glance like an enticement, a tempting glance that promised him pleasure, as if the objects were whispering to him. Look me over, cast a covetous eye over me, contemplate me, feel me, touch me, caress me, put me in your pocket, unscrew me, undo me, take me, take me with you.

The Devoured Father

THE HEADMISTRESS HAD to let the chemist's phone ring for some considerable time before at last he answered it. He made a point of taking all calls himself, since he did not trust his assistant – quite unjustly. The headmistress, aware of Raven's mother's condition, did not want to trouble her with this affair and thought it better to contact Raven's great-uncle, the chemist, directly, since she had met him a few times before and considered him to be a calm, level-headed man, albeit perhaps something of a schemer. She asked him to come to the school for a private chat. He promised to set out early that very evening, straight after closing time.

The chemist gave a great deal of thought to the choice of an appropriate, indeed an extremely flattering, outfit, because the headmistress was, in his eyes, an attractive, yes, an erotic person. What no doubt aroused him was the fact of her presumed virginity and the prospect of some kind of carnal explosion, if things should progress that far. And, he said to himself as he selected an after-shave, why shouldn't I be the one. And with that thought not far from his mind, he took along a batch of lavender soap that had been on his shelves for ages, to be a present for the needy girls, as he presumed those in the school to be. This soap had proved useful over at least five years as a free gift for customers and for casual purchasers whom he would have liked to convert into regulars.

Never let it be said I'm an old skinflint, the chemist told himself and looked around in his shop for a suitable perfume for the headmistress; but he found none and bought a small bottle from the local Avon representative. What scent goes with grey tweed? he asked. The Avon lady sold him her own favourite.

He was not to know that the headmistress never used perfume, or for that matter lipstick, rouge or hair-spray. She became immediately uneasy. She did not seriously believe it, but she did have the feeling that the chemist was giving her perfume because she smelled unpleasantly.

So the atmosphere was doubly tense as she told him about Raven's break-in. And since she did not for one moment think that the chemist could believe or understand the excuse that Raven was giving for his act, which she herself regarded as monstrous, practically blasphemous in fact, she had Bad Luck bring Raven into her office. He appeared neither frightened nor conscience-stricken. He shook hands with his great-uncle with perfect politeness and without having to be told, there was even a hint of a bow, and he spoke only when spoken to.

Did you really break into this office? the chemist asked, trying hard to make sure his voice sounded calm and warm.

Yes, said Raven and, closely as the chemist scrutinised him, he could see no trace of a blush.

And why did you do that? the chemist then asked.

Because I want to find out where my father is, said Raven in a steady voice.

Your father? But he's dead, said the chemist.

No, said Raven.

Nonsense.

He's alive, said Raven. He went bankrupt, fraudulently, and cleared off abroad. He's had plastic surgery and lives in St Tropez, Argentina or Zurich. He has a wife, she's younger than I am. He's got several Jaguars and has changed his name. He's a criminal, a very clever one. When I find out his address, I'm going to visit him and he'll adopt me.

Your own father can't adopt you.

Yes he can. And I'll have my face operated on too.

You can go now, said the headmistress.

Wait, said the chemist, and gave him a cake of soap. Raven gave The Victim the soap as a present.

It was soon clear to the chemist what Raven's problem was. He would have to find a way to materialise, to make visible for Raven, this father who had so suddenly dissipated into the void instead of passing on respectably like other people, even if he had to resort – and there certainly did not seem any other way – to a ruse, to trickery.

He had an old university friend in Great Britain, and in a long letter he described the necessity for his macabre request. He called on the headmistress again and presented his plan, after he had handed over a bottle of toilet water, at which she blushed to the roots of her hair. He for his part interpreted her flushing as the manifestation of an erotic thrill caused by his presence. She thought that although she had been quite diligent in her daily use of the soap, her body odour was still not to his liking.

A few weeks later a parcel arrived at the chemist's addressed to Raven and enclosing a letter in English. The chemist got into his Volkswagen to deliver the parcel to Raven. Neither Raven nor – or so he pretended – the chemist had an adequate command of English. So they asked the headmistress to help. The letter more or less said that the enclosed urn had at last been found again and the British Royal Mail apologised most profusely for the whole incident.

There he is then, the chemist said solemnly.

Raven said nothing and took hold of the receptacle sceptically, moved it about a little to hear what the contents sounded like. Indeed there was something rustling round inside the bronzed aluminium urn.

No wonder, because the chemist had asked his friend to fill the container with something that would sound like a mixture of ashes and particles of bone. Unfortunately, the friend had, for lack of any other material, chosen to fill the urn with, of all things, a mixture of brown sugar and grated nuts used for sprinkling on the top of cakes. This would not really have mattered if it had not been for the excessively inquisitive Fever.

For a short while, then, Raven was freed from his terrible affliction, but Fever, secretly rummaging about as usual in other people's cupboards, found his uncontrollable curiosity could not be satisfied by merely rattling and shaking the mysterious tin, the purpose of which was beyond him.

No, he just had to open it, this urn made of bronzed aluminium. At this, the aroma of cake-crumble rose so unmistakably to his nostrils that he could resist only for a split second the temptation to devour the sweet-tasting alleged ashes of Raven's father before stowing the urn away in its original hiding place.

When, a few days later, he felt the urge to annoy Raven once more, he showed him a newspaper clipping in which it was reported that German right-wing radicals had been the masterminds behind a Nazi-style party in South America. He could well imagine, he said, who the boss of these criminals was. At that, Raven opened his cupboard and took out the urn.

He's not in America. He's in here.

You're crazy, said Fever, his conscience pricking him.

Raven tried to shake the urn to prove it, opened it and found it empty apart from one or two grains. Fever moistened his finger and gathered up the grains, which he drew out and licked off his finger.

Raven immediately felt sick at the thought that Fever had eaten his father. He could not utter another sound.

What's wrong with you, it was only cake-crumble.

Now Raven ran his finger round the inside of the urn and licked it clean. There was no doubt that the ashes of his departed father were made of cake-crumble.

There and then he was convinced that his father was organising Fascism in America. That he was a multiple murderer, a bankrupt, a swindler, a bank robber, a sexual pervert, in short, everything that Fever had ever talked him into believing. And he also believed it when Fever said, Like father, like son.

Then again he tried to fight this predisposition, unable to decide whether it actually existed in him or whether Fever was only trying to persuade him of it.

In the Museum, the First Visit

ONE HOLIDAY, RAVEN had no idea which one it was, they went on an outing to the museum.

In a tired, ancient half-light that was punctuated here and there by the piercing glare of a beam from above, limbs and heads stood mounted on stakes and poles, there were broken-off noses, penises and testicles, and above them stretched, as in some enormous crypt, a vaulted ceiling of white granite. And all the heads were staring at Raven from their stony eyes or the shadows of their empty sockets.

As if he himself had been turned to stone, Raven stood before a colossus, gazing up at it. The longer he stood and stared, the stronger became his impression that the colossus was not standing still but was turning its head slightly, leaning forward and down towards him, in a fatherly kind of way at first, and then this inclination turned into something menacing for the puny little human in front of it. Raven could hardly tear his eyes away from those of the giant, its eyeballs made from brightish stone, its lids from a darker one, and its pupils empty hollows. You could see right into the interior of the stone head, into the colossus, into the dungeon of its skull, that innermost sanctum.

And when he finally succeeded in breaking free from his petrifaction and in fleeing from the crypt, it was only to emerge into an even more enormous vault.

Here, there was war.

How beautiful the bodies were, beautiful and yet at the same time in a state of devastation. The limbs a patchwork of fragments. Smashed in some ancient battle, their beauty concealed latent cruelty. There lay a man, with one arm raised. Another was bending over him, sword in hand, his arm drawn back to strike. And there, a kneeling archer, opposite him a dying man, his body riddled with arrows. In their midst, serene, cruel and composed, immune to all the swords, arrows and spears, her shield merely for decoration, her spear only for support, a huge woman was directing the battle like the cogs of some timeless, irresistible machine that had become a perpetuum. The tip of her spear was pointing upwards to where, as if ready to be set in motion at any moment by a barely perceptible gesture from her, a steel hook swathed in chains hung down from the orange-painted travelling winch, dropping a plumb-line over the war.

Those cogs and levers in this machine, which time seemed to have crumbled and eaten away, were and remain the most gruesome, permitting of no escape, and even if they were absent from the stones, they nevertheless functioned in Raven's mind, accomplishing their work of destruction in such a brutal manner that he could no longer stand the horrifying image within him, it took on colour and sound inside his head to become a butchering and screaming, a merciless, inextricably tangled orgy of killing.

He had seen enough for one day; he ran out in a haphazard rush, with no idea of where he was going, surrounded again and again by the living stones. Perhaps it was the murmuring of the wrought-iron fountain that drew him on, but the ultimate refuge, the one place where he could relieve himself of these images as if answering a call of nature, was the quietest one, the lavatory.

Hardly had he shut and locked himself in the cubicle, reeling slightly from its pungent smells, when he became aware of sounds, confusing at first, then frightening and finally quite obviously indicative of an amorous encounter.

In the next cubicle there was a jostling and shoving, a tugging and fumbling. There was heavy breathing and panting, moaning and trembling as if there were two bells hung next door, ringing out the climax of a union.

Raven did not know whether he should make some movement to warn of his presence or whether he should rush out as quickly as he could, but in the end he considered it wisest simply to remain shut in there and to participate as an ear-witness. When, in the course of the struggle next door, a wallet slipped out of the pocket of a pair of dropped trousers and fell to the tiled floor with a slap of leather on stone and a tinkle of loose change, and when a foot, obviously no longer under control, inadvertently pushed the wallet through into Raven's cubicle, the to-ing and fro-ing next door continued for a while, became slower and more hesitant and finally ebbed away, and during this time Raven was able to bend down to take a look at the bulging wallet, run his fingers over it, open it and examine the banknotes, coins, photographs and the visiting card it contained, before he was interrupted by a loud knocking. He lit a cigarette. After a short pause, there was another knock, louder this time. Raven knocked back. There was an answering knock. Raven took out the notes, hesitated for a moment before taking the business card as well, and slid the rest through the gap back into the neighbouring cubicle. There was a relieved hush, but only for a few seconds, and then a cry of dismay rang out. This was followed by a muffled conversation, although Raven could hear every whispered word. Incredulous, almost plaintive, the voice of the older man: He's taken my money.

And at this the young one, indignant: It's my money he's taken.

The elder one, trying to pacify him: I'll give you a cheque.

The young one, his anger rising: Are you crazy? Come on, cough up, cash on the nail!

There was the sound of a slap. Very matter-of-fact, as if

he had done some quick thinking, the older man: We'll go to a cash-dispenser. Come on.

The door opened and two people left the toilets, just at the moment when an electric bell rang and an announcement came over the loudspeakers that the building was about to close.

Then there was the voice of the older man: Hey, lass, this is the men's toilet.

The younger man's voice: You must be a right little slag, eh.

Andre's voice: Go take a flying fuck at yourself. Arsehole.

There was a knock at Raven's door. Andre said they were all waiting for him. Raven showed her the money and the visiting card.

Can I have that? said Andre.

He gave her a note and the visiting card.

That was his first visit to a museum.

The Melting Face

IN THE DEPTHS of his cupboard, behind all the clothes that no longer fitted him, the few books and toys he was no longer interested in, Raven searched for and dug out a longish white cardboard box, decorated with a cross. In the big garbage bin in the kitchens he found an empty jam tin. He removed the label with hot water and secretly borrowed a spirit stove from the chemistry laboratory, a fine paint-brush from the art room and, from the medicine chest, Vaseline for taking temperatures.

He opened the window in his room, locked the door and

took from the box a Communion candle, which he broke into pieces with three or four karate chops. He lit the spirit stove and carefully melted the white wax that smelt of paraffin. The cross that had been let into it in red wax was the first to melt and then it mingled with the white. Raven took the Vaseline and smeared it thickly all over his face. He dipped the paint-brush in the hot mass and tested the temperature on the back of his hand. Then he poured the wax on to a clean baking tray and filled in the thinner places with the paint-brush. Before him now lay a white skin of wax, shot through with red streaks. He picked it up and laid it carefully on his face, moulding it to his features, bored an opening for his nostrils and waited till the mask had completely cooled and hardened.

Then he took it off and examined it, his wax portrait. It was him, all right, and yet again it wasn't him. There were only smooth surfaces, the little hairs, the small creases between his eyes, everything had been smoothed out and made more evenly proportioned but also more lifeless than his own face. Yet the very rigidity of the mask, this thing, neither living nor dead, endowed it with a certain truth about Raven's face, which would have been incomparably more difficult to read in his face itself. What it was exactly, Raven could not fathom.

At that, Fever knocked at the door. Raven opened it and showed Fever his mask. For a long time, an unusually long time, Fever gazed at the wax face, it seemed to exert a certain fascination on him too, which held him in thrall. You're not anything like as good-looking, he said at last.

Without another word, they went to bed.

During the night, Raven was wakened by the sound of a hair-dryer; Fever had fetched it from the bathroom and now he was sitting by the light of his small pocket torch, slowly moving the hair-dryer over Raven's wax face, which began to buckle, distort, collapse in on itself, go into folds and form bubbles and holes. With a start, Fever realised that Raven was awake.

Raven didn't even give Fever a telling off, he was almost easier in his mind at the thought that that face had now become a different one again.

The Taking of The Victim

IF ANYONE HAD asked Fever's brother why he had set off to visit his young brother that day shortly before Fever was due to sit his O Levels, he would not have been able to say. It could have been because of a blue sky up there above the pall of smog that enveloped the town, or maybe he had no money left and thought he could go out and collect from his brother. Then again, it could also have been that he could no longer stand being cooped up in his caravan with its stench of warmed-over tinned ravioli and propane gas, out there on the car park next to the arterial road behind the central markets, or in the cheap beer bars, with names like THE RIGHT ANGLE or THE PULL INN, or perhaps he could no longer abide the whores who, after prolonged haggling and because of his good connections, were prepared to share the car park with him. The mixture of exhaust fumes and cheap perfume was powerful enough to overlay the sweat of the long-distance lorry drivers which inevitably clung to them. Shagbag Diesel, he called this mixture of odours.

All the same, the thought of going to visit the boarding school out in the country did nothing to make him feel any happier. For one thing, he hated his little brother for the fact that he was now the one who carried all their parents' aspirations; a supposedly good school, then a sound training as a chef, start at the bottom, then a hotelier's diploma, work your way up, get to know the lot, leave nothing out, don't let anybody take you for a ride, no, not nobody! These maxims he had heard from his father, adages he had been so force-fed on that he had grown fat on them.

And for another, he hated, among many other things, the smell of the boarding school, the dormitories, the mixed underwear, the stink of self-abuse, the bathroom mirrors spattered with squeezed pimples. The podgy or spindly girls with all their adolescent problems, most of them two years in advance of the boys in this, and going through agonies. Give him the whores any time, although he kept telling himself how much he despised and detested them.

He swung himself into his Capri, for he was convinced the women were always watching him, he believed that although he was ugly – he was that honest with himself – he had a certain randy, distinctly masculine aura about him, and all the ones around here were itching to sleep with him or at least to get the chance to jerk him off. He was sure it was just that they were too shy. Now and again he did some favours for his friend, a pimp from childhood, supplying this and that, collecting debts with the aid of a piece of lead piping which he had shoved inside a length of garden hose, a tear-gas pistol or a flick-knife. Deep down, he was harmless, a coward. That was the dangerous thing about him. Yet he had never actually hurt anyone so far. It was always enough – his friend called it the first phase, very much in the tradition of the torturers of the Holy Inquisition – just to show them the tools of the trade.

At the third attempt, the Capri started and moved out of the suburban fug.

He neither enjoyed the drive through the open countryside nor was put off by the factory buildings that lay scattered almost at random about it, the power cables, the crows in the field behind the motorway service area where they scavenged on the garbage, the birds of prey, the hawk, the harrier or the buzzard, each of them perched proprietorially on its own fence-post, loftily eyeing the passing traffic and waiting for fresh carrion, for the rabbit knocked spinning through the air like a ball, turning red in flight. Fever's brother was totally indifferent to all this, he squeezed every last ounce out of the Capri and thought, you can bloody well bust a gut, by which he meant both his own engine and the young man in the Golf GTI behind him, whom he was grinningly obstructing. You'll be late for your appointment, Fever's brother thought. He erected his middle finger, licked it carefully and stuck it out of the window, where the slip-stream quickly cooled it.

Very pleased with himself, he left the motorway, drove through a little wood, caught up with a farmer on an antiquated tractor and, once he was able to overtake him, gave him the dreaded finger. The halfwit hadn't reacted to the sound of his horn and had not given way. He took the finger to be a townie's greeting, which he returned, beaming broadly.

Fever was sitting in the basement with the others when, over the racket of the cassette recorder bouncing off the concrete, he heard the crunching of the fraternal gearbox. They were drinking a bottle of apple schnapps, and before that Fever had already smoked a few and been on beer. Raven sat, staring vacantly, on a stool which he had tilted backwards against the wall so that the only thing he had to move was his left hand, the one with his glass in it.

Andre didn't want to drink anything that day, nor to talk to anyone, so she was in her room, reading. The Victim, who could never cope with her school work, was trying to learn some French vocabulary, muttering it quietly to herself.

But how was she, who had never learnt to concentrate even in complete silence, supposed to retain a single word in the middle of this row.

Fever jumped unsteadily to his feet and shoved his cigarette between The Victim's moving lips, because he couldn't go through the building with a cigarette in his hand. He hurried upstairs, but once his brother could see him from where he was waiting in the car park, he reduced his pace to a leisurely and apparently casual stroll.

The elder brother gave Fever an irritated thump on the arm because he had not earned a single penny and had smoked all the grass himself, along with Raven. Fever invited his big brother downstairs for a drink, there were some hot women there, he said. Contemptuously, the former pupil, with the school rules still embedded in the crust of his skull, trod on his cigarette-end and ambled downstairs. This sort of thing would never have been allowed in his day. And the person on duty only came by twice, at fixed times.

Without a word of greeting, the big brother sat down in Fever's armchair and had a schnapps poured for him. No one spoke, only The Victim was murmuring her vocabulary, la ferme – the farm, la vache – the cow. The cassette player was giving out 'Stairway to Heaven', a cassette that Fever had got from his brother. The big fellow drank two glasses and then his watery, normally unobservant eye fell on The Victim's breasts, which stood out even under her loose pullover. Fever, whose eyes were fixed only on his brother, noticed this. He got up, snatched the HB out of The Victim's mouth and kissed her in his usual way. Then he looked over to his brother and smiled, pleased with himself. The big fellow stood up, took his glass of sticky apple schnapps and threw it in his brother's face. This he followed by a slap with the back of his hand, hurting himself a bit too. To The Victim, who was staring at him wide-eyed, he said, C'mon, I'll show you my car.

She closed her vocabulary notebook, took an HB from Fever's packet, lit it and went off after the big brother. Raven filled up his glass and likewise took a cigarette from Fever's packet. Everyone took a cigarette from Fever's packet and when he, with trembling fingers, went to take one, there were none left.

From that day on, The Victim was the big brother's property.

Ordinary Level

THE SCHOOL-LEAVERS' party, still an annual event, was heralded, as ever, by the arrival of a variety of vans: just as in the days when Bad Luck was still the pupil Glück, it would have been an Opel Blitz, now it was a VW Transporter open truck that delivered two young laurel trees, taller than a man, and various decorative flower arrangements.

Then it was the Ford Transit from the wine merchant's, bringing the demi-sec sparkling wine and white and red wine in modest, but nevertheless sufficient, quantities.

Last of all came the black Mercedes van belonging to the piano dealer in the county town. At first sight, the classical, Roman-style capital letters in gold on a black background called a funeral undertaker's to mind, and indeed the piano tuner wore, even in dull weather, dark tinted spectacles. Raven, Andre and Fever hated this particular day even more than all other days. The Victim did as they did. They had all decided at a very early stage never to allow themselves to be numbered among those taking the final examinations, and they did everything in their power to ensure that they would never get the length of the *Abitur*, and now they had achieved their goal.

So they also vented their hostility on the laurel saplings, pouring household cleaner and spirit alcohol into the tubs in the hope that the plants would shrivel up and wither before the evening celebrations in two days' time. The laurel trees betrayed no sign of being affected by these caustic substances, for years now they had withstood their malicious attacks and had gone on making their guest appearances throughout the district, green, upright, rich in their foliage and silent but for a dignified, dry rustling in response to draughts, a barely audible little cough among the aromatic leaves that, to the trouble-making alchemists, must have sounded like an expression of derision.

The one and only person who did not arouse the detestation of the ORDINARIES, as the four called themselves since they had determined to go no higher than the *MITTLERE REIFE*, the ORDINARY LEVEL, was the piano tuner, who had to come and tune the Bösendorfer baby-grand.

Each year they fought out the same conflict with him. Hardly had he and his dark glasses entered the small and only hall in the school, where music was normally taught, when he would demand that he be left completely alone and in absolute quiet. At first the four would hide, he seemed to sense their presence and always managed to flush them out. He would say he was going to complain to the headmistress, but it was obvious to him that this would entail a much greater and more unsettling disturbance than if he simply put up with the four intruders. So they would bring him schnapps and cigarettes, and the tension would go out of the situation at once. And now, the thing they had all been waiting for most eagerly happened: he closed the curtains and took off his dark glasses. Under them was hidden an apparently extremely valuable glass eye, which looked as if he had borrowed it from an outsize teddy bear. He opened his little case, took out his tuning forks and began to bemoan the decline of his craft. With each passing year and each glass of schnapps, his despair became more vehement. As a rule, he would start the story in his own early youth, when he could not even sing 'Hänschen Klein', never mind tell an A from an F sharp. His pianistic abilities as a little beginner under severe duress would have made you weep, but his father, a music shop proprietor with an iron will, had forced himself to prolong the sufferings both of the young music teacher and of his untalented, downright tone-deaf son.

It seems things came to a head on his thirteenth birthday; he had just played a little étude from the *Little Music Book for Anna Magdalena Bach* and once again had been unable to keep the right and left hands apart, had put in the counterpoint in a way it had never been heard before and had transposed the melody by the mathematical brain, Bach, into the flowing, shimmering picture-book brain of a Debussy, when his father emerged from a dark corner of the room where he had been listening unseen, and dismissed the piano teacher, placing the entire blame on her shoulders, since, for reasons based on the theory of heredity, his own flesh and blood could not possibly be so totally and utterly unmusical. Once she had left the house in tears, the father boxed the boy's ears, but, instead of crying, he merely gave his father a defiant glare. This insolent look sent the father into such a rage that he sat down at the grand piano and hammered the étude into the keys as if every note of it were a further cuff on the ear, so that it might engrave itself on his son's hearing for all time and, he hoped, would be picked up as if by some internal gramophone needle.

Now get practising! he yelled, and keep at it till you can play it.

He closed the shutters, unscrewed the bulb from the lamp and left behind only a candle. The lock on the door snapped shut behind him. It was dark and still.

He sat down at the piano and only now did the tears come; he cried for half an hour. Then he took up the music and tried to play. To no avail. That was when he had the idea that was to be his salvation. How, he asked himself, is anyone supposed to be able to play on an instrument that is out of tune?

He talked himself into believing that the piano was completely and hopelessly out of tune. He opened it up and tugged around at the strings. Then he found a tuning key in the sideboard and got down to work. A wonderful music arose, he pushed little bits of paper between the strings, turned the tuning key while he played, he plucked and drummed on the strings to his sheer delight. Enchanted, he listened to the tone of an E-string, struck staccato, as he tuned it higher and still higher, with his cheek half-lying on the strings; the strings were no doubt pretty old, and the E-string snapped, the tension in it was released with tremendous force, the string whipped back, caught him first on the eyebrow, then across the eye and finally down his cheek: one half of his eyesight was gone for ever.

He had to scream, bleed and knock for a long time before his mother opened the door – his father would never have done so – and took him to the hospital. His eye was beyond all hope, he would be left with a nasty scar and he needed a glass eye.

For some considerable time the boy was kept off school, since his parents were ashamed. They assumed the whole town knew how the accident had come about.

It was not long before the son asked his father to have the E-string replaced, so that he could resume his practice.

A further two days later, he was playing the Bach étude with a clarity and brilliance his teacher could not match. His ear improved by the day, until he had almost developed perfect pitch, albeit only when he was in a darkened room. In bright light, his ear was no more than average, in sunlight it was as bad as before. But in the dark, he was an auditory master.

It seemed obvious that he should be sent to a music academy, but where on earth would they manage to persuade the professors that he had to play in the dark. Besides, there was the fact that, because of the scars, his face had taken on the look of a criminal, a queer bird, an unreliable and disagreeable type. He was not accepted anywhere. He became a piano tuner, since there were no prospects of his becoming a piano teacher either. The light was too bright, and the man too ugly.

By the time he had reached this point in his story, he had finished the schnapps and asked for more, or at least for cigarettes. Now he was far enough gone for them to be able to persuade him to remove his glass eye and show it round. He felt more comfortable without the eye, so he placed it on the grand piano, which had a remarkable effect on the atmosphere in the room, for the piano now stood there on its spot and there was total silence until the piano tuner began talking again.

The grand piano, he said, was an all-seeing mechanical divinity, the universe, the ear of the cosmos, all wired up and with its mechanism inside its head, a transmitter and receiver, terrestrial satellite for the soul of the world.

If there is such a thing as a god, the piano tuner babbled aloud, then he will be sitting at his monitor at this moment, or else he will have switched on his video recorder, and my eye is his camera.

By now, the piano had been tuned, the piano tuner smoked one last cigarette and, blowing the dust off it three times, reinserted his eye.

Now if only the other eye were gone too, he said, I wouldn't have to drive any more. Into his black van he climbed, then he drove off for this year, to come back to subsequent school leavers' ceremonies until such time as he would be finally lashed, mangled, throttled and shredded by the tons of force generated by the exploding strings of a big concert grand.

Now the laurel trees had been set up, the floral decorations distributed around the hall, the piano tuned, the white wine and the demi-sec sparkling chilled, the red already in place behind the cold buffet that the headmistress always laid out in cooperation with the cook. Inquiries about vacancies had been made in all the surrounding boarding houses, guest houses and hotels. There were always rooms available everywhere. Now the parents could start arriving. For the male pupils, a tie was obligatory, for the female ones a skirt or dress, and from early morning on, the Ordinaries started to smoke and drink to excess. By the time the ceremonial presentation of certificates started in the early evening, they were all, except Andre who had not consumed so much, in their rooms with a sick-basin handy by their beds. The celebrations for those who had achieved the Ordinary Level were a more modest affair. Only those receiving a certificate were obliged to wear a tie or a dress, the ceremony itself was basic in the extreme. They were asked to come to the headmistress's office, even The Victim, who had gone through endless agonies as to whether she would gain a certificate at all. The headmistress handed over the booklets with their marks in them, not without a certain emotion. Each of them was asked what they wanted to be.

Chef, said Fever.

Druggist, said Raven.

Beautician, said The Victim.

Something else, said Andre.

That was the end of their days at the boarding school.

Brief Career as a Druggist, Funny Little Bottles

DEEP WITHIN THE chemist's being, so deep that hardly anyone could suspect it existed, lay something extraordinarily soft and tender. His childhood and youth had been hard, his mother cold and aloof and his father withdrawn and strict; thus it was that this tenderness and softness had proved a handicap to his development, since he himself came to regard this trait as weakness. Very early on, his voice had taken on a metallic, glassy quality. If he uttered some matter-of-fact remark, and he produced many of these because his parents took him seriously only as an unemotional person and not as a happy and playful child, then he unconsciously imparted to his tone of voice a cold edge that originated from somewhere back in his throat, as if every syllable, every sound were being struck out with a little clapper against some metallic or glassy vessel in his throat. This, in contrast to his large grey eyes which were surrounded by countless little laughter-lines, created, on first meeting, at first hearing, a far from endearing effect, since the impression of warmth that seemed initially to emanate from him was destroyed by this extraordinarily cold tone of voice. It was like jumping into a steaming bathtub in the expectation of a hot bath only to find that the water was giving off cold condensation. To most people he seemed unapproachable, cold, even calculating.

The chemist, for his part, was by no means oblivious to this, he felt he was not appreciated and consequently, like anyone who feels rejected, he did in fact become cooler and more distant. Thus the first impression was reinforced the next moment, and only a very few people indeed managed, after a prolonged and onerous process of getting to know him, to penetrate to the core of this man.

It was no different for Raven: the chemist was surrounded by countless little bottles adorned with awe-inspiring, indecipherable labels and hermetically sealed with ground stoppers. His voice had that metallic, glassy ring, his demeanour was distant and cool. It seemed to Raven as if the master of his future apprenticeship, lord of a thousand and more little bottles, were himself imprisoned in a bottle and might at any moment start beating helplessly against the glass, if only so as not to be left so totally alone with himself. Yet that beating was too tentative, too faint for very many people to be able to hear it; and if anyone did hear it, there was hardly anyone who would dare to respond to it.

The chemist's father had been a grocer and general merchant, who would have preferred to leave his wife to deal with his clientèle. She, however, was not one either for indulging in chit-chat about this and that, and certainly not with the customers who, since nothing bound them to the shopkeeping couple other than the fact that the shop was handy and its range of stock wide and varied, were no more than passing trade. And the chemist's mother certainly did not want her circle of acquaintances to be dictated merely by such chance, so, as soon as his tender years permitted, the son had to take on the job of dealing with customers. This resulted in his last traces of affability being eradicated, for people soon made it clear to him too that they regarded his father, his mother and now indeed the whole family as conceited, snooty incomers (although nobody could remember exactly when they had arrived), whose northern accent made not the slightest concessions to the local dialect. And so sugar and paraffin, confectionery and horn – and later, plastic –

buttons, corduroy and washing soap, shaving brushes and Danzig *Goldwasser* liqueur for wedding anniversaries, all made their way across the counter without anything ever amounting to an exchange of gossip, far less a friendly chat or a joke between buyer and seller. What's the point anyway, the mother used to say, cash for goods and goods for cash, that's what business is all about. Anybody who wants entertainment should go to the circus – it came twice a year – and pay for a ticket. Things went along fine, so well that the father and mother were perfectly satisfied with the prospect of their son also becoming just such a general merchant, as in fact he already was at the age of twelve. The boy, however, said he reckoned he was bright enough already to be a general merchant, he could do that and wanted to aim for something higher, he wanted to learn something else. Fine, they said, so become a druggist, then you'll have to get to know about all the drugs from abroad and from the four corners of the earth, you'll have to do a bit of studying for that all right. So the boy got hold of books about drugs and after a very short time he knew them off by heart, page by page. What's the next step up from a druggist? he asked his teacher. Pharmacist, says he. Right, I want to be a pharmacist, says the boy. Then you'll have to study, the teacher warned him, and the boy studied and read his way through every book the teacher possessed and soon knew more than his teacher who, as a result, promised to put in a good word with his parents in order that the boy might attend a more advanced school. The teacher got the parents' backs up because they reckoned he had put this bee about studying into the boy's bonnet. The teacher could count himself lucky that the parents were not in fact ones for gossip, otherwise he could have been ruined in very short order. The boy still had to argue at length with his parents, who regarded their son's desire to be better than they were as something of a humiliation. So, as well as the obligation that the chemist saw as deriving from his close family relationship with young Raven, this was another reason why he wanted to do everything in his power to help him, for just as he had been a solitary child, so also was Raven a loner – and the chemist did not believe that Raven would be capable of protecting himself with a shell of coldness the way he himself had done.

Only, he could not bring Raven to understand that he had to continue his school career and get his *Abitur* in order to be able to go on, as he had at that time decided, to study pharmacy and to become a chemist.

Raven took the view that he had been at school long enough, the others, Fever, The Victim, Andre, none of them wanted to go on with school, so why should he be any different. No, he was firmly convinced that even the life of an ordinary druggist and general merchant would fill up his days in a very satisfactory manner.

The boy's attitude was driving the chemist crazy. He wanted to offer him a great future, he could become a chemist here, or he could take up a job elsewhere if he liked, he could go in for research, travel, a chemist could work and live anywhere, a chemist was just as indispensable as a doctor. And Raven couldn't be bothered looking beyond the limited horizons he had picked up in the boarding school. What he was was enough for him, and what was waiting for him in life, well, that he knew already; this neither worried him nor filled him with joyful anticipation. It was there, and so there was nothing else to discuss.

Furious, the chemist turned to his niece, Raven's mother, to get her to bring her influence to bear on the boy. He was all the more shaken to see the extent to which this woman's judgment faculties were deteriorating from day to day, and it was equally obvious to him that the drugs he procured for her in huge quantities were bringing this about, accelerated by even greater quantities of alcohol which she procured for herself. She was quite single-mindedly destroying herself. To be sure, she conceded that it would be better for the boy if he carried on at school to become a chemist or whatever, but she said from the outset that she would never, never be able to convince him of this.

The main thing is that he should stand for no interference from anybody. Not even from you. And least of all from me, she said, terminating the discussion. The chemist took three little packets of Valium from his coat pocket and impressed on her not to take them with alcohol, which of course she proceeded to do the moment he had said his despairing goodbye, climbed into his Volkswagen and driven back to report to Raven that his mother would be quite beside herself if he were to leave school now. Raven was silent for a while and then said, So I've to become a chemist, then. Yes, you should, said the chemist. To which Raven retorted, his mother only wanted that so that he could get more stuff for her. Now his mind was made up once and for all. No more school, no studies, no chemist.

Raven had spent a disturbed night. While he had fallen into a deep sleep right away, his dreams were unpleasant, and yet he could not remember any of them. Perhaps he had caught a cold, or maybe the shadow of some worry or fear had settled on his vocal chords; he did not know what the reason was, but when he awoke he could not help noticing that his voice seemed to have deserted him, or at least it had slipped down somewhere inside him, where he was no longer in control of it.

Yes, it was still there, yet it was outside his body, and with every word he had to try to recapture it, to snap after it like a fish, and to force it back into the right place and keep it there. But his voice was not going to stand for that, it wanted out, it was impossible to hold on to, it became rough and hurt when he talked, rough as a bare, whitewashed wall.

He started to cough and clear his throat, he seemed, like

his voice, to be outside himself, seeking, and not finding himself.

He had a dry cough, it hurt just to hear it. He wanted to take something to ease it and looked for throat pastilles or cough medicine. And so Raven came upon the amazing effect of the very palatable cough-mixture. If he took one sip of it, that did no good at all, but it did have a pleasant taste. He felt sure that if he took two, three spoonsful, that was bound to do something to help, yet it still made no difference. So he took more and more of it, using the large spoon instead of the small one, and ended up drinking it, letting it trickle down his throat straight from the bottle, and suddenly he felt a lot easier, felt contented and happy and breathed more easily. He realised he would have to be careful. Soon the chemist would notice that his stocks of cough-mixture were dwindling. He read the instructions enclosed with other medicines. He sampled this and that until one day the chemist had to measure out some 100% alcohol for a customer. An hour later, the customer came back and complained that the alcohol was not concentrated. The chemist held a lighted match to it. The match went out.

Now he left his bedroom door open at nights. And sure enough he heard noises. He crept into the shop, switched the light on and caught Raven in the act of putting the alcohol bottle to his lips.

The chemist gave Raven a good long talking-to. He should just take a look at his mother and what had become of her, the way she was going downhill.

There was only one other solution he could see for Raven. A chemist's life was not for him. He needed discipline. He needed hard work.

Stocktaking

WITH A GROAN, the chemist got into his old Volkswagen to set out on the long, roundabout way to his friend, for he lived to the right of the motorway, while the stonemason lived on the left side. Because of the many kilometres you had to drive in order to cross the carriageways, their visits, which had been few and far between anyway, had become even more infrequent, until the stonemason had finally given up coming altogether and the chemist looked in on him only on special occasions like birthdays, or at Christmas. And yet, even if they had not seen each other for a year, it was as if they had parted only the day before, so calm, sober and undemonstrative was their reunion. They had never called each other friends, it had always been a matter of 'my acquaintance, the stonemason' or, in the other's case, simply 'the chemist'. For all that, the chemist was the only person who knew anything at all about the background, the history or the real character of the stonemason. And what that was, he never revealed. And whenever anyone did succeed in persuading him to have a drink, he would invariably become sentimental and murmur, with glistening eyes, ah yes, my old acquaintance the stonemason, he's been through a lot, or, ah, the stories I could tell. What he had been through or what kind of stories could be told about the stonemason were things the chemist never divulged. Thus the stonemason was surrounded by that aura of mystery that makes a man interesting and gives rise to speculation: was he once famous and rich? Did he commit some crime? Had there been some great, unrequited love? If the stonemason had heard all the rumours about him, he would no doubt have rushed to commit his totally unspectacular life to a single sheet of paper and have it published in the local newspaper. And he had picked out, as a backdrop to the evening of his life, an equally unspectacular setting. In the past, at some time or another, it must, like any other landscape in fact, have had its own particular charm. To be sure, it was flat, bare and cold, a kind of high plateau, yet it was precisely in that very flatness, barrenness and coldness that its charm lay. On clear days you could make out distant mountain ranges, and when the light was favourable you could see the radar scanners of the military installations and the television transmitter masts shining on the peaks. In the last twenty years, though, the plain had become overrun by small factories, pig farms, approach roads, shopping centres, pylons and railway lines which had already been closed again; the people there slumbered in a complacent, muted sadness and went about their business with the minimum of fuss. Anyone bent on discovering any other peculiar charm about this region would have his work cut out to find it. But who would want to do that anyway? Neither the stonemason nor the chemist had ever come across anyone who, after the construction of the motorway, would have expected anything more. And the folk were more grateful than annoyed about the noise of the military aircraft that hurtled back and forth between the mountain ranges in the course of their training and manoeuvres, because it was a welcome excuse for looking upwards, into the skies, and for letting their eyes follow anything that suddenly came into view only to disappear again. In this way, they could reassure themselves that there was a life beyond the one they saw on television, namely out there where the planes came from, and presumably over there where they disappeared from sight again. The scene was particularly dreary when, as now, it was blanketed by a thin covering of snow. This was the reason why the chemist had also brought a gentleman's umbrella with him, which he used as a walking-stick. He was convinced that if ever anyone of his age were to slip, then there was a definite risk of breaking a bone, and that would not heal without complications. So he took the utmost care as he got out of his car at his friend's workshop and looked around, inspecting and counting off the stacked-up stone slabs and blocks and comparing the figure with the number of those who had passed on in the previous year. He came to the conclusion that the stonemason had provided a headstone for all but one of them. His curiosity as to who that was and why they did not have a stone from his friend's workshop standing on their grave made him smile at himself. I haven't one foot in the grave yet, he thought, although I'm well along the way to it. With that thought and with the intention of finding out whether his friend was in a similar frame of mind, he opened the red-leaded and rust-flecked iron door.

There was not a sound to be heard and very little light inside the large shed, the day was dull and the sky-light was still obscured by a light dusting of snow, an indication that once again there was no heating on in the workshop. Once his eyes had grown accustomed to the half-light, the chemist took a few cautious steps forward, startling the rabbits, of which the stonemason kept a large number in hutches. In their excitement, they bumped against the wire netting of their cages. To the rear of the workshop, the stonemason had used some boards to partition off a kind of cabin which he had hung with blankets and carpet remnants to protect himself from the cold and the dust. This was where he slept and cooked his meals. To announce his presence, the chemist banged his umbrella against the huge blade of a stone-saw, the noise echoing through the shed like the gong in a Tibetan monastery. Even before the quivering din had slowly died away, the stonemason, who appeared to have been asleep, pushed a blanket aside and came into view. Without a word, he fetched from a corner of his hovel which, since the window there was broken, he called his refrigerator, a cardboard box inscribed with blue Cyrillic lettering, blew the ubiquitous dust off it and took out a bottle. The chemist followed him into the cabin. They sat down opposite each other with the bottle on the camping table between them and eyed each other in silence for a while until the chemist had to sneeze. The dust, he said, and wiped his nose. Then, when he had recovered his sense of smell, he complained about the stench from the rabbits. Like in the zoo, no, worse than the zoo, he said. Basically, their meetings always followed the same pattern and year by year they came increasingly to resemble some mysterious ritual. As usual, the stonemason made fun of the chemist's umbrella, which was lying across his knees, and lit a cigarette; each evening he rolled a large quantity of these so as not to waste time during the day. That way, he said, enveloped in clouds of yellowish smoke, he wasn't bothered by the stink.

Exactly, said the chemist, that stuff stinks even more evilly than the rabbits.

Yes, said the stonemason, want one?

Naturally, the chemist always declined the offer of a cigarette, whereupon the stonemason would assure him that his tobacco was pure and unadulterated, for he grew it himself and dried and cured it in his oven. Then he stood up and went to fetch two old mustard jars, and at this the chemist reminded him that he did not drink. The stonemason smiled and filled the glasses, wished him *na zdorovye* and refilled the empty glasses. They carried on drinking this way before another word, other than the stonemason's *na zdorovye*, was spoken, each of them getting through three glasses, three glasses of Siberian vodka, distilled with water from Lake Baikal. What followed was what they both termed stocktaking. As a rule, it was the chemist who set the ball rolling.

Last year he had counted twenty-three stones. To the best of his knowledge, five people had died since then. When he was coming in, he had counted nineteen stones. So what about the stone piled up rough and unworked outside the building? Had the fifth person not died at all, had they been buried in some far distant place, had they even been buried at sea or had they, or perhaps their surviving dependants, been so tactless as to have the headstone made by some other monumental sculptor not locally resident? Aroused by these questions to a fair state of agitation, the stonemason got to his feet and rummaged about in a box for the square-ruled arithmetic notebook which this year was serving as his order book. In fact his entries confirmed what he already knew, namely that he had produced four gravestones. There now ensued a great racking of brains as to who had actually died, what of and whether the death had been expected or had come as a surprise. So now the question arose, had it in fact been five and not four deaths? The chemist arrived at the figure five by counting up all the members of a certain age-group who were in the habit of buying their medicines in his shop and subtracting those who suddenly stopped coming. And he was seldom mistaken about this, although the stonemason, with some justification, accused him of employing a method of calculation that excluded from the outset the possibility of those people making a recovery. If, as indeed did occasionally happen, younger people or children met with a sudden death, for instance in a traffic accident on the motorway, everyone got to know about it as a matter of course, having heard the rescue helicopter taking off and landing or the sirens of the ambulances and recovery vehicles. So the stonemason reckoned he had registered a victory this year because the chemist had made a mistake and the chemist could not disguise a certain malicious delight at an order having eluded the stonemason. To a certain extent, then, honour was satisfied on both sides when the chemist revealed to his friend that a change in his, the stonemason's, life was imminent, that this would be a good thing and was long overdue. It was just not right anymore that he should be doing all that hard work on his own, that he should be drinking his vodka on his own and breathing in the dust and smoking his tobacco all on his own. After a brief moment of amazement, the stonemason burst out laughing and asked whether he was about to be married, or what. And anyway, the woman who could put up with his tobacco hadn't been born yet, more likely had still to be fathered, and he couldn't imagine anyone other than himself being up to that.

Rabbit's Demise

RELUCTANTLY, RAVEN GOT into the chemist's Volkswagen, for he had no way of knowing what fate had in store for him at the stonemason's. Raven thought the chemist would lay down the law on how he was to behave, but he remained steadfastly silent, with the result that not a word was exchanged throughout the whole trip. When Raven realised that the workshop was so far out of town, he became even more uneasy, and with every passing kilometre he began once again to have doubts as to the wisdom of his decision – which had been half-hearted in the first place – to become a stonemason. The chemist brought Raven to the workshop door, but did not shout in a greeting. There it is, was all he said. And how do I get back? asked Raven, horrified. You're stopping here, replied the chemist, I've already brought your mattress out.

Now Raven felt he had been thoroughly press-ganged. He had had misgivings about the interview with this stranger as it was, but if he had known that he had to stay there from the start, his dread would have been even greater. Now, in the imminent conversation, he was going to have to reach agreement with the stonemason at least to the extent that he would let him sleep the night here. The disorder in the place was to his liking and after a short time he recognised a certain hidden order in it. There was a peculiar smell, Raven could not imagine that stones would smell like that. He thought he could make out herbs, thyme, garlic, there was an odour of sweat and manure, oil and tobacco. He could hear faint scraping noises, but there was no sight nor sound of a human being. Groping his way, he moved cautiously through the shed and was startled by the sight of a beautiful white gravestone which seemed to hold some kind of place of honour in the workshop. The date of birth, the name and the letters FREUD SCHÖNE GÖTTERFUNK TOCHTER AUS ELYS were already carved out, but the date behind the cross, the date of decease, was missing. He ran his hand carefully over the smooth stone and wondered where he had heard the woman's name, one ROSAMARIA RIEDEL, before. Carrara marble, Raven heard, and was brought up in alarm by the loud, rough voice. He looked round and caught a movement behind a curtain dividing off a part of the workshop. The stonemason's head appeared from behind it, his hair tousled, as if he had just been startled out of his sleep. And he was yawning expansively as well. Raven well knew how ill-tempered someone could be who has just been roused from sleep and could already see himself making his way back to the chemist's on foot. You think I've been sleeping, said the stonemason. You're wrong. I've been watching you. After all, I have to get to know all about you. Do you know how I make a living?

Raven nodded. And you want to learn about that? Yes, said Raven. Are you sure? No. I live by rabbit hunting, did you know that? No.

Raven sat down opposite the man, between them lay a pile of evil-smelling weed that the latter began to slice and chop with a big knife. Raven watched with interest, the other man said nothing and went on chopping fast and accurately, as if he wanted to arouse Raven's admiration for his skill.

So what is it you want to learn? he asked after some time. Raven did not know what to reply, for he was sure that the slightest mistake on his part would fan the flames of the stonemason's displeasure.

See, you don't even know.

Raven was irritated by his disparaging and mocking tone of voice. Yes I do, he said with a defiance that made him feel much more sure of himself.

Out with it then!

Raven remained silent and was just about to say something when the stonemason cut him short by asking, in a seemingly more conciliatory tone, Do you want to become an artist, maybe?

That seemed to Raven such a strange question and it was put in such a kindly way that he answered affirmatively on the spot and even took a sudden pleasure from the thought of becoming an artist. Why not, he thought to himself, and this agreeable idea brought just the slightest hint of a smile to his face which, however, did not escape the stonemason's eye even though he was keeping his attention mainly on his cutting and chopping. Doubtless he interpreted it as a suggestion of smugness, arrogance, cheek, impudence and downright foolishness, for he threw down his knife, half-jumped to his feet and bawled at Raven in a voice that echoed four times round the workshop, becoming even more terrifying each time. He was shouting, Dammit to hell, an artist. You want to be an artist.

He spat out the word once more, as if it had liquefied in the ferment of his rage and turned to sulphuric acid. An arsehole of an artist, he added, this time calmly and in the kind of voice a doctor uses when breaking the news to relatives of a patient's sudden death.

Raven himself was now less intimidated than angry, for he felt he had been lured into a trap by this man. Hadn't he, after all, directly wormed the assertion that he wanted to be an artist out of him. Of course he didn't want to be an artist, he didn't even know if he wanted to be a stonemason, never mind whatever the man had meant by the word artist. So he reacted by flaring up, raising his voice a little in his turn, and said, Yes! and then rather more quietly, Dammit to hell.

He would have been better to stifle this Dammit to hell altogether, for it took all the strength out of his loud Yes. The stonemason, who had at first been quite impressed by the Yes, resumed his scornful tone. Very quietly, he asked, Like who?

Raven did not want to fall into another trap. The best weapon seemed to be to answer with another question: What do you mean, like who?

Or maybe he should have said, exactly like you. That might possibly have meant that he took the man for an arsehole, or at least he might have taken it that way. He wasn't that sure of himself yet. His counter-question sounded pretty stupid. The old fellow leaned back a little and looked at him pityingly. Well, do you know any artists? Do you know what an artist is?

Raven knew his way around the chemist's bookcase, where, in search of erotica and in the belief that it had something to do with the memoirs of some Italian Fanny Hill, he had come across a biography of the sculptor Michelangelo which he had at first dipped into, looking only for racy bits, but then eagerly read right through. So he replied with an alacrity that astonished the stonemason, Michelangelo.

He was so taken aback that he remained silent. Raven thought he could see a hint of misting in the eyes of the man sitting opposite him, but then his mouth opened and he burst into the most incredible roar of laughter that resounded and reverberated around the workshop in a quite remarkable way. His laughter sounded so refreshing that Raven, too, began to grin, and the wider his grin spread, the quieter the laughter became. When Raven went so far as to let out a sound, the stonemason stopped abruptly. Raven did not notice this right away, because the echo carried on for some time.

Have you any idea who he was? Michelangelo?

Raven had the impression that the atmosphere had relaxed. To be sure, he was somewhat surprised at the sudden seriousness that followed the old fellow's laughter, but his defensive attitude had slackened. So, with the bit between his teeth, he lapsed into a jocular tone that was unusual for him, not realising that he had touched on a sore point.

Well, he's an artist. Dammit to hell. An arsehole.

There followed a silence so icy that it seemed to Raven as if the echo of the laughter had been frozen. The stonemason took up his knife again and chopped away at the weed, very slowly and with a gravity that had the colour draining from Raven's face. He had chopped a good three hundred grammes before he challenged Raven to repeat what he had just said about Michelangelo Buonarroti. Raven thought he would certainly have to walk home to the chemist's now, or at least spend the night in the open. He cursed his stupidity. It's like in boxing. You must never drop your guard, he thought.

Repeat that! said the stonemason in a voice that, as Raven told people later, you could have cut a marble slab with.

That he's an artist.

You said something else.

I take it back.

Say it's you that's the arsehole.

It's you that's the arsehole.

Slowly, the old fellow laid the knife aside, gathered the chopped, stinking stuff together into a little pile, stood up and went to the window. To Raven, every movement was a challenge to him to take up the knife and slit open his own belly. The stonemason came back with a shoe-box, the two mustard jars and a bottle of vodka. He filled the glasses, offered one of his roll-ups from the shoe-box and said *na zdorovye*. Three times the stonemason refilled the glasses, three times he said *na zdorovye* before he told Raven about the water of Lake Baikal, which he had allegedly been drinking. He pointed to the label and said the first thing Raven had to remember was that this was the best vodka of all and that Lake Baikal had the clearest water in the world.

Seals are dying in Lake Baikal, said Raven.

Have you been there?

No.

Then hold your tongue and pay attention. I am no artist. For all I care, you can become one if you like. I'm a stonemason, a craftsman, a worker. And do you know what I make my living off? On average, five people a year will be run over here, along a stretch of twenty kilometres. And often old people die, but three children this year already, one of meningitis. One thousand two hundred marks apiece. Two thousand in the case of the grown-ups. Sometimes as much as four thousand. I work cheap. Far too cheap. Dammit to hell. What are you gawping at? D'you see now, I'm no artist. D'you know what Michelangelo did?

To be on the safe side, Raven said nothing. For his part, the stonemason stood up immediately, without waiting for a reply, went into his cabin made of carpets and blankets where he spent a while searching for something. He came back with a book and looked for a particular place in it. He handed it to Raven. Raven read a passage. It was the sculptor's biography, a piece he knew already. The stonemason watched him with obvious relish and, when Raven had finished reading, ordered him to tell him about it.

He sneaked out of the house at night.

With a knife, the stonemason added.
With a knife, and he went to the mortuary.
And then?
He looked at the corpses.
Just looked at them?
He looked inside.
And why?
To see what was in there.
And what was in them?
Fat, blood, heart, liver, muscles, gall-bladder, shit and the rest.

Raven broke off, because he could not fathom what the other man was getting at. Yet he seemed remarkably determined, and his questions were pointed. Raven took one of the roll-ups, poured himself a vodka and, at the first draw, thought he was going to suffocate, so poisonous did the cigarettes taste. What is that? he gasped between convulsions. The old man nodded towards the pile between them and gave an impatient wave of his hand.

And then what?
Then he stank of corpse fat.
And what was all this for?
Because he had to find out what was inside so that he could draw the outside.
That's right. D'you know how much I make?

Raven tried to work out the amount, taking the number of corpses the old fellow had mentioned. It didn't come to much. But the stonemason explained that he could live on it, since he produced practically everything he needed. Everything except bread, vodka, electricity and margarine. Then he wanted to know if Raven was hungry. He nodded. Let's cook something, said the stonemason getting to his feet. You can't eat stones. He went to the rabbit hutches, which Raven hadn't even noticed, since they were hidden by a tarpaulin, and beckoned him over. Pick one out!

Now Raven realised where the smell of manure came from and that those strange noises were caused by the animals' small, quick movements, their breathing and the rustling of the straw. He pointed to a very large rabbit that barely moved at all and stared at them with cold, amber-yellow eyes. Not that one, said the stonemason, that's my best buck. At random, Raven pointed to another. With a quick movement, the stonemason seized it behind the ears. That's the way you pick them up, he said and, as if he had read Raven's thoughts, whether it hurts, I don't know. He looked closely at the animal; its fur was grey and glossy, its belly was white and the tips of its front paws had light grey spots, its eyes were light brown like strong tea. It sniffed vigorously and kicked lazily with its hind legs.

Has it got a name? asked Raven.

Rabbit, said the stonemason. And what's your name?

Raven, said Raven.

Hold him for a minute, ordered the stonemason and fetched from his workbench a heavy wooden club that thickened out towards the end. He weighed it in his hand.

That's your instrument.

Does it have a name?

Swingle. You hit with it.

He held the instrument out to Raven, who took it in his left hand and stretched out both arms far in front of him. The rabbit looked curiously at the striking instrument, as if he thought it was an outsize carrot the size of a forearm.

How to handle a swingle, that's the first thing you've got to learn. Don't grip it so tight; relax your wrist, keep your arm loose. Now put that down and stroke the back of the rabbit's neck. Like this.

Raven felt the calloused sand-papery hand at the nape of his own neck; with surprising gentleness it was trying to get the tension out of his neck muscles, but was achieving exactly the opposite, for Raven now realised what the man wanted him to do. Like a tortoise, he drew in his head. He couldn't do that, he said, his voice tightening, after all, he didn't want to be a butcher.

If you don't know how to use a swingle, you might as well leave now, the stonemason retorted darkly. Now stroke him for a bit and feel what happens.

Raven put down the club and obeyed. He's going all quiet. He likes it. He's stretching his neck.

And now, wallop, said the stonemason, tickling the back of Raven's neck, very gently, but Raven got the message. The old fellow filled the two glasses to the brim. Raven raised his to his lips with his free hand. They both threw back the vodka in one gulp. Raven could feel it burning in his stomach and the burning rising up his spine, warm and pleasant now. The muscles at the back of his neck slackened. You're getting on fine, the two of you, said the old fellow with a grin. In fact Raven and the rabbit were looking at each other almost like friends.

Did you know they smashed Michelangelo's face in for him? It did him a power of good, said the stonemason.

I don't want to be an artist, said Raven quickly.

Have another drink.

Raven felt the intoxication approaching like a gentle, warm wave, enveloping him and making him think and see clearly and yet hazily at the same time.

I don't like slaughtering them either, said the stonemason. But eating them I do like. Garlic. Thyme. Marjoram. Your mouths are watering, both of you. Rabbit and Raven.

He stood up and went for a carrot for the rabbit, bit a piece off it himself and watched the animal comically nibbling at it.

I'll make buttered carrots with it. Look how happy he is. Now you've got to strike. Wallop. They have a slight flavour of tobacco, you've never tasted anything like it.

Tobacco? asked Raven in bewilderment.

Because I dry it in the oven. Now stroke him again. That's the way. Now take the swingle. And wallop.

Raven swung his arm and he managed to break the animal's neck with the first blow. He noticed a last, fairly violent spasm, but it all happened so far away from him that he did not even see the stonemason screw up his eyes for an instant and give a little jerk himself. He took the animal from Raven's hand, set a bowl on the floor, hung it up by the hind legs on a nail driven in for just that purpose and with a few quick movements pulled its skin clean off, he gutted it and explained that you had to be careful not to damage the gall-bladder. He showed him where the gall-bladder was and told him about the various ways of preparing rabbit and what he did with the skin and it was only later that he noticed Raven had long since fallen asleep. Well, you'll learn all that next time, he murmured as he salted and peppered the rabbit and rubbed down the inside with garlic.

Initiation into the Profession

THE PERSISTENT SMOG that had been lying over the surrounding district for some days broke up. The sun could be seen, the cold of the last few days hung on stubbornly, but after a while the stonemason felt a warmth that had long been absent creeping into his bones. Spring was still a long way off, yet this day had something spring-like about it. It ensured that people did not altogether forget the seasons after the long period when one day so dreadfully resembled the next that Raven was grateful for nightfall and its reassurance that his future life would not pass in one single, life-long day. The old fellow went out of the workshop, beckoned to Raven to follow, squinted up to the sky and then said, Have you ever felt like a woman?

You mean liked to feel? Raven asked in turn.

How you go about it is of no interest to me, said the stonemason. Today we're going to see Rosamaria.

The old fellow stretched with a languorous grunt, went back into the workshop and washed more thoroughly than he had done for a long time, so that the room was filled with the aroma of lavender soap. From the chest he took an old-fashioned but rakishly elegant black double-breasted suit and gave it a good going over with a brush. If anything ever happens to me, have a look inside this suit, he said casually to Raven, who was watching in bewilderment. The stonemason shaved, took the vodka bottle and a mustard jar full of dark-brown powder. He took some of the powder on the tip of a knife and stirred it into the vodka, but it refused to dissolve; black particles formed and rose to the surface.

Want some? he asked Raven, but the mixture looked so unappetising that he shook his head. *Na zdorovye*, shouted the boss and knocked the stuff back. Ready? he asked.

Ready, said the apprentice.

He led Raven behind the building and pointed to two bicycles standing under a plastic sheet. On you get! said the stonemason and pedalled off.

With a following wind and on a day of reasonable warmth, a cyclist would take half an hour to get to the only clearly distinguishable hill in this flat region, on which stood a building constructed in the fifties in a modest villa style. From it, there was a panoramic view which merely confirmed the impression of the surrounding district's featurelessness. The house was called the Villa Panorama and had been leased by a building contractor to a certain Rosamaria, who ran a moderately successful brothel in it. The stonemason had been involved in the building work at the time and had for a while been on friendly terms with the builder, a self-made man, one of the first to get back on his feet after the war, who took a liking to the unconventional and energetic stonemason. So, along with a few other dignitaries, he spent numerous wild evenings there as the guest of the generous builder. A wide drive led up the hill to the house, which by some mischance, however, could be seen into from all sides and so had to be planted all round with fast-growing shrubs. When the stonemason then struck up a friendship with Rosamaria, to whom the host had taken a fancy, the friendship between the men soon cooled off. Rosamaria herself had gained her first experience as a businesswoman after the war, so she had something in common with the building contractor, each of them in his or her own way achieving prosperity through bartering. Soon the builder stopped inviting the stonemason, yet neither he nor Rosamaria was of a mind to give up their occasional trysts altogether, although the stonemason was, after a short period of time, no longer able to afford them. So it was that an odd kind of agreement with the madam came into being, and this too was based on an exchange in kind rather than cash. The stonemason enjoyed what might be termed free bed and board, in return for which Rosamaria commissioned a most becoming headstone in white Carrara marble. After each visit, the stonemason would add one, or, as befitted the occasion, perhaps two letters and, since with the passing years his visits became rather less frequent, partly because he was not keen to meet the builder, whom he could no longer abide, the last seven years had each seen only one or two letters chiselled into the inscription, naturally leaving the date of her demise blank.

Raven's bicycle had a buckled wheel, and he had to pedal extra hard to keep up with the stonemason who was bustling on ahead. In addition, the air was slowly escaping from his back tyre. The boss did not look back, Raven could hear him singing as he watched him recede into the distance, moving, it seemed, faster and faster. Raven was amazed at the strength of the man, and this renewed his doubts as to whether he himself might not prove too feeble for this heavy labour. What the devil's driving him on like that? he asked himself and cursed his crippled bike. In the last few days he had complained of the constant cold, but now he was bathed in sweat and, like his tyre, he was getting short of air.

The steep track leading up to the Villa Panorama seemed to drain him of his remaining strength and he had to dismount and push, whereas the stonemason stood up on his pedals and pressed on up the slope at an enormous rate. It was as if he had been rejuvenated and his eyes shone with a roguish glee at his strength and in anticipation of the coming delights.

He would not have gone so far as to say that he was in love with Rosamaria, indeed he had never in his life uttered such a, to him, dangerous, sentiment to anyone; all the same, he was always delighted to see her, to chat with her, and he immediately became more talkative and charming than Raven had ever seen him. She, for her part, was enchanted by him, she loved his strength and his leathery skin and he adored her magnificent backside and her luxuriant dark hair which, she maintained, had never yet been touched by dye.

Under her gaze, under her hands, men became obedient, affectionately carnal animals which she could at will tame, break in, chastise, praise with a pat and angrily scold, and for all this they were grateful to her; to them she was something between a whore and a mother, and if one of her clients displayed any hesitancy or even embarrassment, she had the knack of turning him, with a few words, into a long-yearned-for lover, as if he had returned from a long journey and she, her backside, her breasts and her thick tumbling hair had been waiting for this one man alone. Her voice was warm, and Raven felt a tickling in the pit of his stomach when she spoke and he was sure he could feel his champagne glass vibrating gently. The Deafman would love her and that voice, he thought, and he resolved to visit the Villa Panorama with him one day.

The three of them sat at the little bar, drinking champagne and vodka, the room smelled of cold smoke and stale alcohol, and yet Rosamaria wore a heavenly perfume that coupled with this foul-smelling mixture of the remains of countless nights of dissipation in such a way as to make you think your nose was situated somewhere in your loins. After only a few minutes' chat, there was nothing that either of them wanted more than to plunge into, to become immersed in, this sea of odours and flesh, to run his hands through her thick hair and to get to work on that backside with at least the same stamina and dedication as if it were a block of Carrara marble; indeed the stonemason was already conjuring up in his mind's eye a pneumatic drill as the image of his manly prowess and his sexual designs on Rosamaria.

Although she had hardly paid Raven any further attention after her friendly welcome, having eyes only for the older man, his feelings were no different and his pulse, which had already been racing after his cycling exertions, was now positively whirring, and his agitated breathing could neither be slowed down nor disguised.

Rosamaria took up the internal telephone, pinched Raven's already burning cheek and asked for someone called Natasha, whereupon the stonemason raised one eyebrow, gave a knowing grin and finally closed one eye in a wink of complicity.

Natasha will be down for you, Sonny, said Rosamaria, and things began to stir and throb in his trousers, so much so that he was embarassed at the thought that the two others might notice it. And notice it they did, so that, hardly had Raven left the bar hand in hand with Natasha, than the stonemason and Rosamaria burst out in gales of laughter.

Natasha was small, slim, with an almost boyish figure, and since she had dark eyes, Rosamaria had cast her in the rôle of a little black demon. Also in the house were little blonde cherubs, big, cool, Nordic ladies, voluptuous, obviously peroxided women reminiscent of Reubens models with the first signs of a paunch and folds of fat. Each of them was meant to represent a specific type, so that any man could find a playmate exactly suited to his very own personal desires. Natasha had brought out the little demon effect by an ensemble in black and red and with a sharp black line on her eyelids and long black-painted nails, and indeed she exuded something childishly salacious, depraved and at the same time cutely wicked, which was what distinguished this little demon from the blonde cherubs and the real she-devil herself.

The girls never betrayed their true names, and Natasha spoke in an accent with distinct Eastern tones and a soft rolling R, so that no one would ever have thought for a moment that she might not actually be called Natasha. This had all been carefully conceived and tried and tested, so that Raven, too, was in no doubt whatsoever that this creature leading him slowly upstairs was a little black demon from the East. And since Raven himself had something black about him which at times hung about him like a cloud, Rosamaria had quite deliberately put together a black little couple for each one to have its pleasure with the other.

In Natasha's tiny room, the windows were wide open; the air was pleasantly fresh here in contrast to that in the bar. The wallpaper was an infernal red and the bedclothes black satin, only the shower cabinet spoiled the effect somewhat, since it was sky-blue, but then again the shower curtain was fiery red and moved in the light draught like licking flames. Amazingly, there was no smell of sulphur. Although that soon changed when Natasha lit up a cigarette.

Natasha closed the window and studied Raven with a

smile, and she too saw immediately how things stood in his trousers; she would have been happy to bring him immediate relief, but first of all he had to undergo a thorough cleaning process, that was the practice there, and anyway Raven was completely coated with the finest stone dust which had penetrated the fibres of all his clothes and clung to every part of his body. So she took a paper facecloth and carefully unbuttoned his dusty trousers, so as to begin where the need was most urgent.

What have we got here, she cooed, everything covered in dust, where does this dust all come from?

It's from polishing at the stonemason's, answered Raven, although in his excitement he could barely move his lips and was beginning to tremble.

What kind of stones do you polish? she asked.

Granite and pink marble, said Raven.

She was amused by the idea, since she was doing a bit of polishing here too, and took a close look at everything. Raven, too, was looking at himself and tried to think of the morels in the Deafman's mushroom book to calm himself down a little, but it was no good.

Brown, this granite, with a tracery of bluish veins running through it and with a little head of pink marble, how warm the marble is, we'll polish it carefully and wash it and, oops! she said, for she must have been rather too careless in her washing and polishing and now the morel was turning into a timorous and hastily retreating little toadstool, Raven was reminded of the Bohemian Wrinkled Verpa, a very tasty edible specimen. Now the little mushroom was wrapping itself more and more in folds, ageing rapidly and simply desperate to sink back into the moss. And no matter how hard she tried, with her most suggestive plays on words, with her quick, hot tongue and with her deft, hand-cream fragrant fingers, this game ended in stalemate, he had shot his bolt too soon.

Let your sweet little black demon come on top and ride you, she tried to tempt him, and other endearments flowed in an unceasing stream from her so bewitchingly R-rolling tongue. Nothing worked.

His shame at his over-eagerness ensured that reloading was now quite out of the question, so the two of them went back downstairs to the bar, drank demi-sec champagne and waited for Rosamaria and the stonemason. They had a long wait, and Natasha promised Raven all sorts of exotic delights if only he would try again with her.

When the stonemason and Rosamaria finally did come down again, cheerful and exhausted, it was already getting dark. The stonemason eyed Raven inquisitively, but he merely bowed his head, and Rosamaria instructed Natasha with a glance to whisper in her ear and tell her what had happened upstairs. Raven blushed as Rosamaria gave a quiet laugh. The stonemason guessed what it was all about, ordered a vodka and started to tell his tales.

Russian Flies

I TURN MY face to the East and there I see a fiery glare, orange-red, over the lake. The lake is boundless, an ocean to those people who have never in their lives seen anything bigger than this lake. And if you look down into the depths when you go out in a boat, you can see forty, fifty metres down, so clean is the water.

There, in the little town of Listvyanka, where the Angara flows out of Lake Baikal, lived two beautiful twin sisters. They were my lovers, and worked at the Institute for

Limnology. I loved them both; if I went with one, then her sister wept, if I went with the other, her sister wept. Why don't you take us both? they would ask. Well, let me tell you, to satisfy one of them took a lot of doing, a man had his work cut out and it was quite a feat, and another achievement was that each was every bit the other's equal; I was a hero in everyone's eyes, and the priest gave me a wink, inviting me into his church, where he advised me not to drink too little and, above all, he said, not to drink in moderation. You would do best not to drink at all, he said, either that or you should drink a lot, and then take them both. I didn't want to see anyone disappointed, so I drank a great deal and tried to take them both, and at that they both wept and I, for shame at my failure, I wept along with them. The houses were log cabins, the wood tarred black, the shutters white, green and blue, the roofs made of corrugated iron, and the corrugated iron amplified our wailing and the priest must have heard it.

The next day, I met him outside his church, and he said, You didn't drink enough, you mustn't be mediocre and do anything by halves. Have a look at the way the bears do it. And he named a place at the lakeside where you could watch the bears. The people of Listvyanka know the bears well, they're often in the forest collecting mushrooms and berries.

The glare came from the oil refineries in the town of Irkutsk, the lake is so huge that every slightest bit of pollution gets spread everywhere. There are seals living there too, ringed seals, and the great sturgeon, *zig*, the Russians call it, and the *omul*, and the *golumyanka*, a fish caught for its oil, a deep-sea fish. I climbed up into a tree by the shore and kept still. Soon the first bear came along, sniffed around, caught my scent, but it wasn't bothered a bit, it just gave me a look of contempt, went down to the shore and lifted its nose in the air. Then it began waving its paws around, as if it were trying to send a signal over to the other shore, which you couldn't see from there. It beckoned with its paws, waving them about, made snapping movements, grunted and generally acted as if it had gone mad.

Soon a second bear arrived, gave me the same contemptuous look and went over to the shore, some twenty metres from the first, reared up, waved and snapped.

Soon after that a third bear came along, rather bigger than the others, took up its position between the other two and behaved exactly the same way, as if every bear around had gone crazy. This went on for the best part of an hour, then suddenly they stopped, dropped their snouts into the water, all at the same time, and started to drink. It was then, I'm telling you, that I understood what the priest had meant. The biggest bear took his muzzle out of the lake, went over to the bear on his right, which must have been a she-bear, bit her in the back of the neck and took her from behind. The other female kept on drinking and drinking, now and then looking over at the other two, giving a grunt and then getting back to her drinking. When the bear was finished with the first female, he went over to the other, bit her in the nape of the neck and gave her the same as the first. How about that, then!

You're having us on, said Raven.

It's the truth, said the stonemason. And believe me when I tell you the whole thing was repeated three times. Him with the first, him with the second, him with the first, him with the second, him with the first, him with the second.

And then? asked Raven in disbelief.

Then he lay down and the other two lay down as well, just where they stood, they just dropped down and fell asleep, snoring, so that I was able to climb down out of my tree and have a close look at the bears. I swear to you I could hear whole swarms of flies buzzing around in their bellies.

I told all this to my twin sisters and they said, Catch a fish and eat it raw, the way the bears and the Japanese do. So, off I go and catch a fish, cut it into thin slices and eat it raw. But that wasn't the secret.

So what was the secret? Raven asked sceptically.

Catching the flies! said the stonemason. The bears eat the flies during the mating season, they stand at the water and wave their paws around in the air, you reckon they're crazed, but they're catching the bear-flies and eating them, by the kilo, that makes them randy, randy as a bear can possibly be. If you eat just one of these flies, you'll get as horny as a Russian bear.

The water of the lake is so pure, so clean, that they make the best vodka with it, Siberian Baikal vodka, that's the very best, it'll never give you a hangover or a headache, it leaves you with a clear head and you can see tremendously far down into the lake and look into the eyes of the mermaids. Listen, swallow some bear-flies with it. Then you'll make love like a – what am I saying! – like two, like three bears. And then you'll sleep for a whole day, as if you were dead.

And where am I supposed to get these bear-flies from? asked Raven.

In the jar by my shaving things. That's powdered bear-flies. I get it from the chemist.

He yawned, his speech was getting thicker.

If you want to sleep like a corpse, then drink a whole bottle in one go, and you'll sleep for a whole day and a whole night. People will take you for dead.

That's the way it was with the twin sisters. I slept under the big ash tree outside the priest's house, woke up, bought a bottle of vodka and brought it to the priest. I did it the bears' way. That's how you have to do it – like the bears and no half-measures.

He closed his eyes, fell asleep and started to snore, his snoring became quieter and the rising and falling of his chest was barely perceptible.

And the powder, he had concluded his story, you'll find it in the shaving cabinet.

He had no sooner said that than Raven was already astride the stonemason's bicycle and tearing down the road, virtually flying along the road to the workshop. He leapt over to the shaving cabinet, took out the mustard jar and sniffed at the bear-fly powder. No half-measures, he said, swallowed the powder down and ran back to his bike.

He woke with a start as if from an anaesthetic. His first thoughts were, water, the pond, coolness and plants. Then his conscience hit him, causing him endless torment, pangs of conscience such as he had never experienced. Fornication, laziness, excess, these words flashed through his mind and brought him bolt upright, as if they had released steel springs inside him. Hurled to his feet by one single, violent movement, he found himself standing there, wide awake. Where am I? Here I am. Who am I? I'm me. Just me?

His legs were rushes and wobbly stalks among the reeds; straight away, he lay down again and closed his eyes. Cascades of geometric patterns, snake-skins, the curtains in his mother's bedroom, lightning-flashes, all of them, with a terrifying regularity as if they were being hurled out by some machine, flashing around in the damp sky, the space between his eyeballs and eyelids. Then he sat up, he could sense it with his eyes closed, the workshop was in motion, even though it was built of stone, its double doors and the rails for the hand-crane made of steel, the roof beams of wood and the foundations of concrete, dug solidly a metre deep into the ground. Now all this was moving, running as if on wheels, travelling to the right, over towards the little wood and probably crushing the two bicycles over which, despite his drunken state, he had thrown the plastic sheet, then it came to a stop and moved off left in the direction of the motorway, and that was where the granite and the marble slabs stood in neat piles. He was sure that the ones that lay on top at least would topple off, would fall far and hard and would splinter, tumble one over the other and shatter. That would be a huge loss, the thought flashed through Raven's mind, how would the boss cope with that? Would he get furious with Raven, rant and rave about the boy who, after all, could do nothing about the sudden movement of the workshop? Or had he in fact brought it about through his debaucheries, for it to come thundering down about him like some summary judgment? What had been the exact nature of his debaucheries anyway? For no matter how much he tried to rack his gummed-up brain, he was unable to remember, he could only conjecture.

And hadn't the boss actually led him astray into this debauch? He wasn't the only one to blame, he would say if he were to be called on to defend himself.

All these thoughts raced through his mind while the trundling workshop carried on with its demolition work, crushing here and grinding there and gradually going into a slow spin. For all his terror, for all his confusion, he nevertheless felt compelled to open his eyes, just to show himself that all this was not really happening. This was so infinitely difficult, everything in and around his head was firmly stuck. He pulled himself together and opened his eyes a crack, let out a faint groan and wished he hadn't done it. For opening his eyes, it seemed to him, had immediately accelerated the spinning of the workshop, he felt himself sucked up from the spot, knocked about and squashed by some whirling force. He squeezed his eyes firmly shut, as if this pressure could put a brake on the gyrations, but nothing slowed down, he felt a growing ache in his head, the roof was revolving as if it were trying to screw itself upwards, to lift off into the grey morning sky and spin away and, so rotating, leave the earth's orbit, fly towards the sun and burn up. But why had all this still not torn the old fellow out of his cubbyhole, what kind of a skinful had he had, what kind of a hangover must he have, such a head on him that it has him pinned down on his bed for ever, that's what it must be, otherwise he would have been long since hurled out of there and wakened up.

What must he have done to set off this premature purgatory, and why did it have to descend upon him today of all days, after such a night which he could only dimly recall? Now he was sitting in the centre of the workshop-sized spiral which was soaring upwards at such a furious speed, and what he saw was no more than flecks which then gradually began to condense, he could make out configurations of skin and flesh, folds and wrinkles, moist and with small hairs around them, then quite distinctly the pinkly shimmering areola round a hardened, erect nipple, a glistening slit, an enticing abyss under the black-coloured pudenda, a mouth of monstrous red that, as a groping tongue emerged from it, worked its way all down his body. Had the mouth opened to lay bare palisades of teeth in rows? Had he bitten into it with a sudden lunge or with slow and deliberate relish? There must surely have been some pain then. At the end of it all, he had awakened emasculated. He had thought of Fever and his fear of being chewed to pieces and mutilated. But this great, red mouth had tasted, had played gently with his penis, bitten softly and sucked until, and here his memory cleared, it had bucked violently then melted away and become tiny. Was that the way it had been, he asked himself, or had there been even more?

He wanted to open his eyes to let this despondency pour out of him, to open up that sky, but the motion of the workshop was still as wild, the doors were humming and booming and, he could see it all through his closed eyelids, they had taken on a reddish-yellow glow like a piece of iron ready to be forged.

I must put an end to this whole crazy nonsense, he told

himself, for he could only hope that the whole thing was a drunken hallucination. He opened his eyes and looked over at the table, on which a steady ray of sun fell, mellowed by mist, stone dust and clouds of condensed breath, the light was soft and all was peaceful in the shed, the rabbits scuttered quietly in their hutches and a faulty fluorescent tube buzzed and flared briefly; that had been the lightning flashes.

On the table, in his black suit, his best and one and only suit, his features somewhere between yellow and white in colour, lay the stonemason, his hands folded over his chest like a corpse. A corpse that must have laid itself out on the bier, both feet neatly placed, one shoe touching the other, the skin on the hands leathery with dust, cold and wind, the fingers interlocked over the navel. That man, lying there like someone deceased, was the centre, the focal point of the wild spinning which was now slackening and coming to a stop. Anything that might have tried to approach him would have been repelled by him, hurled against the wall and smashed, to stick there like some squashed insect, a fly, that dries up and turns back into dust and powder and, with the passage of time, crumbles off the wall.

Now everything was calm, the dizziness had gone. Raven got to his feet quietly so as not to waken the old fellow, he opened the shed door, touching it carefully to avoid burning himself, but it was as cold as ever, wood, steel and iron were all resting as before on the concrete foundations, outside the door, to the left, in the direction of the motorway, the granite and marble slabs were still stacked up, awaiting their destiny as gravestones, while on the right, over towards the little wood, the bicycles, standing unscathed under their plastic tarpaulin, were slowly losing the last of their air, from the motorway came an incessant drone, the rails of the hand-crane ran their horizontal course and, perpendicular as it should be, there hung the rusty chain with its massive hook.

Raven felt weak, now he could see the world in that

mixture of clarity and garish, comical and absurd moments that is the drunkard's delight after an enormous skinful. At times, self-disgust welled up, to be dispelled by a sense of mischievous pride in the enormity of his excess, the true course of which he still could not recall. It would give him all the more pleasure to tell the stonemason everything about it and to cut four or five more letters on Rosamaria's headstone. And even if he was a bit careless with the truth, he reckoned that the ladies must be governed, like doctors, priests and tax consultants, by a strict oath of confidentiality where the performance or the shortcomings of their clients were concerned.

The mist was lifting slowly, the sun coming through more strongly, perhaps it would be another fine day. Raven sat on the bench behind the building and warmed himself drowsily.

Why was everything so quiet in the workshop, why were there no footsteps to be heard, no coughing, no hawking and spitting? Was the boss still asleep and, if so, why was he not snoring as usual? What was that hair-raising story he had had to listen to? The bear, the she-bear, the fish, the Limnology Institute in Listvyanka, the beautiful twins and the bear-flies. He would have to think up a few questions about that, questions that would expose it for the hoax it all was, otherwise the old fellow would try to go on conning him with one bear after another.

Raven went into the workshop to see whether the boss had changed his position or whether he was at least letting out some kind of a sound, but nothing had changed, it was quiet, the rabbits were eating the grass that Raven had scattered in their cages, there was a stink of tobacco and alcohol, and the stonemason seemed to have become even more pallid about the face. The more agreeable the surroundings seemed to become with the spreading sunlight, the colder, more waxen, more corpse-like he appeared. Raven approached him cautiously, listened for the sound of breathing, peered closely at him to see whether there was the slightest twitch or tremble in his body, but there was nothing to be seen, so he laid his ear on the motionless chest – and heard nothing. That's not possible, thought Raven, he's got to breathe.

There he lay, was he warm, was he cold, you couldn't tell, for his body temperature had never been up nor down. He was like a lizard, he was never affected by cold and he was as warm, or rather as cold, as his workshop, his tools and his stones.

If he's dead, he'll have to be washed, thought Raven. That gave him such a scare that he could think of nothing better than to lay himself down and to remain equally motionless in the hope that the boss would awaken from his paralysed state. What would become of him, Raven, if the old man really were dead, where would he go, these were questions that never even entered his mind. What am I to do with him, do I wash him with soap or even with schnapps, do I touch him with gloves on or not at all, do I fetch a priest or a doctor, or the chemist? It was all these thoughts that tumbled over each other in his befuddled, overhung head, which was now beginning to throb gently. He fell asleep. Thinking he had been roused by a sound, he woke with a start. He might well have imagined the sound, but the boss was now lying there with his mouth hanging stupidly open, his chin had dropped on to his chest and a thin thread of saliva had dribbled on to his shirt-front. Raven felt slightly sick at the sight of this, he looked round for a cloth, a scrap of rag, found nothing and went to fetch a roll of broad adhesive tape that the boss used for all kinds of repair jobs. With rapid movements, so as not to touch the old man more than he absolutely had to, he bound his chin back in place with a strip of the crepe tape which he then wound round his skull.

After he had twice left the workshop and then gone back

in again, Raven swung his leg over the stonemason's bicycle and set off to the chemist's to tell him the stonemason had passed away. It never occurred to him that he could also have telephoned, and that was perhaps for the best, because you don't break news like that over the phone. Along the way, Raven's agitation increased, he went faster and faster and his heart raced along with him.

He hammered loudly at the shop door, which was already closed, then brushed the assistant aside and said, The stonemason's dead.

They stowed the bicycle in the Beetle, Raven squeezed himself in beside it, and they rushed straight back to the workshop.

Raven had hardly left the workshop for the third time when the stonemason's chest did rise imperceptibly, pause in that position and then subside again. After some time, it rose again. The rising and falling became more regular, a sound could be heard. Breath, drawn with a faint rasping through pharyngeal passages congested with phlegm. The noise became louder, stronger, more rhythmical. This was, quite unmistakably, the stonemason's gigantic snoring which could set the blade of the big masonry saw vibrating. He snored so loudly that the rabbits began hopping against the wire mesh of their cages. As sleepers do from time to time, he opened his mouth with a smacking noise, then closed it again and, as he did so, the sticky crepe hampered him disagreeably, but not disagreeably enough to waken him.

Nor did he awaken when the chemist's Beetle drew up with just a suggestion of tyre-squeal on the rough asphalt. The chemist leapt out of the car with unaccustomed nimbleness, while Raven had to disentangle himself from his bicycle. The chemist did not want to rush straight in, so he waited for Raven at the big iron door. Raven opened it and went in hesitantly, already straining his ears for any sign of life, while the chemist kept his eyes shut, preparing himself for the worst. But he, too, recognised the stonemason's signal call.

This is your idea of a joke, I suppose, he said in a voice as hard as Toledo steel.

He went over to the stonemason and with one tug ripped the adhesive tape from his head, tearing out some hair and plucking at the leathery skin. The stonemason coughed twice, then sat up and fingered the new bald patches. The sticky tape was still dangling like a scalp from the chemist's hand.

Slowly, ever so slowly, the chemist's hand moved out in Raven's direction. Raven could see quite clearly that it was trembling. Very quietly, the chemist said, He told me you were dead.

The stonemason said nothing. The chemist said nothing. Raven said nothing.

The stonemason stretched and ran his hands through his hair. He stood up, went over to Raven and asked, Is that what you did?

Raven nodded. The chemist said very quietly, it was hardly more than a murmur, Oh yes, oh yes.

The stonemason hardly drew his hand back at all, yet the cuff he delivered was enough to make Raven struggle to keep his balance. He held his left cheek and said, My ear's whistling.

The stonemason swung his left arm and caught him on the right cheek. Is that one whistling too? but by this time Raven couldn't hear a thing.

For four days he was as good as deaf. For the first three of them, the whistling just would not stop, nor even diminish, it remained steady and painful. On the fourth day it began to subside and then, towards evening, it was gone.

The stonemason noted all this without the least concern. On the fourth day he asked Raven in a loud voice, Are you ever going to do that again?

No, said Raven, and now he knew how the Deafman felt.

Flesh and Neck

AFTER THE CHEMIST had returned, only half-restored, from a lengthy spell in hospital, with his head, which he normally held erect anyway, stiffly corseted by a surgical collar that looked like a ruff, the talk going the rounds was of some mysterious traffic accident in which the Villa Panorama was somehow scandalously involved. Each time, in an effort to pose as the most suitable person to shed light on the rumours, or even to add further rumours, people would talk about it in confidential tones, always stressing from the word go that they of course only remotely ever had anything to do with that establishment; one claimed to have at one time given a helping hand with some building work, upon which his explanations and expositions, sounding less and less credible from one sentence to the next, were interrupted by the question as to whether the work involved drilling and in-filling. He fell quiet, there was an outburst of mirth, then a lengthy silence.

Another insisted he had seen a public figure up there, well known to all. Immediately, the question was raised as to whether he had identified this public figure positively and distinctly. That he had; next question: had he seen them from a distance or close to? From close to, of course, came the reply, otherwise I wouldn't have recognised them so clearly, would I? Whereupon his narrative was nipped smartly in the bud since, for one thing there were no prominent figures in the district at all other than the ladies of the Villa Panorama themselves, and for another would he please explain what he was doing there anyway, since he had been able to observe everything so closely.

These and similar conversations were of common occurrence, especially when the chemist in his ruff happened to be within earshot. If, on such occasions, he happened to be sitting there, he would stand up and leave; if he was already standing, he would just depart, erect of bearing and fiery-red of countenance. He had spent almost two months previously in a full-length plaster cast in the District Hospital. He had been talked into a night out with the lads by two colleagues, the building contractor and the stonemason who, after an interval of two years, had gradually made up their differences, and since he did not drink, he had declared his willingness to act as chauffeur to the two gentlemen. They started their escapade one late Saturday afternoon, shortly before dusk. On the Sunday afternoon, the chemist had the chance to have a nap for an hour in his VW. Late that night, the stonemason and the builder were agreed that the time was ripe for them to pay Rosamaria a visit. On the Monday, then, when they emerged, elated and uplifted, from the Villa Panorama into the light of dawn, they found the chemist curled up, sound asleep, on the back seat of the car. Without further ado, the builder got in behind the wheel where, accustomed as he was to a vehicle with an automatic gearbox, he confused the forward gears with reverse and, being a man of some dynamism, put his foot down hard, crashed through a spruce-wood rustic fence and a cypress hedge, carved a swathe through the rhododendrons and fuchsias, uprooted a holly bush and landed with a crash at the foot of the hill in the roadside ditch, where the car came to rest on its tail like a rocket on its launching pad.

After a brief, shocked pause, the stonemason stated that he felt like Gagarin shortly after the lift-off of Soyuz 13, put a hand to the back of his head and fingered a slight laceration.

The builder, after a somewhat longer pause, rejoined that it felt to him like the lift-off of the space-shuttle Challenger, only rather better. He got off with slight concussion and a broken middle finger. The chemist, for his part, still curled up in a ball in the rear of his car, uttered not a sound. Convinced that he was asleep and not wishing to wake him, they went about their business as quietly as possible, even while, with the assistance of three of the girls, they were getting the sitting-up-and-begging Volkswagen back on to its four wheels. On their arrival at the District Hospital, they were almost outraged to find that a deal more care and attention was bestowed on the chemist than on themselves and their clearly evident injuries. Although the paths cut by the Volkswagen very soon became overgrown again and the flattened shrubs were righted by the caring hands of the ladies of the house, the incident remained a topic of conversation for a long time afterwards and gave rise to an endless stream of new stories about the chemist, the builder and the stonemason, the VW Beetle and their visit to Rosamaria's.

So many secrets were thus woven around the hill, proliferating as rampantly as the plants on it, that the Deafman was torn and tossed between his curiosity and his fear of the unknown.

To the Mount of Olives

How often in the past had the Deafman looked pensively over from his tractor seat towards the so-called Mount of Olives; had tried to peer through the fuchsia hedges and the rhododendrons, the gorse and the holly bushes, in an attempt to imagine what went on up there in the Villa with the exotic name of Panorama, what was hiding behind the fast-growing, indeed luxuriant, shrubs.

Mount of Olives was the popular name given to the Villa Panorama, and any time someone spoke about it, they would do so with an odd smile on their face.

Raven was visibly surprised when the Deafman drove up on the Bulldog to pay them a visit. The stonemason told Raven to kill a rabbit.

With a smile, the stonemason noticed how the Deafman suddenly stopped eating, a forkful of food suspended absent-mindedly in front of his face, his mouth hanging unprepossessingly open, ready to bite, his gaze fixed on some far horizon, going right through the stonemason and his amused grin. That day, the rabbit had proved a particular success, the tobacco flavour was stronger than usual, and the dried thyme had especially tickled the Deafman's palate. Where could one's thoughts stray to in the middle of such a meal, if not towards the perfumes, the melodious tones of a woman like Rosamaria? So the stonemason poured out three vodkas, clinked glasses, thus waking the Deafman from his reverie, and knocked it back. Straight away, he poured a second one for himself and drank it. This was followed by a third which he drank in two sips, and his eyes took on a contented shine. So you're going up then, are you, he said.

Raven answered with a gesture, rubbing thumb and index finger together, indicating that it was all a question of money.

Rosamaria, said the stonemason, loves nothing so much as me and her dog. She's forever sitting there, working out human age in dog's years, inquiring after and inviting sexual partners for her bitch, examining them in every last detail and sending most of them away again, she spares no effort to make sure her bitch lives in even greater comfort than her mistress. At night, she'll burst into tears if she has worked out again that her dog is already twenty years older than herself. When will she die, how long will she live, is she healthy, will she be spared an unpleasant death, where shall I bury her? Things like that are aways going through Rosamaria's beautiful head early in the morning before she goes to sleep. Now, outside, I've got a small block of white Carrara marble, an off-cut from Rosamaria's stone. Raven, tomorrow you're going to start by cleaning it up. That will open your account at Rosamaria's. As for today, you and your friend can go along on tick.

He stood up, fetched the bear-fly powder, sprinkled a generous dose into their vodkas, poured a fourth one for himself and drained it with the others. Then he laughed and said *na zdorovye*.

Raven got the rabbit bones to gnaw, the Deafman got another tasty piece off the saddle, just to build up his strength, and the stonemason had a bit off a hind leg. While Raven did the washing up, the stonemason and the Deafman sat across from each other, in silence but getting on famously. When Raven had served up the Nescafé and they had drunk it down rather hurriedly, the stonemason went and lay down on his cot for a smoke while the two others wrapped themselves up well, climbed on to the Bulldog and set off for the Mount of Olives.

Two Noses

AT THE BOTTOM of the steep drive, which for so long had stretched out before him in his mind's eye, the Deafman stopped, turned the Bulldog and reversed up the hill, in case the brakes should fail. He certainly did not want to end up like the chemist with a ruff as a legacy of his visit. On this occasion, the brakes held.

The moment he entered the room, the aromas began streaming into every cavity in his body, filling the wings of his sphenoid and his cranial cavities, round the ossicles, the tympanum and even the temporal pyramid. There, the smells, and the excitations they aroused, flooded along the corridors of his consciousness right to the depths of his cerebellum. Delightful tickling sensations were set off which were unfamiliar to the Deafman, so unfamiliar that they bothered him. Were they trying to lure him somewhere, from where he would be unable to find a way back, did they want to show him a world that he would yearn for, unfulfilled, for the rest of his life? To be sure, he had often experienced states of excitement vaguely similar to these in the past, but he could never have told what it was that had triggered off his desire. The sensation that something in the pit of his abdomen was stirring in direct association with his twitching, searching nose had struck him on entering the bar, but there had been too many off-putting distractions there. After he had become used to those, however, he realised that the special quality of these aromas came about precisely because of the close proximity of the disgusting and the appealing.

Here, though, in Rosamaria's room, where the velvet-covered furnishings and the curtains had absorbed so much that they had become heavy with them, the perfumes brought him to such a pitch of trembling anticipation that he could barely control it.

While all the ladies of the establishment were meant to represent something and had a particular rôle to play, Rosamaria, the madam, on the other hand, was so much her own true self, so through and through and from head to toe lady, ideal woman, girlfriend or anything else a man might hold to be the epitome of femininity. She entered the room in a blue satin dress that was far removed from the vulgar charms of the other girls' slit skirts and transparent negligées. Only at the back was it cut low, down to below her shoulder-blades which stood out discernibly in the ample flesh around them, reflecting every slightest movement of her arms, even of her fingers, in a stretching or contracting. Without a word, she sat down on a red armchair, diagonally opposite the Deafman, smiling a barely perceptible smile, yet the Deafman was sure he could feel the room immediately become a few degrees warmer. Whenever she raised her voice, the cats began to purr contentedly, the dogs stopped barking and lay down at her feet, the singing birds fell silent, listened and replied. When the church bells which the Deafman could feel in his gut began to ring, the sound of their chime was made of bronze, but when Rosamaria spoke, the sound was an amalgam of silver and flesh. For a long time, she remained silent, sitting erect but comfortably on the red armchair; cold was the blue of her dress, warm the velvety tones of the armchair, and hot the rising anticipation of the Deafman, waiting for her to open her mouth, for Raven had told him of the magical enchantment of her voice. For this reason, in fact, the Deafman had decided against wearing his ribbed vest – without which he would otherwise never venture out of doors, even in summer – so that the thrill of her voice might get through unhampered right to his diaphragm.

She reached out for a book; the Deafman could not read its title but the picture of a dog was clearly visible on the front. She began to read. The Deafman laid his hand against the cognac glass on the little table beside him and could feel it vibrating gently. He fixed his eyes on her lips, which were opening and closing almost languidly, now he could hear her within his body, could hear her faster and slower, depending on whether he tightened or slackened his diaphragm. He heard the voice of Rosamaria like the bells of the little church, heard it slowly if he relaxed, then the bells were of bronze, he heard it quickly if he tensed, then they were bright, as if made of silver, then the DONG became a DING, the great bell became a little bell, the chiming a tinkling. Her nose dilated and made her nostrils flare, lustingly, they were pulsating, no less, wide open one moment, narrow again the next. He was on the verge of brimming over with sounds and smells, and her arousal was growing too, for this was a game she was unfamiliar with, one of the few that were new to her, who thought she knew every game in this world.

This was a game, an interplay at one and the same time from the remotest distance and in the most intimate proximity, and the nearness could not be nearer nor the togetherness closer except at that instant when two people touched.

And so she found herself doing something she had not done since she was thirteen years old, she had slid her left hand under her left upper thigh and under the madonna-blue satin dress, pushing it right up to her behind and letting the little black hairs slip through her fingers, twisting and curling them, caressing and pressing the soft lips, searching further and finding still other things again which gave her intense pleasure.

For some days afterwards, she was still reflecting upon how that could all have actually come about. They had used up great quantities of paper tissues, each of them sat in his or her velvet armchair. It was as if they each had a nose located in their loins, the way they lingered, waited, worked away until two noses had to sneeze with quite elemental force.

Time and Tide

SO THE DAYS passed, and the months. The chemist's cervical vertebrae recovered from their trauma, the strained muscles regained strength, and the cartilage and ligaments bound themselves firmly round the vertebrae.

When the chemist was able to leave the house for the first time without his surgical collar, which had come to be a stigma for him, people once again burst into peals of laughter almost before he had gone out of earshot. No sooner had they come to terms with the man in the ruff, which they regarded as the price he had to pay for his sinful way of life, than this new transformation occurred. Once again the incident became the object of public interest and the subject of the most diverse and prurient speculation.

These were the signs of the times. In Asia, revolutions were being conceived, planned, carried out and put down, people were starving in Africa, in the distant Soviet Union, in the Ukraine, an atomic pile was threatening first to explode, then to melt down and mingle in one vast glowing mass with the earth's core, here a spy was exposed, there another was smuggled into place. A conflagration destroyed the city of Lisbon. The holy men were sending children out into battle armed with the keys to Paradise. Raven learned his trade, pointed chisels and flat-bladed chisels. Fever learned his trade, garnishing, reducing. The Victim learned her trade, teasing, touching up and bringing off. Andre waited for some novel experience, and in San Francisco the threat of an earthquake was still imminent. Cooks boiled away and so did volcanoes, face-workers hammered away, whirlwinds whirled, and typhoons raged off Hong Kong. Time applied tiny chisels to many things, hammering merrily here, thumping resoundingly there, it seemed to pass and nevertheless to stand still. Everything was crumbling, flaking, yet dust remained, which solidified and became stone once more.

Scarab

DURING THE NIGHT of his birthday, it wasn't the biting January cold that woke Raven. The stonemason's hammer blows were reverberating piercingly through the big shed. Raven woke with a start. The exhaustion from the previous day's labours still ached in his bones, his chapped hands were still stinging. The fine, sharp stone splinters in his knees had still not festered and worked their way out with the pus. His heavy working trousers, which he had kept on in bed because of the cold, were sticking damply to the two wounds. His limbs still ached as they had done some hours before when he had lain down. No single part of him had recovered. A dreadful tiredness pressed him to his bed. Only with considerable effort did he manage to struggle into a sitting position. The hammer blows hurt him. The hammer strikes the head of the chisel, that causes a shrill clang, metal on metal. The point of the chisel strikes the stone. The stone is singing, the stonemason would say. The stone is screaming, Raven thought. He pushed the heavy blanket aside so that he could stand up. He was looking forward to putting on his shoes. These shoes made him feel better. The toe-caps were fitted with steel tips which had already protected his toes from falling lumps of stone many a time. When the stonemason had bought them for him, they had struck him as clumsy and ugly. You'll stand firm in these shoes, he had said. From below, you're protected by four layers of leather, and on the top the iron acts as armour plating; what more do you want? Raven soon had to agree. The clanging and banging was punctuated by the stonemason's coughing, which was what drove Raven to get a move on. The coughing had got worse and worse, and just when Raven believed it could not have come from any further down in his lungs, it barked out even more explosively and alarmingly through the echoing workshop. Is it because of the dust or the cold? Is it because of old age, or the cigarettes? He grows his own tobacco, he sews his own clothes, and he even slaughters his own rabbits himself. He doesn't sleep any more. He ferments the tobacco in the oven, the tobacco smell and the smell of stone in the workshop make you cough. He roasts the rabbits in the oven. The roast rabbit tastes of rosemary, of garlic, of tobacco, of stone. He sits nights at his table. He smokes, he scribbles in the dark. And often, when the first light comes into the room, he notices that he has ruined his paper. He presses down too hard on his pencil. He doesn't sleep any more. My sleep is in the stone, he'll say. A few months ago, he lost the knack of sleeping, but this is the first time he has ever worked on his stones during the night. Right at the start of Raven's apprenticeship, he warned him against working at night. If he were to work at night, he would waken his sleep that lies inside the stone. No man can live without sleep.

Raven woke himself up with some icy water. The water was not much colder than his own skin. He listened, trying to make out whether he could hear the winter birds outside. He listened between the regular hammer blows. Only the steady, distant rumble from the motorway could be heard.

He dried his face and looked at the grey smears on the towel. The stonemason was coughing wretchedly. He interrupted the regularity of his hammering to cough. Then he spat and rubbed the mucus into the stone dust with his boot. The floor all round the stone was covered with tiny dots, as if dung-beetles had been creeping round him, rolling their little balls.

The scarabs in my chest are rolling their pills. Do you know what a scarab does? He rolls a nest of dung for his descendants. The sacred beetle of the Pharaohs. The death beetle. He began telling stories about the Egyptians in such a quiet voice that Raven was not sure whether he was supposed to listen or whether the stonemason was talking to himself, his stone or his dung-beetles. He went on about superhuman exploits, about stone blocks as tall as three men, which the Egyptians or their slaves had cut, hauled over long distances and stacked up on top of each other, and all this thanks only to a pound of garlic which was their only source of nourishment. And when Raven contradicted him and insisted that the Egyptians had also eaten wild honey and locusts, the stonemason shouted at him that it wouldn't be daylight for another two hours yet, that he should be asleep at this time of day, if he didn't mind, and that he would call him if he required him. Raven went off to get water for the coffee. Would he be so good as to make sure that the coffee wasn't yet again full of the dust that he allowed to flake from his hair, and anyway he should wash a bit more thoroughly and not go about the place like some zombie. It was a fact that his skin had taken on the colour of damp clay, which made it barely distinguishable from the colour of any other object in the workshop, the colour of his clothes, his hair, the blanket on his bed or newly-dressed stone. His skin had the smoothness of polished granite, while the stonemason's looked like the surface of a block just blasted out of the hillside, criss-crossed and marked by the furrows of the shot-firer's bore-holes, fissured and splintered by the force of the explosion, the tearing loose from the mother stone and the impact of crashing down on the rubble-strewn floor of the quarry. How am I supposed to sleep while you're thumping away, Raven thought to himself. His sleep, too, was in that stone. The stove was not even creating enough warmth to bring the water for the coffee to the boil. Raven ran up and down the shed in an effort to warm himself up. He rubbed his hands together, he hugged himself, he massaged his hips, his thighs, his chest. He stuffed his hands inside his pullover, felt the cold, bare skin and sought warmth under his armpits. He sniffed at his hands, stuck them in his trouser pockets and held himself between his legs. Where it's warm, that's where I want to go, it's got to be warm.

Give your knees a good washing out, or else you'll be stuck in those trousers for the rest of your life, use soda soap, the boss called to him.

Raven went to the stove and grasped the heated kettle, using the hem of his pullover as a pan-holder. The water hadn't come to the boil, it was only simmering feebly. He made two cups of Nescafé, cut a flake off the soda soap and dissolved it in warm water in the basin they used for mixing plaster. He dipped his knees into it and pulled the encrusted cloth off the two abrasions. Streaks of blood spread through the soap suds.

Take the vodka and pour some on them, said the stonemason, who disinfected all his cuts and gashes in this way. And put some vodka into my coffee, he added, then go over to my bed, there's something for you there.

Raven pulled aside the curtain in front of the boss's bed. On it lay a roll of gauze bandage and a small parcel wrapped in drawing paper. The stonemason watched with a smile as Raven undid it. Two oval pieces of leather, roughly trimmed to size and fitted with elastic bands. Raven bandaged his knees, wrapped a strip of plastic film over the bandages, rolled his trouser legs down again and fitted the two pieces of leather over his knees. Gingerly, still behind the curtain, he knelt down and tried crawling about on his knees.

Is that better? called the stonemason. 'S better, Raven replied.

The stonemason was standing by his block of stone, his chisel still in one hand, his cup in the other. He sipped and gazed upwards. The stone was a good metre taller than himself. He swallowed loudly and complained about the coffee being too cold, he could hardly taste it, in such cold, an insipid brew like that was a downright affront. Raven held out the vodka bottle to him. He added some and said, with a gulp, that Raven should go and eat some bread, bread and margarine. Raven did as he was told and sat watching the stonemason as he chewed laboriously. There was still no light penetrating the workshop, just a dim lamp dangling above the stone. The stonemason worked on, feeling his way with his chisel. He would have been able to work even in complete darkness, and he always required Raven to watch him. Even if Raven was crouching over flat slabs of stone, polishing their surface, he made sure the boy was watching him. He maintained that that was how the lad would learn what a stone really was. Never mind if Raven was down on his knees polishing away, he had to crane his neck to keep looking up at him and his stone. Raven polished and watched the stonemason. His knees weren't hurting so badly now. The pains in his hands were anaesthetised by the cold. Polishing made the dust fly and set up a shrill noise. The dust was bound with water. The water was cold; it soaked the sleeves of Raven's pullover and was softening up the leather of his knee-pads. Raven went on polishing. Raven could hear the winter birds as they hesitantly began their throaty song. The steady hum from the motorway was getting louder too. In half an hour it would get light. The birds and the rising noise from the motorway heralded the softly lightening, milky daylight. And the stonemason said, There you are, it's light already, even though it was still too dark to put out the lamp. He chipped and chiselled away with all his might, interrupted only by coughing fits. Raven went pale as the thought struck him that the stonemason's time, and his, Raven's time, was about to run out. Everything had changed. It couldn't last much longer.

Raven was not very tall, his eyes dark, his chest, despite his long, hard labour, still narrow. At the start he had thought he would never survive the time ahead with the stonemason. The latter had made no allowances whatsoever for Raven's obvious physical weakness, even on the very first day. He had issued his instructions, the way people do who devote their lives to their work, whose very lives seem to depend on their work. Instructions like these were commands, which Raven had to carry out if he was not to be inevitably overcome by the conviction that he had forfeited any right to remain anywhere near this obsessively industrious man. Raven would have despised himself if he had left then, and quite apart from that, he would have had no idea where to go or where he might have ended up despite himself.

For four days, the stonemason worked on with barely a pause. Nor did Raven find any time or peace to sleep, and whenever he tried to, the noise and his galloping brain thwarted his efforts. His slight body developed considerable strength which would have surprised even the stonemason if he had still been in a fit state to notice anything going on outside the small pool of light around his stone. The moment Raven closed his eyes, armies of dung-beetles crawled, or hovering lumps of stone danced, past him. Through lack of sleep, he fell into a state of over-alertness, a kind of euphoria, a delirium, that was half crushingly exhausting and half ecstatic, and was heightened further by the uniformity of his movements. They stopped eating, only smoking roll-ups and drinking Nescafé with vodka.

On the second day, Raven came out of the workshop, blinked in bewilderment in the dust-free, clear air and cycled out to the big shopping centre that stood next to the motorway like some stranded battleship. The stonemason had sent him for new stocks of vodka. The best, the Siberian, was what he wanted; distilled with water from Lake Baikal.

Raven had become so estranged from everything outside the workshop that he did not even notice the way the few customers in the huge supermarket were looking at him. There must have been something ghostly about him, certainly something exotic and unreal, for wherever he went people stood aside and left him far more room than he needed, as if some animal, on a leash but still unpredictable, were being led past them. Or maybe they just did not want to come in contact with the clouds of dust that Raven gave off around him. After Raven had finally discovered the right vodka, he jumped when a small boy, who was probably just learning to read, spoke to him and asked what kind of funny letters those were printed on the cardboard carton. So it took Raven a few seconds to think up the answer that it was Russian. The little boy ran off to his mother, who had been warily watching the scene from a distance, and said with a laugh, Look, look, the Russian man's all dusty.

Raven had never known the stonemason to stagger about, babble or talk nonsense when he had been drinking. Sometimes he would tell stories, or lies. Now Raven was laughing at himself making his unsteady way through the shed. The stonemason watched him with a smile and then suddenly started singing, at the top of his voice, Russian drinking songs that he had probably learnt during his army days. He sang, coughed and drowned the coughing with a drink. Raven noticed that his eyes had a feverish gleam in them.

That sweat was caking the dust on his forehead. *Na zdorovye!* shouted the stonemason, he sang, set up a murderously fast rhythm with his hammer and chisel and then began to dance around the workshop like a drunken bear. He threw away his tools, grabbed Raven and danced with him, singing loudly. Raven had to laugh as he had not laughed for a long time. Then the stonemason asked for a chair. His brow was hot. Raven brought him cold water and a cloth. He was quite breathless from so much coughing. He waved Raven away. Raven did not leave, yet did not dare remain close by him. So he went and sat down at the far end of the workshop and watched the old fellow turning into an old man.

Watched the veins on his neck, his forehead, his hands, protruding even further. Watched the dust being washed down in the streams of repeated outbreaks of sweat. Watched his eyes, wide open, yet with such a vacant stare, as if they could see nothing. Watched his skin taking on a bluish tinge and his hands gripping the arms of his chair for all they were worth. Raven was afraid the old man would bite his tongue. Saliva dribbled from the corners of his mouth. And so he sat there on his chair; down at the other end of the workshop sat Raven. Between them stood the unfinished stone.

Raven stared at the leather pouch lying on the stone and after a while, when he felt that everything had gone perfectly still, he took out tobacco and paper. And while he made up the first cigarette, rolling the coarse tobacco into the small rectangle of French paper, feeling the stinging taste of the tobacco on his tongue as soon as he licked along the edge of the paper, he pictured the dead stonemason's hands and tried to work out how many cigarettes he must have rolled in his lifetime. But since he had no idea of the stonemason's exact age, he abandoned his calculations. He smoked two cigarettes, the tobacco set off a burning on his tongue, a biting in his throat and a stinging in his lungs. Raven carefully stubbed out the second fag-end, stood up and went over to the old man. He gripped him under the armpits, slipped his arms round his chest and dragged him over towards the big table, where he propped him up against a table leg. From the cupboard, he fetched a large sheet of clean canvas. Thick, stiff canvas. He spread the canvas out on the table and hoisted the body on to it. He undressed the old man, went to get a sponge and the pot with the warm water. He washed the dust from his body. To do so, he used a piece of scented soap, a gift from the chemist to the stonemason years ago. This soap left a nice smell on the clean laundry in the cupboard. Lavender. Since the deceased had never used shaving foam, only soda soap, Raven lathered up the lavender soap on the skin of the dead man's face and shaved him with a new blade, and without nicking him one single time. And so the body of the deceased smelt of lavender. Even the suit that Raven fetched from the cupboard, and the shirt, everything smelt of lavender. From the inside pocket of the jacket he took a yellowed envelope. In it lay three one-hundred-mark notes and two ten-pfennig coins. No letter, no message. On one of the banknotes, in the top left-hand corner, was written the letter C, and after it a four-digit telephone number. It was an awkward job, dressing the dead man. His body resisted the suit that he had been so reluctant to put on throughout his life whenever he had unfinished work on hand. Raven ripped the shirt up the back. Now he tried to knot the tie, an art he had never learnt. He finally made do with threading the tie through the collar and leaving the rest to the chemist. He took the tobacco pouch, his own two shirts, three of the stonemason's ones and a pair of trousers that the deceased had sewn together himself. He went over to the rabbit cages, scattered some grass that had been kept in a plastic carrier bag from the supermarket and stuffed the clothes into the bag. The only thing that did not smell of lavender was the dead man's shoes, which Raven had dubbined with margarine. Raven oiled the chain and crank-bearings on his bicycle once more, hung the bag on the handlebars and set off, enjoying the smooth surface of the road. He still had given no thought as to where he intended to head after he had made the telephone call. He hesitated, stopped his bike, turned round and rode back to the workshop. The bicycle ran almost effortlessly. Back in the workshop, Raven made straight for the rabbit hutches and opened the doors. He took off the stonemason's right shoe once more and laid a drawing-pin inside it. None of the animals wanted to leave their cages. They huddled together, fearful and trembling, as Raven tilted the cages forwards.

On the way to the telephone kiosk in the shopping centre car park, Raven gave some thought to what exactly he was going to say in the call he was about to make. And so the trip seemed very short. He put in the two coins and dialled the number written on the banknote. And exactly as he had rehearsed it, he told the chemist, who, as usual, took a long time in coming to the phone, the stonemason has just died, and now I've got to go away. He said a polite goodbye to the chemist, who was speechless at first, and then hung the receiver back on the hook despite the man's shocked appeals for him to wait.

Immediately, the chemist chased his assistant, whom he did not trust, out of the shop and told her to wait outside the door to pacify urgent callers with the assurance that he would be back soon. He got into his car and drove the roundabout route to his friend's place. Half-way there, he noticed he had forgotten his umbrella, but his high state of agitation prevented him turning back. He turned off at the shopping centre to take a quick turn round the car park, for he knew that that was where the stonemason and Raven normally made their rare telephone calls. In vain he looked around for Raven's black bicycle and his dusty figure and he gave a startled jump, suddenly jolted out of his preoccupation by the noise of blaring horns and screeching brakes coming from the motorway, which, as a rule, heralded one of the innumerable fatal accidents there. But he heard no sound of an impact, thought no more of the uproar and went on his way to the stonemason's workshop. This'll be Raven, up to one of his stupid tricks again, he thought as he parked the car and stepped out. He was so worked up that, contrary to habit, he did not notice a gleaming patch of ice that had formed on the damp ground. He only narrowly missed it in his bafflement at the gaping metal doors. His heart was beating unusually fast, but he drew some comfort from the noise of some falling object coming from inside the workshop, followed by further sounds of lively movement. His heartbeat was also eased by a familiar aroma, the smell of lavender. And at once he recalled the lavender soap he had distributed to all his customers many years ago as a Christmas gift. For an instant he thought his heart had stopped beating altogether when he caught sight of the stonemason's corpse lying in state on its bier. He went over to the large table and, in his confused state, tried to round up the rabbits which were running excitedly round the dead man. It was no good. He gave up the attempt and went and stood, calm now and reverent, before the lavender-perfumed corpse. What a fine-looking man, he thought as he carefully did up the tie in a Windsor knot. Half an hour later he left the workshop to go and inform the doctor so that he could make out a death certificate. But this did not happen until late that evening, since the chemist now slipped on the patch of ice and badly sprained his left leg. So the doctor had first of all to x-ray and attend to the injured chemist, who had survived the return trip only with great difficulty and in excruciating agony, before he could get on with the other business.

On the Road

NATURALLY, THE CHEMIST could have had no idea that the squealing of brakes and the hooting of horns that had given him such a scare shortly before had been caused by Raven, who had been trying to cross the motorway on his bicycle. Since drivers took that particular section of the motorway at very high speeds, Raven had assumed that the cars, which he could see only as tiny dots, were very far away, and so his action had forced them to slam on their brakes. He himself was not the least alarmed, on the contrary, he had waved cheerily to the furious, deathly pale drivers and had turned off on to a track across the fields leading to the secondary road. Now, without a care in the world, he was riding along it, recklessly zig-zagging about and enjoying the way the plastic bag hanging from his handlebars swung back and forth. He steered into even tighter curves, trying to set the bag swinging in a complete circle. He braked suddenly and laughed as the bag shot forward and seemed to be trying to go on without him. For years now, since the start of his apprenticeship, he had never really been alone. He had never left his more immediate surroundings, seldom went into the little town on errands, since the big shopping centre sold everything anyone needed to live on. At night, too, he had been separated from the stonemason only by a few blankets and odd bits of carpet serving as curtains. To him, the motorway had become something of a natural frontier. He had been taught that a river, a mountain, a marsh, a gorge or a lake could be natural borders, but it seemed to him that it would have been easier to cross rivers, gorges, lakes, marshes and mountains than that four-lane highway. He could hear it constantly. Depending on the direction of the wind and what the weather was like, its noise would be louder or quieter. And when it was raining, it sounded to him as if the lorries' tyres were singing their loudest. Now, though, he was cycling along a country road past forests of leafless deciduous trees.

Nobody uses the country roads any more, he thought. And after he had passed through a small village with a Scandinavian-sounding name, he was surprised to be overtaken by a heavy stream of traffic. The drivers passed so close to him on the narrow road that he had to reckon with being hurled into the ditch at any moment. He got the feeling that they were all directing some inexplicable fury at him, or that the drivers he had forced to brake so hard some time earlier had set these others on him to wreak vengeance for the fright he had given them. It seemed to him that hardly had he had the chance to savour the brief feeling of being on his own when here he was, hemmed in and threatened by all these cars and lorries. He, too, became suddenly angry, feeling powerless, no longer alone but lonely and abandoned in a hostile country. He grew increasingly frightened, angry, and began cursing out loud, which of course no one could hear, and the few drivers who did take the time to notice could only wonder that here was someone going along on a bicycle and talking loudly to himself. And almost as a sign of their contempt, the stink of their exhausts became even more overpowering. The lorries were crawling along in low gear and the dark, almost black, clouds billowing from their exhaust pipes blotted out Raven's vision, brought tears to his eyes and took his breath away. Many of the private cars had their headlights on high beam, so that any time that Raven fearfully looked behind, he got an agonising pain in his eyes. The headlights were intended to force the driver in front to move over towards the verge, but the road was too narrow and crowded to allow any overtaking or giving way. And all over the drivers' faces was written the raging frustration at the fact that their tried and trusted weapons were suddenly useless, that their powerful engines, their piercing halogen lights were doing nothing to speed up their progress. Raven could see them fiddling with the knobs on their radios as they searched around for more favourable road traffic information. And having noticed how unsteady it made him when he looked back, he decided to keep his eyes fixed straight ahead, looking as far into the distance as possible. At the very moment when he reckoned it would be best to pick out some point in the distance to head for, which would grow bigger and bigger and then take on some recognisable shape, a tree, perhaps, a road sign, a person, he caught sight of such a dot in the distance and he knew that very instant that it was a woman. Although this figure was still so far away that he was unable to make out its outline, and it could just as easily have been a man, he knew that it was a woman.

I know it, because that's what I want it to be.

His fear of falling off, of an accident, gave way to a feeling of satisfaction at no longer being the only human being on this road, for he could not bring himself to associate the distorted faces in the cars with humanity. He could feel her coming nearer, his speed and hers being added together. It was a physical sensation, and his face, reddened by the airstream and the cold, became redder still. His blood surged upwards, he could feel his legs going weak. He could make out that the woman was carrying something, probably a shopping basket, and that her hair was fair. If Raven had had the chance to get off the road at that moment, he would have done so at once, would have waited until she had disappeared from his sight again, and would then have resumed his place in the stream of traffic with a lighter heart. But to his right he was cut off from the little wood by a ditch overflowing with filthy water, while on the left his escape was blocked by the speeding vehicles. Thus, the encounter was unavoidable, and although Raven realised it would last only a matter of seconds, the thought that he would have to come in contact with either her or even just her clothes filled him with an excitement that engulfed his entire body. He felt a tightness in his chest, his breathing came faster, he was overcome by dizziness and felt slightly sick. The woman's shopping basket was empty and she was casting irritated glances at the stream of traffic; her stockings were white, too thin for the cold weather. Around her ankles, they had gone yellowish-brown with mud splashes. Raven's gaze was held transfixed by these soiled, slender calves. Very briefly he looked up to her face, her lips were heavily made up, her hair was thick and looked as if it had just been set in curls by her hairdresser. The corners of her mouth were drawn down as if what was left of the day, or what had gone before, filled her with disgust. Yet when one of the drivers tooted his horn and, from behind the protection of his metal shell, made a fleeting obscene gesture, she looked up briefly, followed him out of the corner of her eye and gave a faint smile. Raven, too, wished he had a metal shell behind which he could have concealed his embarrassment and his agitation.

The stonemason had owned one fat old rabbit. This rabbit was the only one he could never have brought himself to kill and eat. It was the progenitor of the whole brood, and it might therefore have commanded some degree of respect if it had not consistently distinguished itself by an extreme randiness that was exceptional even among rabbits. At every opportunity, it mounted any of the females, and after it had been banished to a small cage by itself, it managed on more than one occasion to bite through the wire mesh in order to get at the object of its lustings. The stonemason had christened this buck Kinsey, and he had a special soft spot for it, whereas Raven found it increasingly disgusting and ended up detesting it. He always gave it a little less feed than the others, yet, if anything, its reproductive urges seemed merely to be intensified by its reduced diet. Now he felt exposed, frantic and as horny as the old buck, Kinsey, felt a throbbing between his legs, where the blood had in the meantime surged back down from his head. For a brief moment, he would almost have preferred to jump into the roadside ditch full of muck and sluggishly floating rubbish. He did not do it, though, and when she was only three paces away, he had no option but to stop, dismount and go on staring at her ankles. She passed by, apparently without even noticing him. There was a strong scent from her newly-set hair as it brushed against his face.

He hurried on without looking back. After some considerable time the feeling of oppression in him began to ebb and he realised he could get back on his bicycle again. He had gone only a few metres when he was indeed dealt a slight, glancing blow by a car. By supporting himself on his right foot, he was able to avoid falling off altogether. He let out a yell, of rage at first, then of pain, and could see in the car's rear-view mirror the smiling face of a rather dandified young man. Stung into action by his anger, he overcame the pain and put new power into his pedalling. The plastic bag swung wildly from side to side until it seemed it was about to fall off. Raven held on to it firmly and ignored the sharp pain in his bruised leg. But despite Raven's fury, despite his efforts, the stream of vehicles next to him was still moving faster than he was. Very soon, the white car would be out of sight and Raven's anger was on the point of subsiding while the pain and the desire to stop and examine his injury were growing, when something he could not see far ahead forced Raven's adversaries to brake. With a surge of triumph, he realised they were all slowing down and that he was now moving up along the right side of the column of cars. His anger boiled up again, fired by his determination to get his own back on the driver of the white car somehow or other, or at least to give him a piece of his mind. He went faster and faster and got closer and closer and now he could see in the rear-view mirror again, could see the man's elegant hairstyle, how fresh he looked and how tanned and flawless his skin was. He took a firm hold on his plastic carrier, slipped it off the handlebars and, as he caught up with his foe and drew alongside him, swung the bag several times against the roof of the car. The blows were soft and ineffectual, at most the young man inside probably heard a faint, dull bump. He stopped his car, paying no heed to the vehicles hooting furiously behind him, and flung his door open. Raven stood there, completely at a loss, with the bag, a totally useless weapon, in his hand. The young man came round the car, disdainfully looked Raven up and down and, without a word, planted his fist hard in the middle of his face. Raven could no longer hold on to stop himself falling. Smiling, the man got back into his car and drove off. The driver behind him – the wild hooting was still going on – leaned across the passenger seat, wound down the window and cursed Raven roundly. He threatened him with a further beating and even opened his door as if to back up his words with deeds. He did not get out, however, for Raven was already lying helpless under his bike and made no move to climb out of the ditch until the motorist had driven on. The icy water, made viscous by all the filth, seeped into his bag, soaking the five shirts and the stonemason's home-tailored trousers. The leather tobacco pouch was virtually watertight. Raven's face was still benumbed after its plunge into the water.

Have a good howl if you hit yourself on the finger, then it'll get better faster, the stonemason had taught him. For all that, Raven had never cried in his presence. He heaved his bicycle upright, climbed out of the ditch and pulled the bag out after him. For fear of further accidents and of another encounter with the young man, and because of the coldness of the slipstream, he pushed the bicycle as far as the next village. This village, too, had a Swedish-sounding name. Of course, Raven had never been to Sweden, had never, as far as he could remember, been abroad at all. He thought of elks and warm-hearted, blonde women, but none of these images did anything to restore warmth to his body. He saw a large limousine turning off and parking in front of an inn. Without stopping to think, he followed the car. He was afraid of freezing to death and was pretty sure that some of his toes had already been frostbitten. The stonemason had had only seven toes left. He once told the story of how, in Russia, the other three had first turned blue, then black. When he had taken off and shaken out his boots after a three-day march, the three toes, along with some small stones, had simply fallen out. Raven was reluctant to believe the story and asked whether they didn't wear any socks in Russia. Footcloths, footcloths, was the answer that finally dispelled Raven's doubts. He fought back his tears, smiled at the people getting out of the limousine and staring at him in amazement, and wondered how cold the water of Lake Baikal had to be to produce such an excellent vodka. Deep inside him, he sang a Siberian song, propped up his dripping bicycle and went into the inn.

He found himself in a simply furnished reception area; there was no one at the desk. When the door behind him swung silently shut, he tried to work out why it was only big, powerful cars that were parked outside, and why it smelled so pleasantly. Anywhere that smells good must be expensive, he thought. In his pocket, wringing wet but still legal tender, lay the three banknotes, a vast amount of money. Shivering and tired, he noticed people sitting eating in an adjoining room, so he went in. The people's faces seemed to him relaxed, as if they radiated friendliness and contentment, and this boosted Raven's self-confidence. One or two of them looked up and watched him, but he sensed no hostility in their glances. Most of them were totally absorbed with their plates, on which the food lay, carefully arranged according to shape and colour. Everything was bathed in a pleasant, not too bright light. The murmur of voices intensified Raven's tiredness and his sudden feeling of well-being. Only when he caught sight of the two waiters in their dark suits heading towards him did he feel the urge to turn on his heel and get right out of the inn. Before he had got that far, one of them, after a brief, searching glance, asked if he had booked in advance. No, Raven replied and, having seen that there was no reason for him to run away, said he would like a room. The waiter led him back to the reception and handed him his waiter's napkin. He gave a bell next to the desk a light tap and said someone would be out in a moment. He did not go away, though, but waited beside Raven and asked him if he had had a fall. Raven nodded, emboldened by the thought that he had money, a great deal of money, in his pocket and that he could pay for everything, any courtesies, the comforting warmth, the waiter's quiet, polite tone. Dirty water was still dripping from some of the holes in his carrier bag, forming tiny puddles in front of the reception desk. From an office behind it a woman emerged and looked first at Raven, then at the waiter who gave a barely perceptible shrug. She looked Raven up and down and smiled as she caught sight of the puddles on the floor. You'll be wanting a room with a bath, I imagine, she said and asked Raven to follow her. How on earth do they know I've got so much money, Raven wondered for a moment. Then he surrendered completely to his weariness. With considerable pleasure he kept his eyes on the lady walking ahead of him, whose voice had already made him feel so contented, whose dress he found as beautiful as her hair, the colour of her lipstick, her perfume and her calves. He very much liked the room she showed him into as well, its furniture in reddish gleaming wood, its curtains in a greyish-blue material with a soft sheen. Would he be wanting a meal, too? she asked. No thanks, he just wanted a bath. She opened the door to the bathroom. The bright, shiny tiles made Raven feel good and, as the lady turned to leave him alone in his room with bath, he reckoned she also had a very nice behind. The last impression he remembered was a slight uncertainty as to whether the heat of the water flooding over his body was pleasant and gratifying or painful. He hadn't even the strength left to make up his mind.

Fish-killers

AT THE VERY moment when Raven was falling into a deep sleep in his bath, down in the kitchens a tubby apprentice by the name of Liebherr was being told that there were advance orders for seventeen carp for the following evening. He was standing at the stove preparing a beef broth when he received this instruction which, even though he constantly had to wipe his glowing red, sweat-bathed face with his sleeve, brought a new surge of perspiration to his brow. It was his job to kill and clean the carp that were now swimming lazily and unsuspectingly around in the big tank, snapping at the rising bubbles. This was a task that nobody relished at all, least of all himself; he had already had to perform it a few times, and it always made him feel sick and brought him out in a rash that took two days to subside. As if that wasn't bad enough, he then had to suffer the jibes of his colleagues who, in fact quite appropriately in view of his appearance, had nick-named him Strawberry. On the first occasions, racked with nausea and with his eyes half-shut, he had lambasted the gasping fish, which caused the proceedings to last an agonisingly long time for both parties. Then he had sworn that the next time he would quietly get himself thoroughly drunk before setting about the creatures with the lead-filled cudgel. So he took advantage of every moment he was not being watched to put the bottle of cooking wine to his lips. The chef urged him to get on with killing the fish because they had to lie for some considerable time in cold water so that the flesh could relax again after the last violent spasm in order to let its full flavour unfold. He kept finding some excuse for putting off the job until he had finally got through three bottles of red wine. He let the potatoes boil dry, the noodles turned out too soft, the vegetables too hard and his hand slipped when he was salting the broth.

Just as Fever's broth kept on forming more dirty yellow scum on the surface, which he forgot to skim off, so equally, three floors above, Raven's bath suds were gradually congealing. Three hours later, he awoke again in completely foamless water. He climbed out of the bath and searched for a light switch, for it had got dark by this time. He was startled by the sight of his skin, which had become bloated and wrinkled like an old man's. He threw his clothes into the bath water, which was now quite cold, to wash them. The scabs on the wounds on his leg had puffed up, and around his left knee he fingered a painful bruise about the size of the palm of his hand, the result of his brush with the white car; one half of his face and his nose seemed to have swollen up, but had not turned black and blue as he had feared. By now, he was feeling the pangs of hunger. Nevertheless, the moment he had lain down between the fresh-smelling sheets, he fell asleep again. He could not have told anyone a thing about his dreams. All he knew was that they were full of colours and perfumes.

This was the first time in months that he had not been wakened by the cold or by noise. The room was warm, there were no loud sounds to be heard. He awoke refreshed. His aches and pains were bearable. Between sleeping and waking he was aware of a sense of familiarity, despite his strange surroundings. For a while he tried to work out what it was that was so familiar here, until he realised that the bed sheets smelled faintly of lavender. Yesterday, or was it the day before, the stonemason had died. His sense of time, of the passing days, that had developed before the stonemason's death with the fixed, immutable passage of the hours and days, the anticipation of sleep and the unwelcome, involuntary awakening, had vanished in a flash. As far as he was concerned, time could have stood still or passed twice as fast as before, it would not have made any difference to him. He stood for a long time staring at his washing as it lay in the bath. He took the things out and hung them on the towel rails. On the murky water, the three hundred-mark notes bobbed about. One of them had left blue streaks, the ink in which the chemist's telephone number had been written was gradually beginning to run. Money doesn't dissolve in water, Raven told himself and lay down on the bed with his hands folded across his chest. It would take at least a day for his clothes to dry. He considered what he might do now, whether just lying there would be enough. Spending a whole day here in this room, lying naked on the bed, would mean he had to pay for another night. The three banknotes looked ridiculously tiny, floating in that big bath. What would a room cost here anyway? A vast amount, a fortune, he said out loud, leapt from the bed, wrung out his clothes as best he could, took three sheets of the hotel notepaper lying on the table and laid the banknotes between them. He pulled on the damp trousers and the shirt, slipped into his jacket and stepped into his shoes which still squelched with dirt and wetness. The rest of the clothes he stuffed into the carrier bag and tucked it under one arm, since it had now become even heavier. Out in the corridor, there was no sight nor sound of anyone. Raven could not recall having been led up anything like as many stairs. He had gone down two floors without being seen, but leaving a trail of drips behind him, when he heard the voice of one of the waiters, followed shortly by the sound of his hurrying steps. In his desperation, Raven could think of no way of escape other than to open the nearest door as quietly as he possibly could and to hope that there would be nobody in the room. But to his horror the room was brightly lit and, from the bathroom, he heard high-pitched laughter and the sound of voices and a bath being run. For a fraction of a second he was about to leave the room again, but by now the waiter would probably be just about level with the door. And Raven's terror grew beyond all bounds when he heard three discreet knocks at this very door. What a mess he had got himself into. For what would be more obvious than the assumption that he had sneaked into this room in order to commit theft or something even worse. And of all the excuses and explanations for his presence here that flashed across his mind, each one was more pitiful than the last. So he prepared himself for the worst as, after a polite interval, the door opened and the waiter stood there before him with an ice-bucket and two glasses. He gave him a surprised, but by no means unfriendly, look and handed the tray over to him without a word other than, Ah yes, the wine you ordered, a remark which he even accompanied with a knowing smile before discreetly withdrawing. Raven stood by the door, transfixed by bewilderment and terror, holding the tray in his hands while the plastic bag dangled from his right arm, dripping ever more slowly. The sound of running water became quieter and stopped altogether, a man's voice struck up a song, a woman laughed and suddenly she was standing completely naked in the room, staring at Raven. Without stopping to think, he told her he had brought the wine. He set the tray on the floor and left the room. It was obvious he had to leave the building by a back door, for there was bound to be someone sitting at the reception desk. He heard noises coming from the restaurant, the clatter of crockery and a vacuum cleaner. In the passage-way he saw a large fish-tank. He stopped and listened. Some of the carp were lying lethargically around a valve from which fresh oxygen was bubbling up. Without really knowing what he was doing, he went through a door and came face to face with a fat lad of roughly his own age dressed in a cook's white uniform. That's it, they've got me now, Raven thought and then found it almost comical that the boy was actually Fever, much fatter now, and that he was holding a fishing net in one hand.

An almost breath-stopping reek of wine, a vacant, slightly squinting stare told Raven that Fever was dead drunk. He took in the forehead gleaming with sweat and the red blotches which disgust at the imminent task had already brought out. He recalled his own drinking bouts and the ones they had shared, and in Fever's eyes he could clearly read the despair of the exploited and overworked, so that Raven was sure he was confronted not with an enemy but with an ally. All he had to do now was convince the other boy, who was staring at him dully, that he had to help him escape. The drunken lad watched his former room-mate with a mixture of indifference and suspicion. His brief initial surprise at meeting Raven here had vanished at once and been obliterated by his now overwhelming sense of resignation. He seemed to suspect that Raven had no business being here, not in this hotel and least of all in this kitchen, which was his domain, even if the others here did take every opportunity to torment him on account of his slowness and shyness and played nasty tricks on him, sprinkling flour on the cold frying pan so that he would use a cloth to pick it up when he didn't need to, and switching a cold pot-lid with a hot one so that his hand was a mass of burns and blisters. As if he were about to eject the intruder by force, he tightened his grip on his fish-cudgel and, holding his fishing net like a halberd, moved over to block the doorway. Raven knew that he had to do something fast, for at any moment someone could come down the passage. Maybe the terrified naked woman had already reported that there had been an intruder in her room and so now, on top of his attempt to run off without paying his bill, would come attempted theft and breaking and entering as well.

No entry, Fever tried to point out to Raven, drawing his attention to the notice on the door.

I'm looking for the exit.

The boy pointed in the direction of the reception.

That's the entrance, and I'm looking for the exit.

The way in is also the way out, the boy said.

What about the emergency exit? asked Raven.

That's for emergencies.

What are you doing with that thing? asked Raven looking at the cudgel. Are you the doorman?

Nah, carp-killer.

Great job, said Raven.

Barrel of laughs, said the other. His interest in Raven seemed to have grown a little and he scrutinised him more closely, taking in his wet clothes and the swelling on his face. From the rest room behind the kitchen, yelling and gunfire could be heard. The cooks had switched on the television. And what about you? he asked Raven.

Bilker, Raven replied, for he reckoned now that he had won the other lad over to his side. He could see his mind was beginning to get into gear and the success or failure of his escape would depend on the outcome of this activity. It was clear to the lad that Raven was perfectly serious. He was not in the least interested in how Raven had got into the hotel, why his clothes were soaking, where he had come from or where he was going. He would have given practically anything if somebody were to take over his task for him, and Raven seemed to him to be just the cool, hard-bitten type he could unhesitatingly entrust with the job of beating to death and gutting the seventeen carp. The other cooks would not be back in the kitchen for a good half-hour, so that Raven could get on with the killing undisturbed. He found an apron being tied round his waist and while the cosh thumped down on the heads of the carp, which put up only a sluggish token resistance, the fat boy trawled around in the tank with his net, brought the required seventeen fish out and passed them over to him, saying each time, Right behind the eyes, now. He handed Raven the narrow, tapering, razor-sharp boning knife for him to slit open the seventeen bellies of the victims, some of them still wriggling, some feebly twitching, a job that Raven was very familiar with from his rabbit-slaughtering days. The tail fins flopped against the steel-topped table with a dull slap and, despite the white apron, his suit was soon covered in silvery shining scales and stinking of fish. And while Raven was getting on with the work, the fat boy became chatty and told him the tale of the best suit. When the lad had come to start his apprenticeship, he had turned up in a new, dark and extremely elegant suit which his parents had bought him on condition that he look after it and not put it on until he was celebrating success in his apprenticeship examinations. But only six months later, when he had put on the trousers to try them for size, they were so tight around his waist that he couldn't even bring himself to try on the jacket. And since he had continued to put on weight, in fact at such a rate that he could almost daily see the difference in the mirror, he was quite convinced the suit would never fit him again.

Shots kept echoing from the television, which guaranteed that none of the cooks would suddenly appear and catch them in the middle of their barter. The boy was so delighted at his bargain with Raven that his red blotches had disappeared again by the time the seventeen fish lay dead and gutted on the table. Twelve of them were completely motionless, the tail fins of the other five still trembled as if fluttering in a gentle breeze. Tears welled up in the boy's eyes. Fanned by his raging inebriation, the flame of his liking for Raven flickered into life again. His tongue loosened by his happiness, he told Raven all the news he could not have heard. Old Bad Luck had belted one of the younger pupils, no, more than that, had given him a right hiding. This had caused a new scandal at the school, and Bad Luck had been sacked. He had found a new job in the town. As for the headmistress, she had given in to increasing pressure from the parents, had handed over the running of the school and gone into premature retirement.

Fever wrote Bad Luck's address in town on a scrap of paper and gave it to Raven in case he ever needed a roof over his head. Bad Luck would be glad any time to have somebody to listen to his stories.

More than anything, Fever would have liked to be able to persuade him to stay and afford him permanent protection. Raven declined the offer, but said there was something he did want. A dark suit, a dry one, said Raven, sniffing in disgust at his fingers and his jacket. Now Fever had in fact hoped that, before the end of his apprenticeship, he might be able to get back to his original girth, so he protested a little, but in the end he told Raven to wait just half a minute before making good his escape, and he went and fetched the suit from his room. He urged Raven to put it on there and then, for he couldn't go out into the cold in his wet, stinking, filthy gear. Raven went along with that, and took the white shirt and the socks which Fever offered him as well. Everything fitted marvellously. He stuffed his old suit into a second plastic bag with the inscription HUEBER – GENTLEMEN'S FASHION WEAR. The boy led him past fruit boxes and garbage bins to the rear exit. Raven gave him one final nod.

Jam

GRADUALLY, RAVEN GOT the feeling that, as he went along his way, the town was becoming more and more of a concentrated mass. At first, he saw large sheds, mostly single storey, in which frozen meat, ripening bananas, printed material, electrical appliances were stored or small and medium-sized industrial firms were housed; there were tree nurseries in the sheds with glass roofs, and then came the first snack bar, a concrete box with a small window in the front, although this was covered over with green plastic film, and then a beer bar.

Here, lorry trailers stood by the roadside, as also did the odd woman in a ski-suit which, when they opened the zip at the front of their anorak top, revealed they were wearing either nothing or a transparent brassière or bodice underneath. Just as when he had met the woman with the newly set hair, he was overcome by a sense of uneasiness, of insecurity. Yet this time it was not a matter of shame at his own unfulfilled cravings, but the realisation that these women were offering themselves, were available, for money, to the public, and to him. It was the fear, the unfamiliar awe at his own power, so it seemed to him, to do what he wished with another person. He avoided eye contact and cycled on with his head down, past these women and their HYMER MOBILE HOMES and their KNAUS caravans.

It seemed to him as if he had caught a glimpse, in the far corner of his vision, of two big eyes, timid, frightened, fearful, yet at the same time apathetically empty and inviting, eyes that he knew well. He looked up and turned his head to make sure, and there indeed, in a salmon-pink ski-suit, was The Victim, standing next to a small caravan that was almost blackened by diesel exhaust, apparently waiting for something, or maybe not. Raven had never known anyone who could, like her, just be there, plump and good-natured, very simple and straightforward, but with a quiet capacity – a strength in her that was not to be underestimated – for standing up to anything, and perhaps, in many years' time, for emerging victorious, by dint of her sheer stamina, her forbearance in the face of pointless struggle, just as sooner or later, shut up in the oyster, the pearl, at one stage no more than a minute grain of sand, dead, mindless, round, achieves dominance over the whole complicated organism. And when the oyster itself has long since dissolved into gas and water, the pearl simply remains, unaware of its victory, its triumph.

She recognised him with a smile. He curved round and cycled across the car park to where she stood.

It made no odds to The Victim whether a client came or not, whether he smelt of cheap aftershave or of garlic, whether he was a Turk or a Greek, a Swabian or a Bavarian. What she really hated was when one of them expected her to put on a pretence of passion. Then she would work her pelvis a bit harder and help out with her hand to get the whole business over with sooner.

Precisely because she expected nothing, because she did not want to arouse any ardour, she was never short of clients. Her eyes, vacant yet so full, surveyed Raven in Fever's suit;

he really cut a weird figure on his bicycle. Landed up among the big shots, have you? All dolled up and on a bike. You look like a trainee solicitor, she said, opening the divided door to the tiny caravan, the upper part of which was almost always half-open for ventilation.

If it's really cold, I stand in the doorway and let my tits hang out over the top.

Raven thought he caught a hint of pride in her revelation of this solution to the problem.

She took a pine-needle aerosol and filled the place with its pungent aroma. On the propane-gas stove a large pan of hot water bubbled away, on the floor stood a plastic bath, an array of aerosol sprays, Sagrotan disinfectant, a tiny piece of lavender soap, various other air fresheners, deodorants, one or two, presumably empty, tear-gas capsules, a ten-pack of paper tissues, cassettes with folk music, a carton full of cans of cola, a bucket that was almost full of cigarette ends and in amongst them a few singed rubber johnnies.

Got any money? she asked, which was her way of saying, How are you doing?

Could be worse.

You're looking pretty posh, she said, swathing herself in another cloud of aerosol spray. Hate it when there's a stink. You hungry?

You bet. For the first time, he saw her as a woman. She caught the look and was immediately on her guard.

Fucking's out, forget it, she said. Want something sweet?

Nah. Bread.

She took out a loaf from under the cooker and cut a large slice, the way Raven had seen the farmers do it, holding the loaf against her body and moving the knife towards her. She spread margarine and blackcurrant jam on it. The tiny seeds stuck in Raven's teeth, the sugar penetrated the enamel and hurt him. She brewed him up a Nescafé.

Just like home, he thought, only warmer.

Raven, who had lived for so long in the cold workshop, found the heat in the confined space almost unbearable. It made him sneeze, and he immediately felt sleepy. There was a knock on the door: The Victim went out to get rid of a client. Raven drank the Nescafé, the sensation of warmth overpowering him, and he lay down on the bedspread with its printed pattern of all sorts of beasts of prey and fell asleep. The movement of the caravan, set up every time a heavy lorry went past, rocked him as if in a cradle. Everything that moved fast, that oscillated irregularly, matched in with the state of his tattered nerves.

In his dreams, rubber tyres weighing tons revolved to the accompaniment of folk music, there were pine needles everywhere, pulsating, growing, bursting, fat drops of green liquid, stinking of pine essence, engulfed everything, suddenly there was again a smell of Nescafé, but the aroma was too faint to waken him.

He sensed a sudden warmth, felt flesh next to him; this was The Victim, who had lain down beside him.

In her sleep, she too seemed to be wanting to draw warmth from him and she snuggled up to him.

If they had wakened, they would have heard a rattling at the door-handle. The rattling grew louder when the door did not give. There was a quick, very quiet knock. This, too, failed to wake the sleeping pair.

There was a brief pause outside. Whoever was wanting in was thinking things through. Why won't she open, why is the place in darkness, why isn't the red light burning inside, for that was the signal that she had a client. Has she finally upped and left, something that was strictly forbidden? What with all this and the fact that he had had a bit to drink and he was out of cocaine, which always made him violent, ill-tempered and depressive, a dangerous mixture, and since he had lost his spare key two years ago, he went to his car and took out a small crowbar and forced the aluminium door open with two quick movements. Even that did not waken the two of them.

He lit the mantle on the propane light and surveyed the scene. The Victim lay on the bed in her men's pyjamas, sleeping soundly and, it seemed to him, blissfully. She had, and this roused him to a particular fury, taken off all her make-up and was not wearing sexy underwear, she lay there looking totally unbusiness-like. Next to her, in the crook of her arm, lay a young man in a wickedly expensive, well-fitting suit.

This rekindled his imagination. Would any suit ever look, on his oddly shaped body, like a well-fitting suit? Had the two of them slept together? If so, why was he fully dressed? Was this some bloke The Victim fancied, was this what he had never been able to find out about, what always niggled him more than anything else? No. He would have liked to let his fantasies run on, but a towering jealousy now robbed him of all reason. All the same, he knew that ranting and shouting would make him the laughing-stock of all the tarts and his mates. His influence, none too great at the best of times, would suffer. No, he had to go about this quietly, be cool, calm and collected.

Raven opened his eyes, for a gleam of light had penetrated his eyelids and roused him from his sleep. Even before he woke, he sensed something ominous, suddenly there was no longer a smell of pine needles but of sour, belched-up beer and other fumes from days and nights of boozing.

Silhouetted against the light of the gas lamp, Fever's brother looked bigger than he really was, but he was not aware of that. Only his fury gave him courage. His voice was trembling, but only he and The Victim noticed that; it would never have occurred to Raven.

Is this private or is it business? the big brother demanded, clearing his throat a couple of times. The Victim awoke. If it was private, then I'll give the pair of you a right sorting out. If it was business, then out with the wallet.

Raven was in fact wide awake, but if he were to give him all his money he would have even less idea of what he was going to do than he had now. So he pretended to be asleep and made no move, said nothing and offered no resistance even when the big brother hauled him upright and ordered him to turn out his pockets.

Raven still did not move, so the big brother pulled the expensive cloth from his body and turned out everything that could be turned, until at last two freshly laundered banknotes fluttered out and spiralled to the floor.

The big brother cast a scornful glance at the pieces of paper, took the trousers and jacket between finger and thumb and threw them out of the door. Please let somebody have seen that, he begged, deep down inside.

Raven reckoned the best thing would be to follow his clothes voluntarily.

Hang on, said the big brother, and forced Raven to take his underpants off as well. And sure enough, another banknote fell out.

What am I supposed to do now? Raven inquired, in a very matter-of-fact tone and in the honest hope of getting an answer.

The big brother looked him up and down, told him to turn round and, to his back, said, Pretty boys hang about the museum.

Once he had noted, much to his satisfaction, that some other lights were on and curtains drawn back, he threw Raven's underpants at his feet, examined the minor damage to the door and closed it behind him as best he could. Raven dressed quickly, it was cold and he did not want to hear anything of what was about to happen inside the caravan.

What did he do? asked the big brother.

Ate bread and jam, The Victim said innocently.

Raven cycled off as fast as he could; already, dawn was breaking. In the early light of day, The Victim was persuaded that it would be better for her never to let an old friend in again. The big brother washed his hands with the piece of lavender soap. She was in full agreement with everything he said.

Inhibitory Reflex – the Second Visit to the Museum

WHILE IT IS true that Raven harboured a secret passion for the sculptor Michelangelo Buonarroti's figures, photographs of which he had repeatedly gazed upon in the stonemason's dog-eared book, he had, however, never imagined that these statues actually existed, carved out of stone, that you could go and look at them or even touch them. Marble was, for him, too mundane, too heavy and too cold ever to be associated in any way with fauns and gods, heroes and the dead Christ. This stone, this material, might well bear the same name as the one he had cut, carved and polished, yet it must be fundamentally different, more flesh than stone. He was also aware that these figures were to be seen in museums, or at least alabaster casts of them, but he had set foot in a museum only once, and then the multitude of images had so overwhelmed him that he had had to spend the time chain-smoking in the toilets waiting till Andre gave him the word that the visit was over. He felt more secure when he had the statues lying in front of him in picture form, when, in his imagination, he could arrange their smoothness, their size, their smell and the way the light fell on them, all according to his own taste. And so it was that, in the entrance hall to the museum, an oppressive feeling crept over him, a fear that he might find his pictures in a different, more imperfect form. The real purpose of his visit was something he preferred to put to the back of his mind, and he hesitated for a long time, wondering whether he should in fact buy a ticket or not, whether someone would approach him here outside and offer him money, or whether these people were to be found only inside. It was only his smart suit that persuaded an attendant to wait a good half-hour before addressing the young man with the request either to buy a ticket or to go away. For there were often odd characters hanging about there, seemingly waiting for something or merely keeping warm or, in summer, wanting to enjoy the cool air. So preoccupied was he with his thoughts about the statues in his imagination and the real ones that he did not notice that a gentleman had been watching him for some time and that, shortly after Raven had counted up his remaining small change, bought a ticket and gone in uncertainly, he had broken off his pretence of perusing a catalogue and strolled into the first room after him. This gentleman's features betrayed no sign of agitation, far less any indication of haste or desire. They were chubby, yet at the same time rather gaunt, dull yet determined. He was one of those people who, while by no means overtaxed by their work and their daily routine, yet because of some faint anxiety which dominates their metabolism, become more carefree, come into their own in their leisure hours or on holiday. Confidence was just as evident in his expression as that perpetual hint of apprehension; his urges surfaced only in those instants which absolutely permitted or called for them. He could, at one and the same time, look a person straight in the eye and yet look right through them. In these steady eyes, which appeared to radiate candour, there lay something almost imperceptibly provocative. His sole purpose in coming to this place was to approach a boy. If, however, he had failed to meet one, he would simply have gone home without any sense of having missed out on something. In all probability he had no plans to go and try some other place in search of a youth. Nor did he regard himself as being homosexual or bisexual, he was, all in all, happily married and had children, his family mattered to him and he detested those, to him distasteful, dirty places where homosexuals gathered, the parks, public toilets, saunas and dark underpasses. In his search for a boy, he never frequented any venue other than this museum, so that he never had to keep his movements a secret from his wife. He would say, I'm going to the museum. And even if she noticed no obvious change in him when he returned home, she did nevertheless suspect that something must have occurred that had touched him deep down, but this suspicion was never strong enough for her to quiz him about it or to look for any kind of clues, like telephone numbers on scraps of paper or hairs on his lapel. And so it never crossed his mind that he might be committing any deceit, that he was being unfaithful to his wife or that he was concealing or keeping anything from her. Raven was not looking at the pictures, nor at the busts. He was simply enjoying the high-ceilinged, cool rooms, the marble floors and most of all the apparatus installed in every corner of each room to measure the humidity in the air and register it, sometimes with a slight trembling, sometimes with an even swing, sometimes again with an erratic flicker, of a needle.

So at first the man followed him at a distance which betrayed not the slightest indication of his intentions, transmitted no perceptible body odours, not a trace of breath, soap, perfume, not even the sound of his footfalls as he gradually fell in step with Raven. He did not stop to look at something at exactly the same time as Raven paused, he would go on a few paces, stop by a little bronze sculpture, walk round the pedestal so as to be able to keep Raven in view without needing to turn his head. He didn't yet know how much money he would offer Raven, whether he would wait until the boy himself brought up the subject or whether he would simply give him anything he asked for. That, he thought, is probably the best way, for it had been his experience that when they fixed their prices, the boys followed a kind of code of honour, or at least a strict set of rules, and that their price structuring was more transparent than that of the supermarkets and big stores. If a boy was in some sort of trouble and needed more money than usual, he would always give a reason, at which he himself would nod sympathetically; it might be something to do with rent, or drugs or a long overdue present for a sweetheart. Now, in the case of this boy, he would give him whatever he asked for, without hesitation, without any show of indignation, he was quite sure of that. He fingered the banknotes he kept loose in his pocket so as to be able to hand them over quickly and avoid the bother of having to open a wallet and so arouse curiosity about its contents, be it the cash or the photographs of his wife and children. He was always very careful to tuck his business cards and his identity card away in his desk before coming out, so that nothing could fall out of his pockets which might give away more about him than would his low moan at the moment of orgasm.

Just at the very instant when the man touched his banknotes and realised that, on this occasion, he had forgotten to carry out his safety routine and that there were some visiting cards in his inside pocket, he increased his pace so as to get nearer to Raven, to get a closer look at his face and see whether there was either a familiar or an unusual feature in it. There might be contempt for him, the suitor, or that restless, forlorn anger in the eyes that was the man's favourite expression, which so provocatively reminded him of the fact that there was another, obviously different, darker world beyond his own. Now the game had begun, the uncertainty as to whether the approach was too fast or too slow, the moment of anticipation, the sudden advance, the vague signs and gestures and the unambiguous ones. The last-minute decision as to what he would ask the boy to do. He walked a little faster, perhaps too fast, he thought at once, looking around to see if anyone had noticed his excessive haste. But no one had seen it, not even the boy, and he punished himself for his mistake by taking a long look at the bust of some scientist or other and trying to remember what great achievement the world had to thank him for. Raven had still not noticed the gentleman's interest; he was trying to find out just how these humidity gauges worked, and he came to the conclusion that inside each of them there was a female hair, stretched out so that, by expanding or contracting, it communicated to the vibrating needle whether it was to swing upwards or downwards. And he stooped so as to be able to examine the machine more closely and was just about to get right down on his knees when he was prevented from doing so by a museum attendant who came up to Raven and said, Please do not touch. It seemed to the man, who had by now strolled over to another exhibit, as if he could sense the physical proximity of the attendant to Raven, as if he himself could feel the hand on the boy's arm. He could see quite clearly how startled Raven was by the contact and he already began to fear that his efforts would be thwarted and an approach would prove impossible. He found himself unable to suppress his rising fury at the man in uniform and he almost had to laugh at the realisation that the underlying cause of his anger was something bordering on jealousy. And immediately he recognised this jealousy as an emotion which had, for a brief moment, robbed him of his position of superiority over the boy. On his lower arm, the thin reddish-fair hairs were standing on end. He broke out in a light sweat, felt his vest becoming clammy, goose-flesh spread from his shoulders down to his wrists. Inside, too, there was something stirring, a terrible pang of conscience, a revulsion at himself, at the filthiness he was exposing himself to, and filthiness it was, he told himself, even if he had chosen this particular place of apparent pristine cleanliness in which to end up in filth. This, then, was the moment of decision, if he did not speak to the boy now, he would have to leave. His shame would grow to such an extent that his voice would stick in his throat. Even now he had to make an effort to reduce the heaviness and the pace of his breathing and to gain control over the trembling in his hands and his knees. Was he already attracting attention? Had the attendant not just given him a stare that was longer than necessary? Had there not been an unpleasant smile on his face, a look full of scorn and contempt?

He kept washing his hands all day. So often that, if anyone had asked him, he could not have told them how many times. Because of his repeated ablutions, the oils had been washed out of his skin, it was showing signs of becoming wrinkled, of drying up. He needed creams and ointments to prevent the skin becoming chapped and developing hacks. Now, at this very moment, he would have dearly loved to have a bath, to shower, to wash his hands, his hair. A shave, the cool after-shave evaporating on the skin. Cleaning his teeth, rinsing the back of his throat with mouthwash. But instead, here he was now, at this very moment, looking for a boy. That was why he had come here; he moved slowly towards the boy.

Interesting machine. Do you know how it works?

There's a woman's hair stretched inside it.

After a few seconds, Raven followed the gentleman. He left the exhibition room, went past the wrought-iron fountain. The air conditioning was humming loudly; on top of that, the splashing of the water on the sheet-metal base.

The gentleman had opened the door of the toilet just a fraction and he looked out to see if Raven was coming. Another man was standing at the wash-hand basin, drying his hands in the stream of hot air. Raven came into the lavatory, hesitated, and then made as if to go into another cubicle. At last the sound of the blower on the hand-dryer shut off. There was the noise of a door shutting as the other man left. Raven followed the gentleman into the cubicle. He bolted the door and stared at Raven's neck because he could not look him in the eyes.

This was it, then, there was no point in hiding anything now, just use the little time available to reveal all that he wanted of him; no false shame, simply take the shortest possible route to achieving that which would make up for all the fear, the embarrassment, the revulsion. He took Raven's hand and placed it where he wanted it. Raven did not want to touch that place, he had never in his life touched a penis other than his own. His hand was guided by the sweating hand of the gentleman who, in the privacy of the cubicle, was panting excitedly, his breath coming fast and loud. Hardly had Raven even touched against the cloth of the man's trousers when the man had a violent erection. Yet no matter how hard he tried, he could not get Raven's hand to open the zip fastener and slip into his trousers. Yet it did not for one moment occur to the gentleman that Raven could be resisting out of ignorance, fear or revulsion. This gentleman thought, on the contrary, that in Raven he had come across an especially crafty operator who was only putting on a show of reluctance, so as to prolong the enjoyment, to play especially unusual and pleasurable games. While all the wrestling of fingers and hands was going on, he was racking his brains until he found, and dared to give expression to, exactly what he wanted. In a hasty whisper, he transmitted his desire into Raven's ear. At first Raven was relieved that that was all he wanted and was convinced he could fulfil this wish with no trouble at all. He drew his member from his trousers and the other man did likewise, pulling down the zip to let his penis shoot out. Now Raven relaxed in order to do justice to the gentleman's wishes, he exerted a little pressure on his bladder, but nothing happened. Not a single tiny droplet could he squeeze out of himself. Some inner tension brought on by the other man's lustful leer was preventing him from carrying out the task, which amounted to no more than simply making water. The gentleman wanted to watch how the body could evacuate two so different fluids along two identical routes. No matter how hard he tried, this exit remained blocked. The gentleman realised this and, for the first time, looked at Raven with a hint of annoyance in his eyes.

I'll have to drink a beer first.

The gentleman left the toilet first, after making sure that no one was watching him. Now, true to his well-tried routine, he had quickly checked that his wallet was still there, but in doing so, one of the business cards he had brought along by mistake had fallen out of his pocket. Raven followed him, a few seconds behind, saw the card lying on the tiled floor and put it in his own pocket. Then he carried on, pausing at the metal fountain to look at it for a while. The gentleman had by this time found a seat at a small marble table in the cafeteria in the main hall of the museum. The gentleman ordered two beers, which they drank in silence. It might well have been because of the chill from the drink in the pit of his stomach, or perhaps it was because of the sheer spaciousness of the vast stone room, whatever it was, the gentleman abruptly paid for the two beers, slipped Raven three hundred-mark notes and took his leave with the words, That's it, I can't do it anymore.

Alive, Alive-oh!

AFTER FEVER HAD ostensibly carried out his duties as fish-killer so efficiently, his standing among the other cooks had risen. Perhaps he wasn't after all the spoilt brat of stinking rich parents, a grease-blob, as they called him because he always sweated so profusely whereas all the others had long since become accustomed to the heat in the kitchens. So had the Strawberry finally turned out to be a real mate? They were in quite a charitable mood and some of them were even kindly disposed towards him all of a sudden.

Over a period of some days, his life in the kitchen became more agreeable, he had almost completely abandoned his plans to get out of there as soon as he could. Special little privileges and treats were put his way, he was allowed to open the jars of caviar and take a sample with the mother-of-pearl spoon, he was allowed to test the quails' legs for the salad, to see if they were well enough done; he felt relieved, more and more at ease.

He could not have foreseen that a touring coach full of Japanese would draw up with thirty well-dressed businessmen from Nagasaki, every one with his NIKON cocked for action. They wanted a meal, fish, the way they were used to it, fresh fish that – this was how they liked it best – was virtually still twitching as it was being prepared. Great was their delight when they saw the carp lazing around in their tank. Secretly, each of them was already picking out his favourite. The order was noted and taken through to the kitchen. *Oui*! shouted the *poissonnier* as an indication that he had understood the order.

Let's be having you, Liebherr, he said chirpily, thirty carp to be got ready.

Fever professed an urgent need to go to the toilet and laid down his knife. He went up to his little room, pocketed his wallet, put on his greasy jeans and his leather jacket and cleared off in the hope of finding Raven at Bad Luck's place.

Non-load-bearing Pillars

JUST AS BAD LUCK had lived during his time at the school in a low-ceilinged attic room, revelling in its lack of space, so now he was living under an even more oppressive ceiling. He loved the lowness of his room, what he hated was its enormous size and elaborate layout. He had curtained off a tiny section of the room with four plastic sheets, a lonely, semi-transparent tent that gave off a blue glow. He slept in there, and his transpirations and exhalations gathered overnight and stuck to the plastic skin in thick, oily drops; he could count them every morning as they slithered their glutinous way down. The ice-cold blue light came from fluorescent tubes that he had set up in three corners of the windowless room and under his tent. The door was a bulkhead of green painted iron, the floor concrete grey and covered in dust.

Habitation of this room which owed its existence only to conditions imposed on the builders so that the building neither exceeded nor fell short of the height of the others in the vicinity was strictly forbidden. Firstly, because it was windowless, secondly, because of the inadequate headroom, thirdly because there were no sanitary installations up there, fourthly because there were regulations laid down by the fire authorities. And, because of all these, fifthly, there was a cloudy mixture of glass-wool dust and suspended asbestos particles hanging in the almost permanently static, stifling air. The air here was highly toxic.

If Bad Luck stretched himself very erect, his back straight, a slight tension at the back of his knees, and his neck at full stretch, then the ends of his hair, all plastered up with brilliantine and assiduously kept in shape, would be touching the asbestos ceiling panels with their veneer of glass wool. If, just for fun, he stood on tip-toe, then his quiff was pressed down, squashed flat and he didn't have to bother about keeping his balance but stood there, wedged in head and foot, carrying the total weight, enjoying his unshakeable solidity where nothing could be budged any more; he forgot the world and became a non-load-bearing pillar.

At last Raven had found the squash centre, a concrete cube embedded in asphalt. He circled round it and saw Bad Luck chasing off children who were playing in a car park.

Although it was Bad Luck's job to clean out the sanitary installations on the basement floor, the showers, toilets, washrooms and brightly tiled changing rooms, and although he had express permission and authority to avail himself of these facilities after the place closed, he practically never did so. His employer, a garrulous, soft-hearted relative, made the point that even he himself did not have such first-class sanitary facilities at his disposal in his own flat. Everything was very new and beautiful, easy to clean and keep germ free. Yet neither the showers or the washrooms nor the toilets tempted him to regular use. His particular preference was to urinate into lemonade bottles, which he then, racked with loathing and revulsion, emptied down the toilet once a week. Doing his big jobs caused him quite unimaginable problems, for his disgust forced him to hold it back as long as he could, which of course did not make flushing it away any easier, and the whole thing was made even more difficult because of his extraordinary aversion to the sanitary facilities which he himself, after all, had cleaned. Inside Bad Luck's body, everything became constricted, turning him into a kind of sausage tied tight top and bottom.

Raven was soon to discover that it was far from being the toilets that aroused such boundless revulsion in Bad Luck, it was the handsome, bronzed young people who used them, with their perfect circulation and acne-free skin. Bad Luck detested everything about them. The teeth gleaming like mother-of-pearl and the lemon-yellow little sport shirts, the spicy after-shave and the aromatic roll-on deodorants, the expensive watches that emitted odd noises at unpredictable intervals, as well as the jocular chit-chat they tossed back and forth over the shower partitions.

No, he would say, he wouldn't have touched one of these females with a barge pole.

There was an inappropriate haste in all his movements. If he were to go over to a corner of the room to fetch something, this would be done at an exaggerated speed and not without him circling the table in the middle of the room at least once, to no purpose whatsoever. His haste caused him to do the wrong things, or other things which he had not on any account intended doing, or forgetfully put off once again things he had been meaning to do for a long time, or things he had forgotten or overlooked in his excessive haste would suddenly come to mind at an inappropriate moment and distract him from whatever important and essential things he was in the middle of doing. His sheer haste made this inevitable, for all it achieved was that he kept wasting his own time.

He talked, he ate, he walked, he bathed, he even urinated and defecated in such haste that the resultant tension merely prolonged all these processes. Words spoken rapidly became garbled and had to be repeated. As he walked, he would trip over his own scurrying feet, narrowly escape falling flat on his face, pause for a moment, and by then he would have forgotten why he was going where he was going.

If at first he washed only very infrequently, later his grooming was restricted to his quiff and he finally gave up washing altogether.

His clothes were unkempt, he seemed to have shrunk into himself, indeed Bad Luck suddenly appeared to Raven to have the build of a dwarf, he seemed wasted away and barely came up to Raven's shoulder. People noticed from a distance whenever Bad Luck approached, for there was a smell, a strong smell, a stink. Later on, Raven could no longer remember what the man's real name was, in fact he doubted whether the man had a name at all or whether he had lost even his name in some catastrophe, through carelessness or as a result of some piece of villainy. Probably Bad Luck was his name, Raven concluded. He smelt quite abominably, and nobody could have said offhand of what. He smelt as if he carried about a piece of Harz cheese in his pocket, and yet he didn't smell of Harz cheese. He smelt as if he had some mackerel in his other pocket and small sponges soaked in cats' piss sewn into his armpits. There was a vague stench of garlic, but it was as if the garlic smell had mated with that of babies' dirty nappies. Raven was not sure whether smells could mate, like rabbits, and he made up his mind to ask Bad Luck why he smelt so exceptionally awful. His breath, his clothes, his hair and his very skin itself stank, even his collapsible umbrella stank, so that you prayed it wouldn't rain.

This man had a sharp eye for his own misfortune as well as for other people's. He could tell right away that Raven had not a penny to his name, that he was afraid of having to spend the night in the open, and he hoped he could persuade him to stay the night in the squash centre.

Raven, however, was sickened by the stench. He was not squeamish; at the stonemason's there had been a stink of rabbit droppings, of tobacco, of all manner of detritus, but the cold had taken much of the edge off the odours. Whereas the stonemason would never have tolerated any kind of dirt other than the dust off the stones and everything else rolled off him as if he had been proofed against it, Bad Luck on the other hand seemed to attract all kinds of filth and to suck up all kinds of smells into his pores and combine them there into some nauseating amalgam.

Raven promised to return and then set off in search of a place for the night. Bad Luck had advised him to use public transport and, if he were to come across a ticket check, simply to run away. Raven reckoned this was not a bad idea, for he knew that in the towns a bicycle was regarded as common property that anyone just took as and when he needed it. He rode his VATERLAND bike to the station, where he asked a group of bystanders whether they wanted to buy a bike cheap. No one showed any interest, one said the bike was an antique anyway. But suddenly a small, stockily built man in black leather shorts detached himself from a villainous-looking group. He drew himself up in front of Raven, his legs apart, his stomach sticking out. What you think you're doin' with my bike, he said in an accent that was meant to sound matey but actually conveyed some unpredictable threat.

Raven said he must be mistaken, but this was his bike,

there was no doubt about that. The man beckoned to his friends, who all came over too.

Whose bike is this? he asked without taking his eyes off Raven.

Yours, they said as one man.

Raven took consolation in the thought that he intended using public transport anyway. Only, he had no idea where he wanted to go. It did not occur to him that, because of his appearance, he gave the impression of being well off, and as a result was arousing the hostility of everybody hanging about there, all the cadgers, drunks, runaways, tramps, sharks, irredeemable alcoholics, drop-outs, down-and-out immigrants, jail-birds and violent thugs. Only after a time did he notice the way these people were looking at him, and when he saw two men in black uniforms repeatedly jabbing a tramp in the stomach with a rubber truncheon in a dark corner of the Underground station, he decided it would be better to go back to the squash centre on foot. He ran along the smart streets of the town centre, reached the outer suburbs, the outskirts, and then at last he could make out the silhouette of the squash courts in the low autumn sun.

He prepared himself for anything: the smells, the dreadful stories about his sad fate that Bad Luck loved to regale people with, rounding them all off with some such aphorism as In the end, everything will sort itself out, it'll all be for the best.

One thing, however, that he would not have reckoned with in his wildest dreams was that he would find a snoring Fever lying in a corner on his leather jacket, obviously spark out. Maybe he should just sneak away again, back to the station, anywhere else. It was getting dark, and he would have to keep a very sharp eye on the money the gentleman had given him. All the same, he did not want to meet Fever again.

He tip-toed out of the room. Downstairs he met the squash

players, perspiring, yet still immaculately groomed, who had come here to relax after work.

At the station, he bought two six-packs and sat down in a quiet corner; next to nobody came past here and the railway police were otherwise occupied. Raven was so engrossed in a group of drunken, bawling and singing army reservists picking quarrels with anyone and everyone who happened to be passing, but, it seemed, particularly with obvious foreigners, that he did not notice two young men approaching him from the opposite direction. Then they were standing right there, and it was too late for him to move away. He recognised them as two of those who, that afternoon, had testified that his bicycle belonged to the stocky man. Raven feared the worst. They sat down beside him and said nothing for a while.

Abruptly, so suddenly that Raven expected to see a weapon, one of them pulled a hip-flask from his pocket, drank from it and held it out to Raven. It was almost empty. Without a word, Raven offered them some beer; one of them could open the crown corks with his teeth. Raven said he would like to learn how to do it, too.

Listen, you still need your teeth, the other said with a grin. He should know, for he was missing three incisors and all the rest were mere black stumps.

Raven could not help laughing, because it struck him as a good joke. The others obviously did not think so. In grim silence, they drank Raven's beer. The toothless one stuffed the metal bottle-caps into a pocket already bulging with them.

Get some more in, he said to Raven when they had finished the last of the beer. Raven got to his feet. The other two rose as well and, keeping him between them, made towards the kiosk for another two six-packs. The toothless one was desperate for a banana. Raven bought a small bunch of bananas, which were fiendishly expensive.

They're from Kenya, the sales assistant said proudly.

Raven would have loved to be there at that precise moment.

They devoured one banana after another, the way chain-smokers smoke, and mixed the beer in with the pulpy mass in their mouths; anyone who was off solids could probably manage for a good while like that. Did they want anything to eat, Raven asked, something decent? He was convinced he could only get rid of them by bribery.

Why eat when you can drink for the money? said the man with the solid mouthful of teeth.

When the last beer had been drained, what Raven had been fearing happened. The two of them had something important to show him.

Won't it do here?

They both shook their heads slowly. His only hope was that they would be easier on him because of his generosity. Again between them, he had to go down the stairs into the Underground station. There they steered him into a corner, and Raven was pretty sure this was the same corner where the two black-uniformed officials had done their duty earlier. All at once, the toothless one had grabbed one of Raven's arms and twisted it up his back, while the other one already had his jacket open and was rummaging through it, almost delicately. All he found was some small change.

That's all I've got.

And you wanted to buy us a meal out of that? Now that's just not done. He drove his fist into his stomach.

Raven, the breath driven out of him, could not utter a word. To the question as to where his money was, he could give no answer. Nor did he have to. They had already pulled down his trousers, taken his shoes off, searched in his socks and found all he had. And of course they accompanied all this with another two pile-drivers and several thumps about the head. They took Raven's shoes with them.

Most people in the station were in such a hurry that they did not notice Raven passing them barefoot. He left the station buildings, which had now assumed such menace for him, and threw up in some bushes. In those same bushes he noticed, after he had pulled himself together, a pile of cardboard boxes, with two feet sticking out of it.

If that's not a corpse, there's somebody sleeping in there, Raven thought. He took a good look at the heap, which moved gently with the sleeping man's breathing, estimated the size of the shoes, bent over, carefully untied the laces and whipped both shoes from the sleeper's feet.

It was weird how, in his vastly oversize clown's shoes, he now aroused the mirth of the passers-by. On the long road back to the squash centre he thought, it's just as well I'm used to pain.

Reluctantly he climbed up the steep stairs and opened the bulkhead door.

Fever had wakened by this time and was tucking into a white sausage from the nearby snack bar. They had apparently taught him some manners at the restaurant. He was sitting on a beer crate with the paper plate on a large handkerchief across his knees. He sat ramrod straight, had speared the sausage with a fork and was slitting the skin open to peel it cleanly off the sausage.

Well, here I am, said Fever.

Raven sat down, rolled a cigarette and said nothing.

Fall downstairs, did you? Fever inquired and dipped his sausage in the coarse-grained, sweet mustard that was to accompany all the great variety of different sausages, their staple diet in the days that followed. A buxom Yugoslavian woman smilingly doled out generous amounts of it free along with her sausages.

For several days they sat in the room, doing nothing. They didn't even chat or play cards or read. Raven hardly slept at all, while Fever seemed to do nothing but. On the third day,

Raven, who had not left the building because of his battered appearance, had hatched a plan. He roused Fever and asked, Where's Andre?

With a yawn, Fever told him to look in the telephone directory. As far as he knew, she was living with her parents.

I can't.

Why not?

Anybody in the state I'm in will just get another dose.

Fever had to concede that. From Bad Luck, whose recompense for their presence was the fact that he could relentlessly regale Raven with the string of disasters in his life, he borrowed a few marks for sausages, beer and mustard and went off to the telephone box.

Do you know where I got these scars from? Bad Luck asked.

Yes.

Raven's answer did not put Bad Luck off his narrative stroke. He told the tale of his eldest sister who had gone into a coma after an accident. It was obvious to Raven that he would not be able to stem Bad Luck's endless monologue even if he were suddenly to lapse into a coma himself. Bad Luck droned on. Raven kept an ear cocked, but not towards Bad Luck's narrative.

The sounds of the people playing or torturing themselves down below came up as no more than the rhythm of a high-pitched, double clicking. A first thwack as the small hard ball struck the racket and was hurled violently away by it. A second thwack as the speeding ball smashed against the walls.

After a while, Raven could tell from the thwack alone who was playing, which of the cars out on the car park belonged to whom, and he even knew the colour of the hair of the woman waiting at home for each of them. He could tell by the power of the stroke whether the player had had a good day or a bad day. In fact, he even tried to draw conclusions from the players' rhythm and stamina as to what their sex life had been like the night before.

Remorselessly, Bad Luck was talking on and on. Fever's return at that moment came as a great relief to Raven. They ate their sausages in silence. Bad Luck seemed shattered by the memory of the fate of his other sister. Fever produced a scrap of paper with Andre's telephone number. Raven remembered how Fever had once announced his intention to give Andre the same treatment as he had given The Victim.

Arsehole, he said for no reason at all. Fever seemed used to it.

When the swellings on Raven's face had subsided and the worst of his cuts had healed, he got on with his day-to-day work.

Fever carried on as before, sleeping and fetching the sausages from the motherly, well-endowed Yugoslav woman. By now he was bringing the mustard in large cola tumblers, two varieties of it, one particularly strong and one sweet. They ate the fiery one with the sausages and the sweet one for dessert.

Even while they were eating, and without prompting, Bad Luck poured out his dreadful life stories: Then there was that business with my other sister . . .

Raven interrupted him.

Next week we're going to invite Andre for a meal.

His day-to-day work consisted of going along the tram lines early every morning with a screwdriver, raking about for dropped small change. The tram drivers never rang their bells till the very last moment.

In telephone kiosks, he would spit into the slot for returned coins. When the money dropped through, it would stick in the glutinous gob or people would be put off by the disgusting threads of spittle.

He stole small articles from the supermarket, but always had the feeling he was being watched.

What are we going to cook?

Sausages, said Fever.

Rabbit, said Raven.

Only two streets away, there was a shop with Pet Shop above the door. Raven and Fever asked about the price of a rabbit. The salesgirl offered them very young rabbits, especially sweet little things with red, barely opened, eyes. Raven asked if she had an older, stronger animal. The salesgirl was delighted to get rid of a frighteningly big rabbit that was unsaleable because all the children were afraid of it. Old Shop-soiled, she called it. She gave them something off the price.

They called Andre's number. Her stepfather answered and was amazed that anyone wanted to talk to her.

This is Raven. Want to come for a meal?

You're no use at cooking.

Fever can cook.

She promised she would come.

We must make sure he has a wash, Raven told Fever who himself had not washed for some considerable time now. Bad Luck had still not got round to describing the fate of his second sister. They borrowed two blue dustcoats from him and, from the Yugoslav woman, a small trolley for shifting beer crates.

On a square near the station there was a fair-sized department store. The bathroom fittings department was in the basement. They used the lift marked SERVICE LIFT – FOR STAFF USE ONLY.

The department supervisor gave them a friendly nod. They found one of those portable shower cabinets still in its original packing. The supervisor came with a book in which

Raven wrote RAVEN and a number like the ones written beside the other names.

They managed to get the package, which was taller than either of them, to the subway station, but couldn't wrestle it down the escalator. They decided to walk. Raven was used to carrying bulky loads. Nevertheless it was difficult to get up the steep, narrow staircase. They fetched the hose meant for cleaning out the showers and connected up the cabinet. There was nowhere for the shower cabinet to stand in the low room and Fever and Raven finally had to set up the little glass construction immediately under the skylight, which proved an extremely tight fit. The trouble was that Raven could no longer surreptitiously ventilate the place.

Bad Luck stared at the transparent foreign body in amazement. But he seemed to be pleased and relieved by the thought that the skylight, which he had always regarded as some kind of disturbing menace, could no longer be opened.

Arrival, Boredom, New Language

TO THE DEAFMAN, the jolting of the train, recurring with every joint in the rails, came as a sawing, agonising throb. The journey had already taken so long that he had forgotten how many hours he had put behind him and how many still lay ahead. His body was in a state of painful vibration, the likes of which he had never experienced even after his most hectic tractor rides. The railway line was smooth, the joints occurred at regular intervals, so regular he could feel them in advance; driving a tractor was uneven, jerky, unpredictable, yet in the very smoothness and straightness, in the apparent security, danger lay hidden, lying in wait, you could do nothing about it, and so he sat, so hunched up he seemed a good twenty centimetres shorter, his muscles knotted with tension, a bundle of neuroses, in a second-class compartment, as far away from the window as possible.

His eyes could no longer focus on one single spot, his nostrils dilated, smelling this way and sniffing that, so rapidly that he did not have time to look round when first there was a smell of cheese, next there was a stink of manure, and then of diesel, and then again there was a hint, a whiff, of woman, and immediately after that, of horse, and by the time he caught the sixth odour he no longer had any idea of what could be giving off the smell. He looked behind him, behind the train, in his distress he hung his head as far out of the window as he could manage; his fellow-passengers were by now watching him anxiously, but he could not discern anything that might be the source of the smells, everything interwove before his wildly darting eyes into a stinking carpet whose weave told him absolutely nothing any more, he would have had as much chance of telling from the smell of a doormat who was in the habit of going in and out across it. Before he had even stepped down from the carriage, he found himself being met and received, practically taken into solicitous custody, by a young man. This young man presumably recognised him from the photograph he had had taken and which had set off on the journey two weeks before him. And even back then, when his sister-in-law had gone out to post his picture at the pillar-box, he had experienced an unfamiliar excitement. That's travel nerves, his sister-in-law told him when she came back and found him lying in a muck sweat in his room.

The young man had a strand of hair that persisted in falling down over his forehead, and he had to keep sweeping it back across the top of his head with a quick flick of a hand. In fact he was perpetually waving his hands about in agitation, making strange signs and signals, for he had a command of the deaf and dumb language and assumed that every deaf person understood it as well. To the Deafman, however, it amounted to nothing more than just a flailing about, which only perplexed and unsettled him more. The Deafman and his family had their own system of signs and gestures to help them understand each other. Their daily routine and the tasks that had to be carried out were so regular, governed by the time of day or the seasons of the year, that mutual comprehension was virtually automatic. Whatever had to be done was simply done, without any great to-ing and fro-ing.

But how could this young man recognise him from the photograph, in which he had not even recognised himself and which had set his family off in loud hoots of laughter. How could he know that he wasn't semaphoring to the wrong man altogether, grabbing hold of him and his luggage, leading him out of the station, bundling him into a taxi and, after a fifteen-minute drive which was spent open-mouthed, bringing him to an elegant, old-fashioned but by no means hostile-seeming house.

But the very harmlessness of this house filled the Deafman with new, unknown fears, for he had expected that everything here would be smooth, bare and rubbed down with surgical spirits so that nothing unwanted, nothing forbidden, could get a hold. Yet here it was altogether different. Nothing smelt of surgical spirits, nothing was bare and smooth, it was bright but not glaring and it smelt of, he could not make out exactly what, but it was nice, welcoming. Was all this a trick, a trap? They all gave the impression that they were his friends, wanted only the best for him, but everything in him was trembling with the uniform, sawing rhythm of the joints in the railway lines.

So frightened and exhausted was he that he fell asleep immediately after the young man had shown him to his bedroom, his accommodation, they called it here, which he was to share with a man who would be arriving in the next day or two; wall-to-wall carpeting, he thought, he had read about that, but that there should be such a thing in his room, that was awesome, so awesome that he fell asleep.

During the night he was wakened by a thunderous rumbling that he felt in his abdomen, as if someone were pummelling it with their fists. He had no idea whether he was dreaming or awake, where he was, whether he was alone or someone was in fact there, punching him. He did not know whether he was lashing out, or shouting, or whether, in his thrashing about, he had hit the light switch, but there, by his bedside, as if he had sprouted out of the wall-to-wall carpet, and looking extremely sleepy, which right away calmed him down a little, stood the young man.

In amazement, he watched the Deafman holding first his ears and then his abdomen and moaning softly, as if a deaf person could hear the noise which was in fact being made by a helicopter that had been hovering very low over the building for some seconds.

The roar of a helicopter was something familiar to the Deafman, for whenever the vibration of the rescue helicopter's rotors cut loose in his stomach, someone would be in his death throes or had already died or at least would be lying seriously injured, trapped or run over on the motorway.

On the bedside table stood a glass of water, which was moving slowly, a few millimetres, the mirror was rattling faintly and the pigeons, which spent the night on the window-sills of the toilets, were cooing in agitation.

The young man could see by the new patient's distraught expression that he was in the throes of waking from a nightmare caused by the vibration of the rotor blades. But that's just our Minister of the Interior, he said and waited a while till the Deafman had fully wakened from his nightmare and become aware of his surroundings, and gave him a Valium tablet. Then he switched on a small television set standing next to the wall cupboard. On the screen, a brightly lit building could be made out, with a helicopter just landing beside it. Some men got out, among them one who looked particularly corpulent and perspiring. They went into the building, surrounded by photographers and cameramen, flash-bulbs flared incessantly; the people looked exhausted, grey- or red-faced, and they seemed to be doing a lot of talking and the ones who were being most self-important were talking most of all. The Deafman stared at the little set for a long time and the young man stayed with him. When the Deafman's eyelids drooped shut, he had fallen asleep without noticing.

Next morning, a nurse woke him, and shortly after that the young man came in again and brought him a newspaper with pictures showing a portly Minister of the Interior. A Minister of the Interior on a big game hunt, a Minister of the Interior with a fine-looking black man, a Minister of the Interior standing in front of a massive oak cabinet that was insured for fifty thousand marks, and there he was again, pictured next to a Federal German Army helicopter. True, he was wearing an anorak in military green, but the Deafman distinctly recognised the rosy face he had seen on the television. So that's how the Minister of the Interior travels about, thought the Deafman. Then, at midday, he saw the building next door, where the helicopter had landed, for here, close by the centre for heart patients, with the landing area marked out in yellow, stood the central headquarters, the cradle, of the Minister of the Interior's party. So that's how the fat man flies around, and what a colossal oak cabinet he owned, and on his very first night he had seen such an important man. He would certainly not be bored here.

Solferino

IN EVERY TOWN there are squares which have an air of such obvious wretchedness, such unmistakable misery and such undisguised dreariness about them that even the casual visitor senses at once that this is the most miserable, the most wretched, the dreariest square in the whole town. This feeling comes over all the more clearly when, for example, the trees are in blossom in spring and the air is heavy with their fragrance, the weather is exceptionally good and the people hurrying by have a cheerful look on their faces. All the more deep-seated does the hatred, the embitterment seem in the faces of those who have to remain in these squares. And the Deafman had picked just such a square for his meeting with Raven. In the most gorgeous sunshine stood a little beer garden, right in the middle of a traffic island, there was a fragrance of linden trees, for the stench of the heavy lorries, buses and cars pressing along an arterial road leading to the motorway to the north was something everyone's nose had become so accustomed to that they hardly noticed it any more. It was in this part of town that all the hospitals were situated, this square was called Solferino Square, and here stood the clinic in which the operation on the Deafman's ears was to be performed, and the home where he would learn to talk and to cope with living with the sounds of the world about him. Looking out from the garden of the pub, then, you could see the nurses' home of the Solferino Hospital, and Raven watched the women coming and going. That was the hospital where a particular bone disease was treated.

As a rule, the treatment consisted of the amputation of the affected limb. The hospital was particularly well suited for all these amputations because it incorporated a crematorium, the brick chimney of which no longer towered over the new hospital wing the way it had dwarfed the original building. Only two tram stops further on was the hospital of the Brothers of Charity, which in turn was renowned for its urology department and, here too, amputees went in and out, but they wore foreign-looking clothes and turbans, for this was where men who had lost limbs in the minefields and their skin in chemical warfare were given treatment. They went about on crutches or supported by their wives, or they were pushed in wheelchairs if both legs had been blown off or their wounds still caused them so much pain that wearing an artificial limb was out of the question. Their skin was corroded away, their lungs, their gullets, their windpipes and the insides of their mouths, their eyes and their scalps, so that their hair fell out in clumps. And all these symptoms were given first-class treatment here, thousands of kilometres distant from the scene of hostilities. Just as in this country all the means of inflicting these wounds could be manufactured, marketed and sold in the most efficient fashion, so also were to be found here the doctors who were most expert in healing these far-travelled wounds and in teaching the invalids how best to get through life on one leg, on two stumps, with one hand or none at all, with half a lung and flayed skin. Several times daily, helicopters flew over the square, delivering coronary cases to the heart centre that stood only three bus stops further in towards town and a Minister of the Interior who was ready at any time to fly back to the cradle of his party for discussions. In that direction too lay the eye clinic, the home for the blind, a rehabilitation centre for drug addicts, four old people's homes, eight firms of undertakers and the very home itself, established in an old villa, where the Deafman was living. The beer garden was a meeting-place for the one-eyed who guided the blind until, in the beery haze, arguments arose, here the one-eyed and the deaf stumbled over the crutches of the limbless, the newly circumcised and those relieved of their phimosis talked their randiness back to life, although their fresh wound took the pleasure out of their lustings. Here lay the dog belonging to the inebriated man sitting there seemingly sound asleep; it looked so mangy and starved that Raven threw it his half-eaten sausage, but the dog spurned it and growled at him belligerently and the man opened his eyes, laughed to himself, drew up one trouser leg to reveal a reddened stump and said, pointing to his dog, He's been fed today already, and then could barely control his mirth, quaking with inward laughter until he shut his eyes again and took a gulp of his beer, to hold his peace for the remainder of the day. The dog lay down again at his master's foot and fixed Raven with a steady, malevolent stare.

Blind Man's Trap

AT A CROSSROADS with six sets of traffic lights stood a man with a white metal stick; the Deafman, who was on his way to meet Raven, watched him fascinated. Hat, spectacles like two black traffic lights, but one thing was missing, a dog to show him the way. At least I'll not get bitten, the Deafman was pleased to note. Because of the proximity of the eye hospital, the lights had been fitted with acoustic signals to help the blind.

Several times the blind man held his stick aloft. At first, he wanted to draw attention to himself, to magnify himself and his affliction with the aid of his stick. None of the vehicles was ready to be distracted. None stopped. There was no deviation from the straight line, just like the Federal Railways, each one of them followed its track as if on rails. The Deafman stood still and settled down for a long stint of observation.

The man with the glasses threatened and cursed, waving his stick. Even this brought none of the unseen motorists to a halt, the traffic noise simply rolled on past the irate blind man. He pulled on his stick, which could be extended like an aerial. No one received the signal from his aerial. He cupped his ear, first to one side and then to the other, then left again, and right: the road had four lanes, wide ones, with four sets of rails in the middle, where the trams presented a gliding menace, the buses were unwilling to brake, the traffic lights buzzed, flashing a simultaneous hail and farewell. None of them could make up its mind on a particular colour, on a buzzing tone; for the deaf man it was like the flashes of an autumn thunderstorm, for the blind one a buzzing of angry bees.

The Deafman saw the man with the stick setting off, and certainly the light next to him was green, something the blind man couldn't see, but he did hear it sending its buzzing sound temptingly across to him, heard the enticing siren buzz of the traffic light mingling with the imperious howl of the ambulance, the screeching of the trams, the subterranean rumble of the Underground trains, the distant roar from the urban motorways and from the building sites, all combining to lure the blind man into a wrong move, in amongst the traffic, out in front of the radiator grilles and under the wheels.

Now, it seemed to have got just too much for the man in all this noise, he stretched his stick out in front of him to spear and run through a car. The traffic lights indicated that the little man up there was quite red with terror, something else the blind man could not see, so he stepped out. He would have walked on, been squashed flat several times over, if the Deafman had not stopped him. That's my good turn for you, my new-found friend. But for me, you would be as flat as your sunglasses. Maybe that will be my last good deed before I go under all these knives tomorrow. Like the cow, that's how I'll end up, and there'll not be so much as a calf left over from me, he thought, and grabbed the advancing man's hand at the very last moment, long before any one of the drivers had even given the slightest thought to putting a foot on the brake.

Next time I go out for a walk, the blind man said to the deaf one, who nodded in reply, I'm going to put wax in my ears, for this is a murderous trap for the blind.

Perfect Pitch

AT FIRST, RAVEN saw a hat, the Deafman, then two hats, then two heads above the fence. One of them was the Deafman's. Next to him, walking at the same slow pace, came another man, his eyes concealed by a pair of large dark glasses that covered more than the usual area of his face. Both men were wearing hats which, from a distance, looked distinctly smart. The two of them made an eye-catching pair and could well have passed as exhibitors at a fashion trade fair, for there was no one else around dressed anything like them. Their arrival was, in fact, something of an entry that many an actor would have envied. The one with the glasses was carrying a long white metal stick, holding it clumsily in his hand, like some irksome appendage. He could not have been blind for very long, he was relying too heavily on the Deafman's guidance for that. His steps were uncertain, often he turned his head and put his hand up to his dark spectacles as if he were about to take them off in order to be able to see properly again. In a fury, the little dog started barking at the Deafman, the blind man flinched in fear and did not want to go any further while his deaf companion, showing no consideration because he had not noticed the animal, dragged him along over towards Raven's table. Rather bewildered by all this, Raven looked at the blind man who, in some inexplicable way, seemed familiar. What it was that reminded Raven of some other person, he could not say. Was it the way he moved, the little of his face that was visible, his mouth perhaps, or his ears? The Deafman pushed the blind man into a garden chair, touched Raven lightly on the shoulder by way of greeting, took out his Complications-Notebook, laid it on the table and sat down. Without any introduction, greeting or hint of shyness, the blind man started to talk. He cursed in a quiet, monotonous tone of voice, having, presumably, not the faintest idea as to whom he was addressing, or why.

More than an eighth-tone off key, he murmured quietly, yet in considerable annoyance, and then if the other one starts up on top of that, there'll be a disaster, then there's the fire engine as well, without touching bottom G in the bass.

The man pulled a tuning fork out of his pocket, hummed a low note, presumably bottom G, compared it with the A on the tuning fork and hummed his way down from the A to the bottom G. And hummed again, to demonstrate how dreadful a bottom G that was an eighth out could really sound.

When it buzzes, I'm supposed to set off, that's what they told me. So it buzzes, and off I go. The note is off, and that hurts. Then the fire engine on top of that. If he hadn't stopped me, and he gestured vaguely in the Deafman's direction.

Next to the beer garden was a tram stop, and more often than not private cars would be blocking the tracks, so the tram driver would give a vicious ring on his bell, which was painful even for ears that were not so delicate. Now, though, right next to this blind man's apparently highly sensitive ear, this bell, this instrument of torture just had to cut loose. He leapt from his chair, held his hands over his ears and yelled, E or G, E or G? And his voice rang with the expression of extreme agony.

When quiet had been restored, he struck his tuning fork once more, its fine, silvery tone barely audible. And he shouted, You can tear off my ears if you like, but I've got it now!

He groped for his beer glass, which the waiter, indifferent to it all, had placed on the metal table while the dreadful clanging was going on, struck the glass with his reversed tuning fork, drank a mouthful, struck it again, drank again, until the glass was empty. Then he ordered wine and went through the same procedure again with the wine glass, which had a clearer tone, then he ordered champagne and was blissfully happy.

I've got it, I can hear it, he kept repeating, his speech becoming increasingly thicker.

The Deafman had paid him scant attention but sat bent over his Complications-Notebook, busily writing.

The blind man gave him an infuriated poke in the shoulder, so that the deaf man gave a startled jump.

The blind man held out the tuning fork to him and said, Here, a present.

The Deafman looked baffled, gave a laugh, looked at the blind man and snatched off his glasses to try them on himself.

Raven could see the blind man's scarred, ugly-looking eyelids and now – at last – recognised the piano tuner.

Up till now, Raven had not managed to get a word in. All he said now was, Do you remember me?

At this, the piano tuner was silent for a second, raised one finger as if to let Raven's voice resonate in his ear, just as a wine connoisseur rolls a sip over his tongue to let it wash over even the remotest of his taste buds.

Raven, the Ordinary, he said. And without evincing any great surprise that Raven should be sitting here with him he recounted, in a few words, the story of how, on one of his trips with the black delivery van, over-tired and a bit tipsy, he had nodded off and – quite slowly, thank heaven – had smashed into the motorway crash-barrier. All the same, the collision had been severe enough for his good eye to have been so badly damaged by splinters of bone that he had lost it as well. So now everything's always just dark, he said. Sometimes red, sometimes blue.

But now he had achieved what he had always dreamt of, perfect pitch.

Hardly had the piano tuner come to the end of his tale when the Deafman handed Raven his Complications-Notebook. In it was written, in a different, scrawly handwriting:

A joke for the Mutt and Jeff

This blind man comes into a big store with his guide dog at his heel. He picks it up and whirls it around through the air on its lead, scares the howl out of it. Up comes the store detective and says, Stop that. Cruelty to dumb animals. Surely, says the blind man, I can have a look around, can't I?

In gratitude, old Gig-lamps had written it into his book for him, in an unsteady hand, guided from memory, told a joke into his book.

When they got up, they were so drunk, especially the piano

tuner, that two of them would not have been enough to find the road home. Raven walked on the piano tuner's right, the Deafman on his left, their staggers took up the whole breadth of the pavement as, like all good reeling drunks, they covered just about twice the actual distance.

Snails, Horse-shoes, Stirrups

AMONG HIS LUGGAGE was the copy of the Meat Inspection Regulations, in the 1960 edition. The Deafman was convinced that, with the aid of the knowledge he had acquired, he would be able to keep one step ahead of the doctors, or at least to know what they intended doing with him. And if all else proved fruitless, he would write down his demands, for one thing he had learnt was that the written word was of more lasting effect than the spoken.

Prior to his operation, he asked, by means of just such a WRITTEN REQUEST, to see the Meat Inspection Regulations relating to humans. The friendly nurse was somewhat baffled but then, when the Deafman showed him his copy, he had to smile and went off to get hold of an anatomical atlas. And indeed he did find a doctor prepared to lend him his one.

In no time at all, the Deafman became familiar with the interior of all sorts of ears, the secrets of the human head, and knew the passages and the cavities in the skull by their German and Latin names. To be sure, he was none too keen on the Latin words. *Schnecken*, *Hufeisen* and *Steigbügel*, snails, horse-shoes and stirrups, he could recognise.

In addition to the assortment of white and red tablets of

various sizes, there had been two whitish-grey pills lying in his plastic dish, which he swallowed with some reluctance. They were to make sure that he would not come to by waking gradually, but only after being shaken out of his sleep by two strong hands. His indifference was almost total, everything washed over and off him as if he were coated with Teflon. He walked stiffly and as erect as his organs of balance would permit, nothing seemed either irksome or agreeable, his eyes were open, but they looked neither at nor through things. An orderly pulled an operation gown over him that needed tying at the back, and steered him across the corridor into the bathroom, parked him in the corner next to the radiator and ran the bath, the bath salts smelt sharply of disinfectant, the water was very hot but was tested with a thermometer and considered by the orderly to be just right. The sticking plaster in the crook of his elbow, from the blood sample taken the day before, detached itself, floated among the green froth, became saturated and sank, a little of the dried blood forming a tiny streak among the green.

The Deafman did not know if he had ever seen the orderly before, but the man chatted away to him. He dried him off and shaved him with hair clippers until all that was left was a saucer-sized disc of hair like a polar cap on the globe of his skull.

He led him, clad in fresh paper slippers, through darkening corridors and large, apparently airtight doors. He lay down for a short while on a trestle stretcher and was given an injection in the hollow of his left elbow and then he lapsed into total apathy and, almost without him noticing what was going on, they wrapped green sheets round him, no longer faces, but green moons, many moons, above him.

Blood-clock

THERE MUST HAVE been an abrupt change in the weather, at first all that bright and steely blueness, clear visibility and this feeling of ease and lightness. Cheerfully, people were going about, some about their business, others about their pleasures.

For Raven, it was too bright, the people too cheery and bustling; he could hardly wait for the twilight to come, and in search of darkness he went into the cinema, from the steel-blue sky into the steel-blue artificial night. A whole lot of iron was being hurled about, limbs like iron, muscles restrained by metal-studded leather armbands. Hundreds were dying violent deaths in double-quick time. One had a bullet go right through him, yet he recovered again on his own, the machine that automatically switches itself on and off, that supplies itself with energy, repairs itself. He bit open a cartridge with his steel teeth and sprinkled a smokeless powder into the smooth gunshot perforation, set it alight, tiny explosion in the flesh, tongue of flame shooting through the colossal body. But cauterising, gritting the teeth, brings relief, the danger of the body poisoning itself was averted, the man was riddled, a fireworks display in his flesh, the machine once again ready for battle. When the usherette asked him to leave the cinema at the end of the performance, Raven got to his feet and stepped out into the open, squinting through screwed-up eyes.

But something had happened, something had come up. The light, as if filtered through milk and softened, was shadowless. He walked aimlessly and came to the market-place, where his thoughts turned to the Deafman, for here anyone could smell the odours of the whole world, from orient to occident, and, at the fishmongers' shops, the bed of the ocean, and between them, there rose an arctic, icy air. Outside the ironmonger's stood a group of people. There, everything was happening in slow motion, just as in the film a while before, no sound, no gestures, only slowed-down, aimless movements. Raven pushed his way through, the only one moving in real time, and, all at once, before his eyes, a man was lying at his feet, a hole in his head, obviously dead, yet parts of him were still twitching, a leather bank-pouch lying torn open beside him. His blood trickled steadily away between the paving stones; here, the passage of time was regulated by the pulsing of the blood-clock. Raven looked, and turned away, unmoved. Far behind, a man was running, no one tried to stop him. He was the gunman and was carrying a black night-safe canister. Raven went on a few paces, in amongst the fragrances from a kiosk selling spices, there was a whiff of something that didn't belong. It was gunsmoke, and the odour left no doubt that a moment ago, compressed into gas, it had driven the projectile into the man's skull. Now, turned into harmless smoke, it rose, through Raven's unconsciously dilated nostrils, past the exposed olfactory nerves, through the cavities and chambers of the ethmoid bone on the lower side of the frontal lobe. Involuntary movements of the head resulted, the olfactory impressions and the transmission of their stimuli crept along the paths of conscious sensory perception into the emotional spheres of the parietal lobes, over the wings of the sphenoid bone, the frontal cranial cavity and the peak of the temporal pyramid. The palatal cavity, ear-drum, middle ear, os pallatinum. First came the wrinkling of the nose, the idea of escape; the goal was the cavity in the secure depths. The bullet had taken the direct route, through the frontal bone above the nose, and in an instant all the cavities had filled with blood, all sorts of secretions and shredded brain.

He ran into the nearest subway station and had no idea why it was this smell that first made him feel sadness and horror at this man's death. He wept as he had not done for a long time, or perhaps had never done before.

He wept because a man lay up there on the pavement, up above him, outside the ironmonger's. The blood was seeping vertically down to Raven. The man would never get to his feet again, no, he was dead.

Frogs and Fists

AFTER THE DARKNESS there was whiteness, his head was swathed in soft, translucent gauze. The Deafman awoke and his eyes were already open. The whiteness was dazzling, a slight pain, perception sharply registered its return after the memory-less, dream-void hole of the anaesthesia. Why am I here? he kept asking himself over a long time. He saw himself in a snowy expanse, flakes were fluttering and dancing before his searching eyes, a mist between them, or smoke, as from slowly smouldering birch logs. If only he knew what a dog's bark was like, or even the way it howls, then this would be Siberia, not too cold and not too warm.

Then came the soft, warm touch of a woman's hand, immediately after that the needle-prick in the crook of his arm. A slight bump against the bed, now the gauze bandage slipped and a corner of the room appeared in the picture, two nurse's legs stepped into it and paused, supporting leg and resting leg were exchanged, and then they left again. So he was being looked after by nurses. Why? Yet what tortured him more than this question was thirst. At first he felt something growing in his mouth like a thick fur. He fell back into sleep, and the sleep had transformed the fur into a desert, criss-crossed with cracks and jagged lumps. He was roused from this renewed sleep as a small sponge, saturated with a mixture of peppermint and camomile teas, was moistening his lips.

A sense of contentment set in, all questionings became insignificant, both the painful dryness in his mouth and his disorientation in this hospital room of which he knew only one corner, and that was immediately forgotten again.

Overnight, a sudden, piercing and clammy cold had descended over the town, above it hung, as if held in place by wire cables, a dirty low cloud cover that allowed nothing to penetrate it, neither to escape nor to enter.

Anyone stepping out into the street wearing the same clothes as the day before had to do an about turn, provided they had the time, to put on something warmer. In the dampness, the cold took a firm grip and crept and sucked itself insistently into hair, clothes, into the very pores in exposed skin and inside the bodies themselves, through noses and deep into the remotest branches of bronchial tubes. The Deafman was glad of the white bandages that still covered up the two small wounds and now provided warmth. He borrowed a cap that under normal circumstances would have been far too big for him, left a note, BACK AT 4 P.M., and went out of the building, alone and with no real aim in mind.

In the sudden cold snap, not only the odours of objects and people altered, but also their colours. Some of them took on a fresh, reddish complexion, others became grey with the tinge of blue that marks out people with stomach trouble.

On the streets a special kind of sticky dust was accumulating, covering the cars, the big blue buses, the advertising hoardings and the walls of the buildings with a dirty grey film.

For reasons that were virtually incomprehensible to the workmen who had to do the job, the responsible authorities had decided now, of all times, after the onset of the cold spell, to renew or to reinforce the foundations of the tram lines. The orange paint of their machines was no longer shiny; through streaks of grey dust and splashes of tar he could see, if he looked hard enough, Japanese geishas smiling at him, and wooded landscapes under swiftly changing cloud patterns appeared, bright rays of sunshine fell through early mists, the odd demon limped across the landscape here and there, especially where the rising tar vapours introduced a particularly black shading to the picture.

The machines – some of them were still standing idle at the side of the road – were of varied types. Under tar-smeared sacks, buckets of especially runny asphalt formed peculiar layerings, as if rotting, decaying corpses lay beneath them. The Deafman had no way of telling what the real purpose of the appliances was simply from looking at them.

He was half alarmed and half amused when he saw how one machine, a rammer, which had till then been standing harmlessly at rest on one ungainly leg, was now, like some violent, one-ton frog, shaking to the marrow the man operating it, relentlessly jumping into the air and – the hairdresser's windows were now beginning to vibrate – smacking down on the asphalt surface to smooth it out, and as it did so, everything that got in the way, accidentally or on purpose, was stamped into the black, steaming mass, to disappear not to be seen again in a hurry.

And he himself felt each thump of the frog from the soles of his shoes to the roots of his hair like a blow from a giant fist under the ground.

Apple Fragrance

BEFORE THE REAL cold of winter had properly set in, the Meat Inspector, an avid consumer of apples, was able to buy at an incredible bargain price a leftover stock of red-and-green, pleasantly fragrant russet apples, whose leathery skin particularly appealed to him.

His back was giving him considerable pain, some time ago his hands had begun to shake more violently. In contrast to earlier years, the trembling persisted even after he had drunk one or two schnapps. The schnapps no longer agreed with him the way it had, but gave him heartburn. In the past, he had been able to combat the excess acidity with warm milk, but now that no longer helped; on the contrary, the milk seemed to form spongy lumps in his stomach which sucked up even more acid and gathered it there.

Smoking his cheroots, without which he just could not live now, made his tongue more and more furry, almost feelingless, and this deadness had been spreading to his lips, his face and into his nose, down over his throat and windpipe and into his bronchial tubes. Increasingly often, he was racked by agonising coughing fits, dry and biting.

Previously, he used to be able to soothe this cough, which occurred only infrequently, with inhalations of extracts of camomile and sage. Now it would get dangerously hot for him and he would become giddy under the towel draped over the steaming basin. He had to sit still for a long time before the dizzy turns subsided and the heat inside became bearable.

He put his faith in the healing powers of the apples, whose aroma itself seemed to liven him up.

To prevent them from starting to rot, he stored them in his bedroom, which he never heated. So there lay the green-and-red apples, spread out carefully one by one – on no account were they to come in contact with each other. They surrounded the cherry-wood bed in the form of a spiral, since he had laid them out, down on his knees, stretching and turning, with himself as the focal point and axis. That cherry-wood bed, which he had inherited, was his prize piece of furniture. At the head of it stood his sample-case with the microscope from Leipzig, his most treasured possession.

So he had gathered every object that he cherished around his bed. In his little kitchen cum living room stood, humming, a large chest freezer and a rusting stove which he had not fired for a very long time now. He brewed his feeble tea with an ancient immersion coil which, encrusted with calcium deposits, looked like some implement from the Stone Age.

For the first time in his life, he took leave of absence outside the usual holiday periods. He stayed at home. He stayed in his bedroom. He stayed on his cherry-wood bed, surrounded by the spiral of apples, their aroma growing in intensity and filling him with a feeling of contentment. It was getting colder, there were no more flies. The apples were changing colour from green to red. He lay in his cherry-wood bed and did not leave it. The scent of the apples became more important to him than the daylight, which was now fading pretty early anyway.

The chemist came to visit him once and brought him a mixture for his bronchial troubles. He thanked him, although he had no intention of taking it, for he was convinced it would do him no good. Proudly he showed his microscope to the chemist and asked him to pass the instrument on, in the event of his early death, to the Deafman. On the chemist's second visit, the Meat Inspector hastily stuffed the unopened little packet of medicines under his pillow and said, Ah, if only as a young man I had taken up another profession.

When the chemist was getting ready to leave, he stopped him at the last moment and said, Take the whole lot with you now. If I get over this, I'm going to pack in the job anyway.

The chemist loaded the box for the Deafman into his Volkswagen and drove off.

During the following night – it was exceptionally cold – the Meat Inspector passed away in the middle of his spiral which had been brought into some disorder by the chemist. The scent of apples could not have been more delightful than on that following morning once the sun's rays had fallen strongly through the little window on to the fruit.

Earwigs

AFTER HIS WALK, the Deafman returned to the home at four o'clock on the dot and wrote in his Complications-Notebook:

I am aware of a distant stinging pain, first under the left ear, then under the right one. The earwig that crawled into me once when I was a child will have hatched out its larvae. A family of tiny earwigs is now merrily earwigging and tickling away and having a merry and jolly time and multiplying at a furious pace.

The earwig crept into the ear, there it remained still, then it was aroused and the cavities of the ears became its breeding ground, you could almost talk of a culture. They ought to cut out samples in slices and present them for bacteriological analysis. Doesn't §36, Section 2 deal with mentally defective earwigs, have they, by multiplying, excluded themselves from fitness for limited duties according to §32, Section 1, No. 15, and without exception at that?

No, the doctors will no doubt have discovered them, if in fact there were any earwigs there, with their sensitive magnifiers and their deadly elegant glasses.

So up I go, and take a look at the yellowish-red muck-spattered machines, with a few club-footed demons on them.

To the examination by trichinoscope after the extraction, at least three minutes should be devoted.

I should really ask the respected doctors whether the extracted material and anything else found in my old napper (above the lymph nodes)

1. gave off a fishy-oily or blubbery odour and/or further

2. any other moderate differences as regards odour, colour and taste, composition and durability were present.

Such and similar moderate differences are present particularly in cases where there is superficial decomposition, perceptible urine odour, seminal odour, ugh, yuck, odour of medicinal and disinfectant preparations, interspersion with perceptible bleeding, calcium deposits or hardened blood vessels.

Make inquiry: was this present? If so, request to be stamped with mark indicating unfitness between shoulder and small of back.

Yet in the end, what stung me was the cold and the chilled humidity, the dust in the air completely frozen into tiny, hover-light cold-dust-trichinae, pellets that really should be more closely investigated.

And so it came to my ears, the trams, which strew sand under their own drive-wheels in order to brake, colossuses, so heavy that no high-pressure hydraulic brakes can bring them to an immediate halt on their own.

And the tar that TB patients have to inhale. They all went along to the building site, those with the mark of death on them, with their grey-white skin, and greedily they wheezed in the tarry, sticky vapours in the hope of a cure. From the rampant tubercles, subdued by tar, tarred and feathered and stuck together so that no further harm shall they do and, thus delivered, they then perish for want of fodder.

So the earwig has gone from one ear straight through my brain to the other ear, in order to lay its eggs on both sides, and who knows what devastation it has wrought in between.

Now however there is a channel there, which is not present in other people, so that certain appropriate thoughts can come shooting through like an express train and there are flashes of inspiration there such as hardly anyone else can spark off.

Not even the photographer with his unhealthy skin, were he still in the land of the living, could have set off such a flash.

Let them plant a grain of barley in my ear and let all the doctors pee thereupon till it germinates and sprouts and then stretches the passages of the ear, three semi-circular canals, the external auditory canal and the snail-like cochlea, let them beat on the tympanic canal, set the system of levers in motion until the root wanders into the skin-like labyrinth, that delicate construction suspended from ligaments so that between it and the bony shell lie cavities filled with fluid in which the osseous snails can twist and turn to their hearts' delight. Then the young plant can serve as nourishment for the little pet, and when it is big enough, all the canals and cavities are widened, the snail alert and fattened, then the auricular barley shoot will be uprooted and the roar coming from the world can make its entry into my little head.

There were also machines there with blue flames licking out of them, operated by the man with the black walrus mous-

tache puffing on the fat cigarettes, and smoke billowed out of his nose. Yellow and orange his overalls, so that he could be seen even in the worst fog, his cap multi-coloured.

Both, man and machine, are like dragons in the big town, they wait to burn something up with their smoky, fiery breath. Ultimately, in order to conclude matters in accordance with the regulations, as dragon slayer officially appointed by municipal and local authorities.

If the human dragon turns a yellow lever, then a tongue of flame, suddenly yellow and red, shoots out of the machine dragon and licks its way into the melting tar.

If the human dragon turns a second lever, bound with blue tape, then a toothed gear-wheel is lowered and starts turning, spitting sparks from every orifice, that's the fault of the teeth which are meant to crunch up the little stones into the warm tarry glaze. They grind their way through the road surface faster than any high-speed plough can dig into the soil, deeper and deeper they bite in and chew stones, spit sparks and teeth, till one day the frog, which is sitting down below, stretches out its froggy head and gawps with its froggy eyes and darts out its froggy tongue at the human dragon and his machine and hey presto! – like flies they disappear into the belly of the earth-frog that goes on just gulping and gawping.

Roar of the World, Pain of the Newest Kind

TODAY THEY UNWOUND *the bandage from my brain, so that now the cold is blowing very hard around my sore ears.*

Then came the pain when they screwed two little grey frogs in behind my ears, forcing tubes into the snail-spiral thread of the cochlea, paying no heed to my Ouch!, for Ouch! is something I've learnt to say in order to alert the doctors to my pain.

Yet they have given me no peace at all.

They put things on me and gazed through their glasses like the fish in the aquarium in the waiting room.

At the early-morning meal there are soft-boiled eggs with little woollen bonnets.

The bandage is the place between ear and ear and brain, the egg-cosy for the soft-boiled feelings of anxiety.

Now even my thoughts are getting cold and solidifying and I'm having trouble changing the gears in my little head-machine brain, where now and then the gearbox jams so that everything starts juddering. Then there might be a crunch. Presumably the others hear it, there was a crunching then, it came from the things on my ears, the headphones, close to me, a pain, a pain of the very newest kind.

Right into the Marrow

RAVEN HAD EVEN remembered to pick some greens for Old Shop-soiled. He was now living in the cardboard box that the shower cabinet had come in and was thriving mightily, becoming quite friendly and letting himself be stroked.

What's all this in aid of? Bad Luck inquired.

You'll find out, said Raven.

At a greengrocer's stall, Raven had got an enormous carrot

as a last meal for the condemned rabbit that both of them had become quite fond of.

Raven let him have a lollop around the room, he felt quite at ease among them. From Bad Luck, he borrowed a pipe-wrench, gave Old Shop-soiled the *coup de grâce*, skinned and gutted him and handed him over to Fever, who had been away drinking a beer at the Yugoslavian woman's during the slaughtering. The very sight of the bloody corpse had Fever retching. The Yugoslavian woman declared her readiness to prepare the rabbit *à la* Plitvice.

Must go in microwave, she explained.

She was invited to the meal as well. She volunteered to bring serviettes, plastic knives and forks, paper plates, mustard and beer, and some sausages as well, since Old Shop-soiled seemed a bit meagre for so many people.

They set up six beer-crates in the room, right next to the shower cabinet. On two of the crates they laid some blankets for padding. For a table, they would use their knees.

Fever promised to perform a turn for the entertainment of the assembled company. Strips of pink toilet paper were wound round the neon strip lighting. Now everything was ready.

Only Bad Luck had his ablution still to come, but he was still blissfully unaware of this. They were prepared to use force if need be.

Raven had got hold of a bottle of baby-soap, so as to forestall the excuse that ordinary soap was too harsh for Bad Luck's delicate skin. It had had to suffer so many hard blows from fate that it had become quite thin.

Fever had stolen a pair of socks and two pairs of underpants. Raven still had some of the stonemason's shirts. They were redolent with the delicate bath-salts from the hotel. Fever recognised the smell and began to grouse about his former colleagues. Raven paid him no heed, so he fell silent again.

Bad Luck came through the bulkhead, all unsuspecting. Raven thrust the baby-soap into his hand.

Pregnant, then? asked Bad Luck.

There's something not right with that thing, said Raven, pointing towards the shower cabinet which, standing in the purplish glow of the neon light, had taken on a somewhat solemn appearance, almost like a place of worship.

Bad Luck was very proud of his competence as a plumber, which he had had to pick up during his caretakering years. Without demur, he stepped inside the shower cabinet.

The shower head is loose, said Raven.

Bad Luck reached up for the shower head with both hands, resistance was now out of the question; Raven turned on the water and wedged himself against the door, with Fever jumping to his aid. There was a short, sharp cry of terror inside the shower, then all went quiet, his hands were still raised and he was leaning against the glass door with an expression of infinite despondency in his eyes, as if he were losing, along with his smell, all his memories of his accumulated misfortunes, the only thing that gave his life any meaning.

Without complaint, he pulled on the clothes they had laid out ready, and smeared a new lot of pomade into his hair.

The Deafman arrived; he had brought a bouquet of basil. Andre came, looking no different from the way she always had. She still had her little pimples, perhaps one or two fewer than before. She smoked non-filters and was delighted with Raven's home-grown tobacco. Raven was still smitten with her. His love had nothing to do with physical urges. Maybe that would come later, he thought, looking shyly at her.

The Deafman and Fever smoked some grass as an appetiser.

While Fever had had a certain expertise in the past in blowing smoke rings, he had certainly perfected the art now, in which his thick lips, now in a permanent pout, had proved a great help, so that he aroused general amazement at how thick and firm his smoke rings were, sometimes round as a ball, sometimes egg-shaped, all made to order. He had the knack of blowing the rings in such a way that one could go through another, that they slipped over objects and hung there until a puff of air chased them away, he even had the skill to fit the Deafman with a halo, at which the latter clasped his hands piously and rolled his eyes heavenwards in a pre-Raphaelite expression of rapture.

But his finest trick was performed on the Yugoslavian woman, who had to take up a position as if what was being performed was a knife-throwing act. She was already panting with excitement when Fever ordered her to spread out her hands in front of her. Lasciviously, the symmetrical, thick rings from Fever's mouth slipped round the Yugoslavian woman's chubby fingers which, each of them distinctly divided into three little sections, fitted gently into them as she stretched out each of her hands expectantly towards a ring, as if she could hardly wait.

This was the first diversion that Fever wanted to perform. The second entertainment, too, he had rehearsed some days before.

Outside the squash centre there was a car park. Here Bad Luck had put up a board: POLICE NOTICE – SKATEBOARDING, ETC. STRICTLY FORBIDDEN. Often he would come shooting out of the building, seething with rage, whenever he caught sight of children playing there.

A week before, Fever had taken a skateboard away from a frightened little boy with the words CONFISCATED BY ORDER OF THE POLICE. In the evenings he had tried it out in the car park, but it soon occurred to him that inside the squash courts was an ideal place to practise.

So, first of all, he demonstrated his meagre skills, and then the others had to have a try. To everyone's surprise, the

Yugoslav woman cut the best figure. She was used to having to work and keep her balance in severely cramped spaces.

It was Fever who first started firing the little squash balls at the skateboarders, then the others joined in, taking up rackets and balls to bombard the skater. Anyone who failed to score a hit had to take the next turn on the board and do two circuits of the court. Harder and harder flew the balls, for the marksmen quickly learned how to hit the little balls with great force. The game became more painful and ferocious, for, as usual, things increase in violence, hurt more and become more dangerous and difficult to keep under control, when many people do them at the same time and with the same objective in mind, whether or not all of them know exactly what that objective is.

The Yugoslav woman now asked for assistance in fetching the beer. Fever went along and came back with five cases on the wheelbarrow. She carried in the rabbit in a big roasting dish, in the Plitvice manner, with a variety of sausages woven round it: from Cracow and Debrecen, Wieners, Thüringers, Nürnbergers, and Cevapcici. All this lying on a bed of red cabbage and giving off an aroma of cloves, apples and wine.

Sell-by-date sausages, she called the trimmings.

To accompany this, there was rice with pine-nuts. They ate in silence. Fever complimented her three times. Indeed, as one beer followed another, he was gazing at her with increasing warmth.

Andre was given half of the saddle, Fever got a thigh, Raven ate some belly and the two front legs, Bad Luck got a piece off the saddle and the other thigh went to the Deafman.

They drank and smoked. The air-conditioning for the squash courts murmured cosily, the neon tubes gave off a pleasant hum, one of them beginning to flicker whenever the heating in the shower cabinet switched itself on.

When the five crates had been emptied, the Yugoslav woman personally went off to get more beer, accompanied by Fever. That took quite some time.

Raven and Andre sat silent; Bad Luck seemed to be still mourning for his lost aura.

One of these times, I'll tell you what was wrong with my other sister, he said out of the blue and then relapsed into silence.

Now they had drunk their way through six cases of beer. Andre had been first to nod off, Bad Luck seemed to be sleeping, as rabbits are reputed to do, with his reddened eyes open. Raven had sat down next to Andre in the hope that she would lean against his shoulder as she slept. The Deafman was smoking and staring into the flickering light from the neon tube, the Yugoslav woman and Fever had withdrawn into the shower cabinet, the only intimate corner of this room, and they fitted in with not a millimetre to spare.

It was already getting quite light when the Yugoslavian woman went home, in an hour she would have to be back at work. The others slept on.

Fever woke as the Deafman was pulling the pouch with the grass in it out of his pocket. He seemed to be a new man, no longer slouching about with drooping shoulders, his voice came from deeper in his chest and sounded more assured. He wakened Raven.

We have to make a plan, he told Raven.

He was sick of having no money.

He opened two bottles, they went on drinking, Fever considered possible ways of getting hold of some money. Raven told him of his experiences in the museum. Fever refused to believe him. Raven said he had proof. He searched for the visiting card that the gentleman had lost. It was gone, had probably fallen out of his pocket when the two characters had frisked him at the station.

Queers are always loaded with cash, said Fever suddenly, as if consumed with hate.

Andre woke. She had the visiting card in her bag that Raven had found during his first visit to the museum. They drank some more; the Deafman just sat smoking and grinning incessantly into space.

Dusk had just begun to gather when they set off. Raven borrowed Bad Luck's 'Quickly' moped and went on ahead with Andre to seek out the address. The house stood in a well-to-do neighbourhood. A semi-detached, with one half of the building in darkness. Raven read the nameplate on the door and compared it with the business card; it was the right house. Fever and the Deafman, who was still smiling beatifically and had absolutely no idea what they were about, walked past a building site. Fever swung a kick at a bucket under a tarpaulin, which slipped to one side. He hurt his foot, because a large crowbar was lying hidden there, the kind used by the workmen for lifting the tram-rails.

Raven and Andre came to meet them and reported that they had found the house. They drove back, Andre holding the heavy crowbar. Raven parked the Quickly next to a small garden shed that looked like some kind of a temple.

They waited for the others to arrive, went up to the house and jemmied the door open. The tool made quick work of it. They threw a few things around; the Deafman stared at them incredulously, he could not fathom what was going on, had no idea where they were. The light went on, the man was standing in the room, they made to run away, but he grabbed Andre in a firm grip.

You're a right little bitch. Stay where you are, all of you. I'm going to call the police, you little bitch, he said.

It wasn't the gentleman from the museum. Maybe, if he had known the man, Raven would not have raised the heavy crowbar and said, Let go of her! Now the man was far, terribly far away from him, the heavy implement was big and reached out into the distance, with a hissing sound it struck the man, now gaping in atonishment, on the back of the neck.

The sound when the crowbar landed on the man's splintering neck was not a loud one, no, it was surprisingly quiet, the flesh on the nape of the man's neck deadened the smack of the iron bar slamming into it.

What could be heard, though, and it was something that was to remain in the ears of those who heard it, was a gentle crack as the iron bar forced its way savagely between two vertebrae at the nape, drove them apart, for it was a crowbar after all, splintered them, stretching the gristly strand of the spinal cord and peppering it with splinters and destroying it in such a way that the man could no longer feel any pain, the nerves were instantaneously ruptured or blocked the moment the iron bar, the crowbar, landed on his neck. So the last sensation experienced by the dying man was probably the chill of the metal, a bitter taste in his mouth, then nothing more, blackness, blue-blackness, and nothingness.

For a long time afterwards, Raven had to struggle to regain composure enough to look Andre in the eye. He was looking for some kind of help, or a promise. He saw no sign of this, but he did glimpse in her eyes a new elation, her gaze had become more alive, as if something enormously heavy inside her had evaporated, had fallen from her, dissolved and dissipated itself. For all that, her face was almost expressionless. Raven could make out no sign of alarm, no terror, no fear, no disgust at the deed but also no approval of it, no revulsion at the corpse or the thin thread of blood running from the inconspicuous laceration on the back of the neck, trickling over the throat to drip, in a few seconds, down on to the carpet. There was no movement, no jerk nor even the slightest twitch, from Andre, there just seemed to be a lightness about her. Fever was the first to have to light up a cigarette.

The Deafman had noticed this change in her too, and it filled him with horror, he stared at her, stared into her eyes, as if waiting for the relief that the merest spark of consternation in those eyes would have brought him.

One thing was clear to Raven: they would have to split up, for they were so conspicuous that anyone would suspect them right away. And even if people did not connect them with the murder, as he hoped, their general appearance was striking enough to prompt any policeman to make a spot identity check. Andre ran off with an expression of boundless, mute happiness, her step was light, like a fleeing fawn. She'll run to the squash courts, Raven thought.

Fever was next to leave. I'm off to Plitvice, he said.

But how could Raven leave the Deafman in the lurch, just standing there, incessantly nodding. He went over to him, the Deafman stared at him and stopped nodding and abruptly came to his senses. Raven had no idea how long this stare might have lasted, but then the Deafman seized him by the shoulder and gave him such a kick in the arse that it hurled him forward and left a blue-green bruise that was to remain visible for a long time to come.

Staggering, half-falling, Raven now ran out. He, too, felt like some animal, a head of game, and perhaps it was for this reason, or perhaps because he wanted to find himself a place where some kind of silence reigned, that he ran towards the little temple which stood not far from the house. Gasping for breath, he stood behind the little building, caught sight of the bronze stag inside it and then could see beyond, between its antlers, out across the dead-straight canal and beyond again, under the arches of the two bridges and over them at the same time, through the fluttering swarms of pigeons, right to the fountains on the ornamental rocks and through that, through the mist of spray glistening in the slanting rays of the setting sun, all the way through to the window of the castle, right through the great hall and through the rear-facing window made of crystal glass, through the avenue cut in the wooded park behind that and he could have seen even beyond, but there was a man standing in the way.

At that, he set off running again. In his violent dash he bumped into strollers who hurled abuse after him; he paid them no heed but ran on, to ask the man to take a couple of steps to the side, so that he might see past him, see right through to the end. He was already staggering from exhaustion, but the man was not very far off now, he was only a few more paces away. He was not looking at Raven, he was gazing in a different direction and now he seemed to have been struck by a sudden thought, stepped aside and hurried away. Raven imagined he had heard him singing, but that must have been his own jangling nerves or the rushing of blood in his ears. He imagined the man to be wearing a dark suit, which reminded him of the deceased stonemason, but that was probably an illusion conjured up by his tiredness and the shimmering before his eyes. He stopped, propped his hands on his thighs and, half-bent over, drew rasping breaths until he was able to turn back. He went the whole way back, forcing himself to walk slowly, he went right back to where he could resume his vantage point behind the little temple with the golden stag.

But no matter how hard he tried, or where he positioned himself, he was unable to rediscover the exact spot from which you could have seen right the way through to the end if that man had not been standing there.

Now he turned round twice on his own axis.

Next to the Quickly stood Andre looking at him as if in a state of elation.

They took the Quickly, which Bad Luck was now about to lose as well, and rode off in a different direction. He wanted to drive and drive until he could see the beacon of the refineries in the town of Irkutsk flaring over Lake Baikal. He drove out to the motorway and then along the hard shoulder. He drove through the outskirts, past the caravans where the whores hung about and where The Victim lived.

Andre wanted to stop here. She saw The Victim, leaning against her caravan and dressed in the salmon-pink ski-suit. She went up to her and said, You remember me, I'm your friend.

The Victim nodded and went into the caravan with her.

He rode through the broad-leaf forest and finally across the cold plateau where the shadow of the shopping mall emerged out of the twilight and its outline grew sharper until finally a lot of lights could be seen in the windows sunk into the grey wall like embrasures. There he turned off the motorway.

Raven went into the overheated building and took the lift down into the bowels of the store to where foodstuffs were sold. He bought himself a bottle of the Siberian vodka; he hadn't enough money left for two.

He walked out to the stonemason's workshop, which not unnaturally lay in darkness, the iron door was unlocked, but then what was there to steal here anyway? Besides, a thief would have had to lug away anything that had been worth stealing, and that would have demanded an effort that no burglary could really have justified. He could have stolen and dragged off the block of stone that still stood in the middle of the shed, the crowbars, the chisels and the mallets, the empty rabbit hutches and the evil-smelling mattresses which had become even more soggy as the dampness and mould had now penetrated the scraps of carpet and the tobacco, still laid out to dry but saturated with cold moisture.

It was all different, yet it was the same, and Raven was now a different person, and yet he had nevertheless remained the same, and all that he had learnt was in his head, fixed never to be torn out again: hewing, polishing, sharpening, slaughtering, the mushrooms, the bird songs and living with the cold and the heat.

Gearbox

After nightfall, the oil-stained hand of the park attendant reached out for a finely chased brass lever, a cogwheel clinked out of a whirring gearbox, bringing it to a standstill.

As a result, the fountain, through which Raven had looked, slowly subsided into itself. The purring mechanism, which was driven by a drop in level of no more than a metre and caused the fountain to send its spray into the air, was switched off, the water was run off, the water supply was shut off, so that the canal could be cleaned out and the banks strengthened.

Overnight, the grey clay bed of the canal would turn into a concrete-grey coloured surface, furrowed with cracks, the section of a wasteland on which the swans, the ducks and the crested grebes would waddle around in bewilderment, getting their feathers filthy in their search for water. The occasional carp, which the men wading through the mud in their thigh-boots and with their bright lamps had been unable to retrieve, would suffocate in the mire. The refuse and filth would be laid bare, everything that was normally down below was now the surface, everything was the one colour, the colour of the clay.

He had walked through the half-light until his feet hurt. The cold had penetrated the thin soles of his shoes, chilblains had swollen up and were pinching. He hardly noticed it, though, for one impression was preoccupying him more than any one had ever done before. Was it the sound of the man's neck rupturing, the look in Andre's eyes, her sudden lightness of step?

Gradually the cold was creeping upwards, streaming all through him and seizing possession of his mind.

Without realising it, he had walked back to the canal. I wonder if it's deep, he thought. He knew that, in this cold, jumping into the water would probably mean death; he couldn't swim, but even if he didn't drown, the cold would kill him.

He stuffed his pockets with stones and waited for a moment when the traffic subsided. No one could see him. He climbed on to the parapet and jumped.

He landed with a dull thud, splashed into the glutinous mass of the freezing mud, but it hurt.

He sustained two palm-sized bruises on his back and his side, possibly he had even broken a rib. But these things usually heal by themselves. He clambered painfully up the steep bank, cleaned the mud off as best he could and set off towards the motorway.

Entry into the Machine

HE HAD LIFTED the bonnet of the FENDT and was staring at the pounding pistons, the rotating wheels, the whirring fan-belt, the rods rising and falling.

He could feel the heat, smell the oil, warming up and

slowly burning off, hear the hissing of the hydraulics, see the hoses gently bucking and pulsating. Everything was in flux, was in motion, was fulfilling its purpose, nowhere was anything jammed or obstructed, and all he wanted was to enter into this machinery, to become a part of it, to merge into the muted, unruffled and well-ordered seething of the whole.

Then he filled his pockets with stones, opened all the doors and windows of the cockpit and drove off.

Completion of the Monument

ABOVE THE STONE on which work had been begun dangled the light bulb; Raven tried to switch it on, but it was burnt out. From the box, he fetched a new bulb, there must have been about twenty of them in there. The stonemason had got annoyed so often when, precisely at some crucial moment, the bulb just had to burn out, that he had decided to buy in enough bulbs to last the rest of his life. Raven climbed on to the chair and changed the bulb, and even as he was screwing it in, the new bulb, which came on quite unexpectedly, began to warm up his hand a little.

He took up the chisels, tested their points and cutting edges, sharpened the odd one or two and made a start on the work.

He worked swiftly, making no hasty or superfluous movements. In order to draw back the mallet after every blow, he harnessed the power generated by the metal bouncing back off the stone and so the work became easier, with the sharpened chisels penetrating the stone as if it were soft and yielding. He ate nothing, he tried to dry out the damp tobacco on the flat plate on top of the stove, he smoked and coughed the acrid fumes out again, he drank in small sips. Twice he slept briefly, but had no idea how long, he felt no exhaustion, no hunger and no fear. The cold no longer affected him. He could hear the motorway and in the mornings he would pause in his work for a few minutes to listen to the birds, winter birds already, he thought, and indeed it did not really get light the next day, for snow had fallen on the skylight. It did not bother him, he went outside and let fine, powdery snow fall on his hair and took delight in the yellow tracery he made when he passed water, writing in the snow; Baikal Siberia he wanted to write, but he got only as far as the first word. BAIKAL. Darkness fell early, his work was progressing so well that he started to sing for sheer happiness. Out came songs and melodies whose words had slipped from his memory, or ones he had never known in the first place, songs that the stonemason had sung.

Through the Microscope

OVER A PERIOD of several days, an engineer and two technicians in the glass control room on top of the dam wall above the reservoir had been observing and discussing the drop in performance in one of the power station's five turbines. On the first day, the output had risen briefly, but had then immediately fallen away steeply. Gradually it rose again, without however reaching its set performance. As was usual in such cases, they waited for some time before bringing in divers whose job it was literally to get to the bottom of whatever was causing the fault. Now, however, this expensive step had become unavoidable, divers went down and found foreign bodies and signs of damage. The water had to be drained off and it rushed like a white water torrent down into the valley with a tremendous roar, and there, at the foot of the dam, stood a green tractor, a FENDT FARMER TURBO. And although it had been in the water for some days, it gleamed as if fresh from the factory. With its hydraulic shovel, the tractor had torn off the grid that was supposed to keep foreign matter and dirt out of the turbine. That, then, was the reason for the drop in performance. Of the tractor driver, no trace was found, not on the bed of the lake or in the power station pipelines or, for that matter, in the drainage channel in the valley. It was therefore assumed that he must have got caught in the turbine undertow, had caused a brief drop in performance there but then, not without making a final, farewell contribution to the region's electricity supply, had gone on to become inextricably mingled with the elements and dispersed into his minutest components to enter into the eternal cycle. From a religious point of view, said the engineer, it was a beautiful, a dignified death. All the same, I wouldn't have fancied being in his shoes, said the second technician with a shudder. The owner was quickly traced by means of the licence plate. In fact he had been reported missing. The missing man's wife and brother duly arrived to view the scene of the accident. Without the slightest hesitation, the brother climbed down to the tractor, gave the key, which was still in the ignition, a couple of turns, the engine sprang to life, the wife climbed on board and they drove out of the lake at a point where the bank sloped gently down and lived from then on as man and wife. On many an evening, the Deafman would sit over the microscope from Leipzig examining the water from the lake. However, he never did find his brother. He had mounted Bad Luck's mirror on the accordion, and in this way he could watch what his left hand was doing on the bass keys. If my brother had hit on that idea, he would still be alive today, he thought. And every time he played on the Hohner, he locked his door, so that none of the sounds could escape. Then he looked in the mirror at the frogs on his ears and twiddled two tiny knobs. Only the farmer's wife could make out scraps of the melodies that the Deafman played, but she never heard a complete song. After some six months, the batteries on his hearing aids gave out. The Deafman took off the frogs and laid them in the shoe-box along with the photographs. After that, the wife would tell people that what she could hear of his playing sounded more beautiful than ever.

To Lake Baikal

THAT EVENING THE chemist had an errand to run, he was supposed to take some medicine for the Meat Inspector, whom he presumed still to be ailing, and drop it off at his home, for after all he was on his own, he had no one, knew no one and was still lying there surrounded by his apples.

The Volkswagen skittered and spun full circle when the chemist braked. While he had not meant to look over towards the stonemason's workshop, since he did not expect to see anything or anyone there, nevertheless his eye was attracted by the glow from the tiny bulb working its way through the thin covering of snow on the skylight. The light was pale and diffused, straggly, a few stray snowflakes were dancing around in it and seemed to be hopping up and down, but then the eye is easily deceived. Anyway, thought the chemist, why shouldn't snowflakes bob up and down instead of falling downwards, even in a dead calm. He turned off the road very gingerly, his tyres were worn almost bald; for years now he had been putting off the purchase of a new set. It can't be burglars, he thought, what's there to steal in there. Even as he was getting out of the car, he could hear the regular hammer blows. And supposing a ghost had appeared before him at that very instant, he would not have been scared, he would merely have smiled. And the closer he got to the door, with its red lead flaking off and letting rust patches show through, the cheerier he became and the louder he laughed. He was laughing as he had never laughed in his life when he opened the door and stepped into the icy workshop to see Raven smoking and working away under the light of the dim little lamp.

Hah, he called out, still laughing, you've aged.

You too, said Raven and gestured towards the vodka bottle. The chemist hardly needed a second bidding, he sat down on a chair and watched Raven bringing the stonemason's work to its conclusion. The faces of the stone were now polished almost to a shine, it now had a beautiful surface with a restful, regular pattern and Raven had chipped away most of the original block until he was satisfied with the design. A cube was all that was left over, just big enough for Raven to be able to get both arms around it.

Finished, said Raven. He pulled the overhead crane across and attached the stone with the chains. He went over to the iron door and opened both wings. He tried to start the chemist's car, to reverse it in and load the stone into it. But the car, as if in protest against this unreasonable demand, refused to start in the cold. Behind the building, where the stonemason's bicycle still lay under its tarpaulin, there also stood an old sledge, which Raven now pulled out and positioned at the door. With the hand hoist he pulled the stone up and let the crab move over to hover above the sledge. The ancient wood gave a loud groan under the burden, but the sledge held together and left two rusty brown tracks in the snow. The chemist followed Raven, who, straining like a carthorse between the shafts, was pulling it along, and then went over to grip the stone and help out with a push. They had to go a good hundred metres till they came to a place where, as a result of a serious accident, there was a gap in the crash barrier. There they crossed the motorway, the sledge's runners crunching on the salted asphalt, the chemist got a fright as beams of light approached, but Raven was not even looking; the driver braked, he had been going very slowly anyway, and put on his emergency warning lights and waited till the two of them and their stone had reached the far side of the right-hand carriageway. The cemetery was a good six kilometres away, and it would have been pointless to try to get there. The chemist gasped, You know, he wouldn't have wanted that, a stone like this.

Raven dragged it a few paces further before conceding that the chemist was right. So he tipped the sledge, which would not have held out for much longer anyway, over on its side, the stone rolled on to the asphalt and lay on the left-hand carriageway, glowing in the darkness as if lit from within.

Fine, said Raven, and the chemist had just enough strength left to nod in agreement. Slowly, they went back to the workshop, where they finished off the bottle. The chemist slipped out of his heavy overcoat and gave it to Raven. Raven packed the coat into his plastic bag, saying he would save it until it got really cold. The Quickly started at the first kick, the chemist pulled out his wallet to give Raven his ready cash, and as he did so a photograph of the stonemason as a young man came into view, something he himself had probably not looked at for years and the existence of which had long been forgotten. The stonemason looked very earnest, he was wearing a white camouflage battledress uniform, and he had taken his cap off. He was standing in the middle of a copse of small birch trees. The chemist held the photograph out to Raven, but he would accept only the money. After all, you're all alone now, he said, gave one last wave and rode away.

The chemist got into his car and tried once more to start it, but the battery was now finally too far gone. So he pulled up the collar of his jacket and gazed at the picture of the stonemason; it had begun to snow again and the car windows were misting up. The chemist began to feel drowsy, his head drooped on to his chest and no doubt he had the photograph of the stonemason still before his eyes when he said as he was dozing off, What a fine-looking man.